Novels by Lisa Silverthorne

A Game of Lost Souls series:
Contemporary Romantasy

THE CINDERELLA HOUR
THE PRINCE CHARMING HOUR
THE EVER AFTER HOUR
THE FALLEN HEARTS SEASON
THE RISING SPIRITS SEASON
THE ETERNAL SOULS SEASON
THE ROYAL WEDDING HOUR
THE HEAVENLY HONEYMOON HOUR
THE DIVINE NEWLYWEDS SHOW
THE CELESTIAL COUPLES SHOW
THE ENOCHIAN APOCALYPSE SHOW
THE ANGELIC ANNIVERSARY SHOW
THE PERDITION PICTURE SHOW

Curse and Crown series:
Romantasy Suspense

THORN & BLADE
STORM & STEEL

The Spiral series:
Dark Contemporary Fantasy

BETWEEN
REPRISE
AVENGE

The Resurrectionist Papers
Supernatural Romystery

GRAVE RECKONING

Standalones:
ISABEL'S TEARS
LANDFALL
PACIFIC BLUE TATTOO

Short Story Collections
THE SOUND OF ANGELS
THE MAGIC OF ORDINARY THINGS
TIMELESS
WINTER'S EMBRACE

Science Fiction Writing as L.S. Silverthorne

Experiencing True Purple series:
RECOMBINANT, Book 1
HELIX, Book 2
SPLICE, Book 3

Standalones:
REDISCOVERY

FORTHCOMING BY LISA SILVERTHORNE

FORTHCOMING!

Curse and Crown series:

Flame & Dagger, Book Three

Frost & Foil, Book Four

Curse & Crown, Book Five (Series End)

The Spiral series:

Ruin, Book 4

Descent, Book 5 (Series End)

The Resurrectionist Papers:

Corpses Delicti

Stiffed Again

Science Fiction Writing as L.S. Silverthorne

Experiencing True Purple series:

Cipher, Book 4

Renascence, Book 5 (Series End)

THE PERDITION PICTURE SHOW

A GAME OF LOST SOULS
BOOK THIRTEEN

LISA SILVERTHORNE

LISA SILVERTHORNE

THE PERDITION PICTURE SHOW

A GAME OF 13 LOST SOULS

**Jack and Talia's happily ever after unravels.
An archangel traitor sets Armageddon in motion
As a prophesied villain rises.**

**To halt the final battle between light and darkness
Samael's secret weapon must be eliminated.
Before it launches the foretold ending of Creation.**

Jack and Talia return to Heaven to fight alongside Azrael and the death angel guard as they assault Hell one last time.

Tensions mount over the Maker's rulings as they race to stop Archangel Samael from setting Armageddon in motion, the final battle between good and evil. A forever war that can never be won. Or stopped once it's begun.

The Perdition Picture Show is the thirteenth and final book in *A Game of Lost Souls*, an epic **13-book** *celestial contemporary romantasy series*.

For fans of supernatural fantasy, romantasy, and suspense, *A Game of Lost Souls* is a must read. You'll love this captivating tale of love, sacrifice, and redemption that intertwines a sweeping battle between light and darkness, angels and demons in this epic **13-book** celestial contemporary romantasy.

Dual viewpoint, slow burn series fantasy romance with the following tropes:

- forbidden love
- secret identity
- soul mates
- forced proximity

- redemption
- dude in distress
- dark secrets
- celebrity romance

1

*L*ike smoke, a flock of ghostly angels drifted across Heaven's darkening skies, the haunting lament of the seventh flight echoing like a requiem across shadowy cloud tops. More spirit than angel, they warned the Heavens that the apocalypse's last, terrifying flight of angels would soon take to the skies for Earth—and usher in something far worse.

Armageddon.

The angelic apparitions sang their bleak liturgy, its mournful harmonies aching through Talia as the translucent seventh flight floated past in a holding pattern.

Until morning.

They glided over the terrace, that horrible hymn filling Eolowen's expanse. Unnerving the guard.

Some looked up. Others stopped sparring to stare, looking as horrified as Talia felt.

The devastating possibility of a forever war between Light and Darkness loomed across the Heavens. Talia knew that if seventh flight touched down on Earth, they wouldn't spill the plague of death on humanity. No, it was much worse than that.

They would trigger the end of Creation…Jack's world.

Pain rippled across her dove grey wings. All those innocent humans…

The thought made her hurt all over.

Somehow, she and Heaven had to stop the terrible events that Archangel Samael set in motion when he took advantage of Lucifer's capture in the Maker's throne room. And the only way to halt Armageddon was to defeat Samael and Raum, the beast of prophecy destined to lead the army of darkness against the light. Before the seventh flight touched down on Earth or the Creation would be destroyed.

That bottom feeder, Archangel Samael cowered in the depths of Hell alongside his hell spawn, Raum. Building an army. Daring Heaven to come after them. She and the death angel guard only had two angel days to halt the end of everything. Pause the events that would ignite Armageddon.

And not even the Maker could stop Armageddon from playing out once that fuse was lit.

She and the guard had to get this right.

Talia felt the entirety of the angels' fears and trepidations vibrating beneath the controlled chaos of Eolowen's intense drills as Heaven descended into a state of high readiness, the shock of Lucifer's trial already beginning to fade.

She never dreamed that something far worse lurked in its aftermath. That was just beginning.

"Work harder, angels!" Talia shouted as she hovered above Azrael's dais, overseeing the guard's final drills. "The seventh flight's holding pattern is our constant reminder that we have one chance to get this right. To stop Armageddon. So, show me that you mean it out there!"

The sharp, tinny clangs of Eternean blades slammed harder against shields and reverberated sharper across Eolowen's terrace like drumbeats. Speed and dexterity drills began at a fever pitch as the guard's anxiousness spilled off the terrace and snaked its way across the lower Heavens.

With the entirety of Hell's demons loose and Hell in chaos, barely held in check behind the partially opened Gates of Hell that Abaddon struggled to close, Samael and Raum gathered an army. They expected to face Heaven in the final battle between light and darkness, not realizing the fight was coming to them. Samael had to be betting on Heaven's heavy losses of angels during the apocalypse's sixth flight, believing that his growing army outnumbered the guard and that would lead them to victory at Armageddon.

With only a seraph and a handful of cherubim and archangels left in Heaven, they had to remain behind to defend it. Alongside Archangel Turiel and his death angel guard and Sidriel, who'd sent her guard with Azrael. Talia's jaw tightened. They would gather around the lower Heaven's borders, defending it in case Azrael's guard fail.

A terrifying thought.

Yes, she and the guard knew they were outnumbered. Overpowered with only one archangel among two decimated death angel guards. Racing against a clock that was quickly running out of time. With only a shadowy idea of what they faced down in Hell.

But Talia and her guard knew one thing was certain: this fight was to the death.

It wasn't a search and rescue or a bounty hunt. It was their last chance to save Creation. All of it. That was evident in Archangel Azrael's laser-focused preparations and in the guard's unwavering focus.

She moved around the edge of the terrace, scrutinizing each squad's footwork and sword skills and studying how they fought as a team. Tomorrow, they were only as skilled as their weakest angels. One sloppy formation could let through a killing blow to the guard.

Or let Samael escape again.

Azrael had always been so protective of his guard. And now, they faced so many questions and unknowns. How many greater demons and hell princes survived? How many Nephions had Samael spawned? Were Jack's seraphim powers enough to turn the tide down there? Enough to take down Raum?

As commander of the guard, Azrael carried a heavy burden and as his right hand, she carried part of that load. His grim address to the guard before a final meeting in High House warned Talia and the guard that losses could be heavy down in Hell. And if that wasn't an onerous enough load for Azrael and the guard to bear, an even bigger uncertainty loomed.

Lucifer.

She rose on an updraft, up to the grand hall's rooftop, checking technique and shield work for the angels sparring above the hall.

"Footwork has to be faster, angels!" She sang out, moving past more squads. "Sharper. And our blows must be precise. We can't miss tomorrow."

Under Archangel Azrael's intense eye, as all of Heaven held its breath, Lucifer would accompany the guard into Hell. Talia knew that everyone, including Azrael, was terrified that Lucifer would bite the Maker's hand and rampage across Heaven again, wreaking his vengeance at last. Or that he'd return to his old ways once the guard was deep in Hell's tunnels—and betray them. Switching sides to join Samael's path of destruction.

A betrayal that would wipe out Heaven's remaining forces. Including Talia and her squad.

But without Lucifer, they couldn't win this fight. And she felt it deep within her angelic light's wellspring.

With their descent into Hell only hours away, she and the guard still struggled against Lucifer's assignment to the guard. That order came from the Maker. Talia and her guard were handling the situation. She sighed. By pretending Lucifer didn't exist and instead tightening their dependence on their individual squads and their own skills. Closing their ranks.

And that included Jack.

Her squad was treating Jack with that same silent contempt... because he'd voted to spare Lucifer.

She circled around the hall and focused on the squads sparring in the meadow, urging them to drill harder.

Except for her and Jack, Berith had been the lone exception, treating Lucifer with kindness and patience. Berith knew too well what it felt like to fall from Heaven. Unlike the rest of her guard, Talia knew what that felt like, too. So, she treated Lucifer with patience, too, but like the guard, she feared he would turn on them in the heat of battle.

If Lucifer turned, she and the guard would lose everything in tomorrow's battle. And so would Jack.

"You've got to be faster!" She shouted as he watched more speed drills. "We have to show Samael that he picked the wrong guard to challenge."

Azrael had been curt but civil to Lucifer, doing his best to set an example, but there were moments when Talia felt his suspicion and anger and she worried it would degrade into a duel to the death between the two archangels. Or whatever Lucifer was...no one, including Pravuil, seemed to know the answer to that question. Something about those angel divisions coming later, after the first angels had been created. Lucifer was much more powerful than any archangel she had encountered, including Azrael.

Would Azrael just let go of all that bad blood between them? Eons of it? Regardless, she admired the archangel for being so civil to Lucifer even when the guard hadn't been civil.

But her guard's treatment of Jack worried her—and Azrael.

She could almost hear his thoughts when he stood on the dais. He had to be wondering how Jack, of all people, could vote to spare that monster. She knew Azrael well enough to know that he was probably questioning his own leadership skills, wondering where he went wrong with Jack. She knew that Azrael would let Lucifer sink or swim by his own hand, but the archangel would defend Jack against any ill will from the guard.

Regardless, Azrael had to be wondering how he would ever integrate the Prince of Darkness into the guard as an equal member...after everything they went through at Lucifer's hand. He had to fear an angelic civil war erupting over Lucifer's return to Heaven. One that would dwarf the war that Samael had been waging.

And right now, Heaven couldn't handle another rebellion. But evil never slept, making it difficult for Heaven to heal while it battled that evil.

"Not fast enough!" She sang out to the guard. "Speed drills! Again. Let's go!"

The squads shifted into short sprints and weaves as they fought each other with swords and shields.

Azrael had been there at the beginning of Creation and had a long, dark history with Lucifer. But now, the archangel was being told to forget all of that and just welcome Lucifer into the guard. Like nothing had ever happened between them. She'd always wondered how Berith fit into Azrael's and Lucifer's ongoing animosities...and why Berith chose to follow Lucifer into oblivion rather than stay with Azrael. She couldn't imagine the pain he'd carried all this time. But she hoped she got a chance to hear the story from Azrael someday. And Berith. It had to be some story!

Angels had long memories. None of them had forgotten the trail of devastation and destruction that Lucifer had wrought since the Creation, the Fall, ...and that first wager. Was expecting the guard to forget all of that asking too much of them? Or was it another concrete lesson from Heaven's tenets that now adorned the walls of the Cloud Chamber?

They would find out at first light. When they faced Archangel Samael and his army.

Despite all of it, Talia had seen the moments of good that Jack saw in Lucifer. The vote had been his decision, but she'd supported giving Lucifer a chance at redemption. Even though it went against everything in her angelic being.

But she trusted Jack. Only Jack had sensed Lucifer's deep-seated longing for redemption and Lucifer's hopelessness, knowing such a mercy would never be granted. So, Lucifer resigned himself to his fate —until Jack's shocking vote saved Lucifer from the Lake of Fire.

"Again, angels!" She sang out, returning to the terrace. "Hit it!"

Were Lucifer's assaults on Heaven and the Maker just him acting out his rage? To make a statement? To get his father's attention. To only injure his father...not kill him? Or had he truly been hellbent on destroying every breath of the Maker's Creation. Regardless, Lucifer never dreamed he would be spared.

By Jack's vote, of all people.

She'd felt the love and pain emanate from the Maker that day when they passed their vote to Jack. It made her see a loving side to the Maker she'd never seen before, one that was a parent's anguish who couldn't cast an unbiased vote regarding their own child's actions. She felt the Maker's torturous decision to pass the vote to one of victims and later, the relief, knowing that they made the right decision to pass that vote.

No one dreamed Jack would vote to spare Lucifer. Not even Jack.

But bringing Lucifer into the guard now—while they were trying to stop Armageddon—was horrible timing. And it was causing chaos. She'd never seen the squads so distracted. Or Jack so worried and isolated.

When the time came, would the guard—and Lucifer—still rally behind Azrael and fight as one force deep in Hell's subterranean tunnels? Against Archangel Samael and Raum?

The guard had no choice. Getting to Samael and Raum meant going through Hell. Literally. Together, as one force.

But poor Jack was taking the brunt of the squads' anger and fear.

Most of the guard—and the lower Heavens—was furious at Jack for voting to spare Lucifer, including her squad. And they made sure he knew it, too.

For days, Muriel, Anahera, Kesien, and Deemah refused to spar with Jack. They wouldn't even let him on the terrace. The rest of the time, they shunned Jack in true angel of death fashion. Even though he'd fought alongside them so many times, protected them from Lucifer, and saved them from being erased from existence. Talia didn't quite understand why they were so angry at Jack, but she hadn't had time to discuss it with any of them—especially Muriel.

"That's it!" She trilled in a series of bright angel notes. "Again!"

Right now, Anahera and Deemah wouldn't even speak to Jack. They looked past him like he wasn't there—like they treated Lucifer. Muriel and Kesien were outright hostile toward Jack, like he'd chosen Lucifer over them. Muriel's distance and Kesien's anger hurt Jack the most—she saw it in his eyes. And Talia saw the pain on his face whenever Muriel passed him like he wasn't there. Or did what Jack called a shoulder check, hitting him with her shoulder whenever they passed each other. Kesien was open hostile to Jack and it bubbled over into a glare, shove, or shoulder check whenever they were in close proximity.

Jack just let it go, but it was quickly wearing him down. He'd said more than once that they were just taking their anger and frustration over Lucifer out on him because they couldn't shoulder check Lucifer. So, he dealt with it, something she wasn't used to seeing from Jack.

"All right, back into your squads and spar." She announced in a series of angel notes. "Show me your best blade and shield work. Like the Creation depended on it." She pulled in a breath and landed in the meadow grass again. "Because it does!"

Right now, with the guard so divided, none of the angels of death was functioning as part of a team. Somehow, she had to hold them all together under the grand hall's roof—and on the battlefield—long enough to defeat Archangel Samael and Raum.

But how would the guard fight as one force if they were still fighting each other? And Lucifer. While ignoring Jack?

The crack of swords against shields was constant, reverberating like thunder, every member of the guard began frantic sparring on, above, and around the white stone terrace, tightening footwork, defensive stances, and offensive maneuvers.

She flew over the grounds again, continuing to scrutinize the dozens of angels of death that rushed at each other across the white stone terrace now, wings extended, sword clanging against shields. Swooping, shield bash at the ready, they collided above the willow tree, along the rooftop, and over the lush green meadow surrounding Eolowen. Some angels kept glancing up at the clouds, expecting the seventh flight to glide past like apparitions at any moment—that horrible lament filling the skies—and head toward Earth to usher in Armageddon.

Every time they passed over the hall, it distracted the guard. And Talia, chilling her to the bone.

Azrael had left her in charge while he remained occupied with planning and other matters in High House, so she kept the entire guard busy with drills and footwork—and Jack when he returned from the Archive. She sighed.

And Lucifer.

But she was ready to knock heads together and settle any fights while Azrael was gone. Or stop any of them from killing each other before they even reached the crossroads.

"Pick up the pace, angels! Clock's ticking!" she shouted as she landed back on Azrael's stone dais, wings spread wide, her gold Eternean armor creaking, sword hanging at her side beside a small gold pouch. "We're about to face Archangel Samael and his Nephions —all of them. We're running out of time!"

Some squads lagged compared to the others, taking their time through drills and not challenging themselves. Their responses were slow and apathetic. Like Lucifer's presence had dissolved their determination. Like they didn't care if Archangel Samael took over Hell and started Armageddon.

And that infuriated Talia.

She moved left toward two sparring units and paused, watching their half-hearted sword thrusts and shield bashes. She crossed her arms, glaring at them, her wings unfurling at her shoulders in disgust.

One of the units was her own.

"We're about to face the entirety of Hell's demon hordes!" she shouted, anger setting the white fire in her eyes alight. "And all of Archangel Samael's guard! Not to mention greater demons, Hell Princes, and Nephions...half archangels and half archdemons. And the Maker only knows what else."

The guard cast uneasy glances at her as they continued to spar. Picking up the pace. She gritted her teeth. But it wasn't enough. Not nearly enough to defeat Samael who was trapped down in Hell—and would fight them with everything he had.

"Archangel Samael is holed up in Hell," she sang in fierce angel notes. "Trapped there, knowing that all of Heaven is coming for him.

He will throw everything he has at us—and more. So, we have to be stronger and faster than Samael and his minions!"

She blinked back onto the terrace, studying the squads along its white stone length.

"Do I need to remind you all again that we'll face Hell Princes. Greater demons. Hellhounds and Hell creatures. Not to mention our own kind—angels of death. Samael has an army of demons, damned souls, fallen angels, and angels of death traitors. Plus, the foretold beast of prophecy...and Heaven knows how many others like him. So, we have to be faster. Smarter. Together—as one. So, fight like you mean it!"

The murmur of the nearby stream meandering beside the white stone pergola along the meadow soothed her anger like the scent of roses and honeysuckle as the guard's shouts grew louder and more intense. But it didn't take away her worry.

Kesien, still healing from all of his injuries, was still slower than normal...and weaker, wings drooping, sword thrusts lagging despite his best effort. But she watched his movements quicken, sharpen as he trained harder alongside the unit. Gritting his teeth as he struggled through the drills.

Talia knew she'd never convince him to stay behind. He and Deemah had scores to settle with Samael and their former guard. They had justice to bring and traitors to apprehend. They would not stand down, no matter how much injury they carried. Besides, even injured, the guard needed him in this fight. And Deemah's fearless shield bashes.

She made another loop around the circuit, trying to motivate them somehow. "C'mon, guard! Show Heaven how it's done! Let's go!"

But like it or not, the guard needed Lucifer, too. Even though his presence in the guard had been aloof and distant. He preferred to train alone and Azrael let him.

Talia trusted her squad and the guard with her life. They would come through. But only Jack trusted Lucifer. Somehow, she needed to bring all of them together by tomorrow.

Even if they tried to kill each other.

Her squad would fight alongside her (and Jack even though they were furious at him), watching her back when the guard brought down Archangel Samael and Raum. She'd let Azrael handle Lucifer.

She gazed across the meadow, searching for Jack's light blond hair and silvery grey wings, but he hadn't returned from the Archive yet. From Pravuil's office. Instead, she saw Lucifer's curly sunlit-blond hair.

Beside the willow tree, the air fragrant with jasmine, Lucifer trained alone again, shackles gone. He trained a marked distance from the terrace where most of the angels of death sparred. Talia knew it was on purpose. He wore dark trousers, black knee-high boots, and a double-breasted charcoal grey military coat with gold buttons and flourishes, his black wings shiny against his shoulders, blood-red halo bright and terrifying. He was the tallest angel on the field and his very presence frightened the guard. Set them off balance—even at a distance.

She felt the guard's barely suppressed anger roiling beneath their angelic calm. Lucifer had to feel it, too, but somehow, he'd ignored it, focusing on training.

Tall and lean, those tousled blond curls bright in the sunlight, he drilled with a flaming sword and Eternean shield, his moves sharp and precise, his strength and dexterity as evident as his training. He was deep in concentration and she was surprised that all she felt from him was determination. That deep, intense, almost-nauseating fury he had carried for so long seemed to have dulled. Dissipated.

He paused against the willow tree, wiping his brow as the sword's flaming blade turned cool and the flames went out. He set the gold angelic shield beside two Eternean swords that leaned in the shade against the willow tree's trunk and from the air, he summoned a flaming sword in each hand and began working through another set of drills.

In the Beginning, he led Heaven's army. Against what foes, Talia had no idea, but it was obvious that his prowess with a sword had not suffered from his exile in Hell. Despite her fears, she saw the beauty and precision in his form, in his movements, and she knew that he had a lot to teach the guard who had become Heaven's special forces unit. Even more so since the sixth flight of angels had flown over Earth.

In every drill, even without an opponent, Lucifer's footwork was perfect, his sword thrusts deadly, his shield bashes flawless. He was formidable—and the sight of him made her tremble with fear as he drilled alone. But even without that clash of swords, he was perfection. And she couldn't help but wonder how they'd ever managed to defeat him, especially in the Maker's Throne room. And she knew the guard—and her squad—was thinking the same thing.

"Impressive, Lucifer," she called to him, landing in the grass beside him. "The guard will learn much from you."

"Perhaps," he said, pausing, his enigmatic gaze settling on her, bringing back a flood of bad memories from when he had controlled her against her will.

She fought down a shudder.

"In a millennium or so," he continued in that precise British accent. "If we manage to cross all of this distance. Right now, they are too angry—or frightened—to see me as anything other than their archenemy. And that's on me."

Lucifer knew how difficult his path was now—and the guard's—but he didn't flinch from it. And he was accepting that responsibility instead of blaming the guard. She was surprised. His demeanor had changed right before her eyes.

"Talia," he said and let the flaming swords in his hands disappear in the breeze. "I know how difficult this is for you, and quite frankly, I'm as surprised as you are that I still exist. Much less, my being part of Azrael's guard. I have no good word to offer you or any sort of proof that I won't turn on Heaven without any warning."

That sent a chill through her wings. Was he plotting violence still? Against Heaven? Against the Maker? His own father?

She didn't know what to say to him. They'd been through so much, battling each against other, enemies at every turn—fighting almost to the death. But the angel who stood before her now was not the same angel that she and Jack fought in the Maker's Throne Room. He seemed so different. Focused. Wise. Free. Still, she couldn't help but worry that it was all an act.

"Just know that I intend to see this arrangement through," Lucifer said, bowing his head. "I've never known my father to grant such a mercy before, one unheard of back in the days of the Rebellion and certainly not now. Especially a mercy I did not deserve. And I intend to show him that it wasn't wasted."

This was such a different side of Lucifer. Words without malice or lies. She felt a twinge of relief swell over her.

Above the willow tree, a flash of pale blond hair and silvery grey wings blinked over her head.

Smiling, she looked up.

Jack landed in the meadow beside the willow tree, dressed in faded Levi's, a light green Henley, and those beat-up blue Vans he still wore. He clutched some sort of map in his fist as he turned to Lucifer with that typical bewitching Jack Casey smile, like Lucifer was just another one of the guard. A typical smile that had won over entire guards of death angels and most television-watching humans. A smile she had fallen for the first day she met him beneath those hot Studio 22 stage lights. A smile that made him the love of her life…and her his wife.

"Hey, Tal!" he said, kissing her in a quick peck. He turned to Lucifer and gave him a nod. "Hey, Luci, how's training going?"

For several moments, Lucifer looked at Jack with a mixture of surprise and confusion.

"Hello, Jack," he said finally. "Back from High House so soon?"

Jack shook his head. "Archive. Pravuil needed to have words about Talia's and my marriage. For my Book of Life and Death, I guess."

Lucifer nodded, looking pensive.

Jack folded his wings against his shoulders and held out the map to Talia. "Scribe sent this map for Azrael, Tal."

"Thanks, Jack," she said, wanting to kiss him again as she accepted the map, tucking it into the pouch at her side. "I'll get it to him right away."

Jack motioned at Lucifer's polished angel shield leaning against the tree. "You need a sparring partner, Luci?" he asked.

Surprised, Lucifer's gaze snapped toward Jack.

"You want to spar?" he said, sounding amused, the corners of his mouth lifting. "With me?"

"I know you'll kick my ass all over this meadow," Jack said with a chuckle. "But I can learn a lot from your technique…and how to take a fall. Now that you're not trying to kill me."

Lucifer studied Jack's expression a moment and Talia ached to know what was running through the former King of Hell's head.

Finally, Lucifer smiled.

"All right, Jack," he said. "Let's spar. With some Eternean blades though, not flaming swords."

"What's wrong with flaming swords?" Jack asked, looking surprised.

"Those are for terrifying your opponents. Not nearly as accurate." Lucifer pointed at the two gleaming Eternean blades that rested against the trunk of the willow tree, glinting silver and gold in the sunlight. "With the Eternean blades, maybe I can finally correct that terrible human posture of yours?"

Jack laughed as he ran over and grabbed both weapons. "Good luck. I learned this terrible human posture from the best."

Jack extended the hilt of one sword to Lucifer.

Lucifer accepted it, taking a couple of practice swings as Jack wrapped his fingers around the hilt of the other sword and lifted it into the air.

"I got a crash course in swords when we filmed The Prince Charming Hour," said Jack, almost apologizing for his sword skills. "I wasn't bad—for a complete amateur."

Lucifer sighed. "I remember. That's when I sent that obsessed firefighter at you."

Jack nodded. "Made for some incredible television—even if he did almost kill me."

Lucifer's face had a pinched expression, remorse hovering there. Talia felt it this time.

With a flick of his wrist, Lucifer plunged his sword into the grass and turned away, hands on his hips.

Frowning, Jack stared at Lucifer for a moment and then he cast an uncertain look at her. She shrugged and motioned him toward Lucifer. She had no idea what was going through Lucifer's head right now. If ever. And she knew even less about how to respond to it. To him.

"Luci?" Jack said finally and set down his sword. He walked over to Lucifer and stood at his back. "What's up?"

Lucifer glanced over his shoulder, his glassy light blue eyes flashing red, anger mixing with confusion.

"I don't get it, Jack!" he shouted. "I just don't understand this."

"Get what?" Jack asked, his voice going quiet.

Lucifer whirled around to Jack, anger burning in his eyes that flashed red again.

"You!"

Jack held up his palms, pulling back from the former King of Hell. "Me? Not following you, dude."

"Of all the angels and humans at that trial, you, above all of them, should have voted to throw me in the Lake of Fire! Why didn't you? I've tried to kill you—over and over."

Lucifer began to pace, an anxious confusion that almost looked like fear and remorse to Talia. Or was it guilt?

"I've tortured you. I ruined your life. I sent demons after you at every turn. I tethered your soul. Turned your best friends against you. I ruined your parents' marriage." Finally, he stopped in front of Jack, the anger slipping into exasperation as his voice softened. "I dragged you off to Hell. And I took Talia from you more than once. Why, Jack? Why would you ever vote to spare me? Why?"

Off to Talia's left, all of the sparring had stopped, the terrace falling deathly quiet until she heard every creak of armor and every hiss of whispers.

Lucifer had asked Jack the question that all of Heaven wanted answered, including Azrael. And they needed to hear his answer. Like she did.

Why would Jack spare Lucifer after everything Lucifer had done to him? Even Talia didn't quite understand it, but they hadn't had a moment alone for her to ask him in any great detail yet.

Jack stared at Lucifer a moment, taking in his expression, his mood, almost like he was afraid to speak. He pulled in a breath and fixed Lucifer with his patient gaze.

"Because...every once in a while," Jack said, pointing at Lucifer, "you did the right thing. Every time when I'd written you off as a hopeless monster, beyond redemption—and believe me, that was a lot —you went and did something good. Something protective. Something worthy of the once most beloved angel in Heaven. And you'll laugh at this, but sometimes, I even saw my own life in your eyes."

Lucifer frowned. "Your life?"

Jack nodded. "I know I made fun of your daddy issues. Your feelings of abandonment. Because I saw myself in those wounds. Those old hurts. My mother never wanted me. Treated me like an unwanted family pet. Her love was conditional and after my dad died, she barred me from family holidays on a whim. I was seventeen. I tried so hard to get her to love me, never understanding why she just couldn't love me like she did my four sisters."

Talia knew how painful Jack's relationship with his mother had been. And still was.

"Not the same, of course," Jack continued. "But I saw the same pain in you that I carried. And as much as I tried to deny it, I saw those similarities between us. And then some angels of death decided to give me a chance at redemption. So, I thought you should get that same chance."

Lucifer was stunned.

"I also saw, when I was in Hell," Jack continued, "that no one from the rebellion ever got a chance to redeem themselves. Apparently, the Maker was a one-shot kind of being. But it was obvious that they had regrets."

Lucifer looked surprised. "You saw their regret?"

Jack nodded. "Berith got the chance to show her regret and ask forgiveness. And she asked to come home, but the others never got that chance." Jack sighed and ran his fingers through his bangs. "I just thought that how you got where you were wasn't all your fault. That there was enough good left in you that you deserved that chance. And so do the other fallen who regret what happened."

Lucifer looked like someone had shield-bashed him. He shook his head, a million thoughts rushing across those crystalline blue eyes as the red receded again.

"You, Jack, are the strangest human I've ever met."

"I get that a lot," he said with a smirk.

"And I must confess, I am...humbled by your attitude and reasoning. I don't think you're the only one who will learn from our sparring."

"Have you and your father had a chance to talk yet?" Jack asked.

"Not yet," said Lucifer in a quiet voice. "Not until I have settled into the guard." His gaze traveled across the meadow and around the terrace, startling the angels of death back out of their pauses as they scrambled back to their drills. "Which might be quite a long time away."

Lucifer pulled his sword out of the ground and nodded toward Jack's sword.

Jack picked up his sword and held it out in front of him, setting himself.

"And when we're done here," Jack said, shifting his sword into a defensive stance. "I'll take you around Eolowen. Introduce you to all of the guard. They're some of the finest people I know. I trust them with my life. When you get to know them better, I think you'll like them, too."

Lucifer's expression lightened. He glanced at Talia. "Talia, you do know that your husband is part golden retriever, don't you?"

"I know," Talia said with a laugh. "One of the things I love about him."

"Thanks, Mrs. Casey," said Jack with a smile and turned his gaze back to Lucifer. "Ready when you are, Luci."

A grin rolled across Lucifer's face. "I'm going to enjoy this."

Lucifer landed a lightning-fast blow against Jack's blade that rattled across Jack's entire body.

He recovered, pivoted, and returned Lucifer's blow.

"Not bad, Jack," said Lucifer.

Talia stepped back and leaned against the willow tree's trunk, watching them spar for several minutes until she felt a tug on her sleeve.

Muriel.

"What's wrong, Muriel?" she asked, glancing from Jack and Lucifer to Muriel.

Muriel's gaze hadn't left Jack and Lucifer sparring.

"Aren't you afraid that Lucifer will plunge that sword into Jack's heart the first moment you let your guard down?"

In the back of Talia's mind, she had played that fear over and over until it made her stomach ache. But regardless of her fears and emotions, that voice of reason in her head reminded her that if it hadn't been for Jack, Lucifer would have already been thrown into the Lake of Fire. Right now, Jack should be Lucifer's favorite person in all of Creation.

"The thought has crossed my mind many times," she said as Jack pivoted left and Lucifer rained down blows, their sword blades clashing like thunder. "But then I remember that without Jack, Lucifer would have ceased to exist, something that Lucifer is well aware of."

"How can you trust him?" Muriel demanded. "Even a little?"

Talia's gaze narrowed as she turned toward her best friend. "Because the Maker trusted him. And so does Jack. So, I will, too."

Muriel sighed. "I understand now." Her brow furrowed. "But I'm still mad at Jack."

"For insisting on love freeing all, not just some?"

Muriel grimaced, shaking her head. "For making me see good in Lucifer. Enough to give him a chance at redemption. Happy?"

Talia smiled. She knew Muriel couldn't stay mad at Jack for long. She just hoped that the others came around, too. Even a little. It would make a huge difference tomorrow when they returned to Hell. Fighting as one unit against Archangel Samael would be critical.

A shadow flew overhead and Talia looked up. Azrael. Landing in the grass beside the Willow tree. Muriel blinked away from her, back to the terrace.

Azrael's face was taut, eyes steely grey, mouth set in a deep line. He had news…and it didn't look good.

2

hen Jack saw Azrael, he took a step backward, letting his sword fall to his side as Lucifer stopped swinging his Eternean blade. They gave Azrael a wide berth as he landed between them.

"Uh, what's up, Azrael?" Jack asked as Lucifer's blade shifted toward the grass. "Any word from the Maker on this whole Armageddon thing? We still have an appointment to kick Samael's ass tomorrow?"

"Hello, Azrael, ol' boy," said Lucifer, one corner of his mouth lifting. "Come to spar with us?"

Azrael, grimacing, let his soot grey wings fold against his back as he stared at Jack a moment and then Lucifer, watching them like a nervous L.A. cop at a midnight traffic stop on Crocker Street.

"Dude, something wrong?"

"Everything okay here?" Azrael asked finally, brows furrowed, charcoal grey eyes churning with uncertainty as he kept glancing from Lucifer to Jack.

Jack studied the archangel a moment. Did Azrael think Lucifer was still trying to kill him?

Lucifer's eyes turned steely as he folded his arms against his chest, still gripping the hilt of his sword.

Jack shrugged, his gaze shifting from Lucifer to Talia.

"Everything but my technique," said Jack. "Lucifer's wiping the meadow with me."

Both corners of Lucifer's mouth lifted, almost into a smile. "You're much better with a sword than I remember, Jack."

Jack smirked, leaning toward Azrael. "He's leaving the obvious unsaid. Better than horrible. Think I should stick to murder marbles and Holy fire."

Lucifer chuckled. "You and those...what are they again? Murder marbles?"

"Never gets old," Jack replied, still smirking.

"Oblivion spheres, Lucifer," said Talia.

"Oh, I see," Lucifer replied, motioning at Jack. "Rare angel power. Name has been Jackified."

Talia busted out laughing. "Jackified? Yes, it and many other things."

Jack shrugged.

Azrael relaxed a little, but he was still all kinds of tense as he looked at Jack and then Talia. And finally, Lucifer.

"Did you think Luci and I were out here trying to kill each other?" Jack asked, making Lucifer smile for real this time.

Azrael stuttered a little, a sheepish look on his face as he brushed dust off his gold Eternean armor. "From the air, it looked like it."

"With my technique, that would have taken about two seconds. Or an eternity."

"I must be out of practice then," said Lucifer.

"Why?" Jack asked.

"Two whole seconds?" he said. "I could have taken over a whole country in that time."

Jack chuckled. "Harsh."

"So is your footwork," said Lucifer.

"And that's why I'm an actor not a sword fighter."

"Good thing that," Lucifer said, still smiling. "You play a better sword fighter on television than that bit I just saw with your footwork."

"Says the angel who's full of hot air," Jack replied. "Can float and sting and all that."

"You're just now discovering this, Jack?" said Lucifer as he uncrossed his arms and let the sword dangle at his side. "Spoiler alert. All angels are full of it."

Jack snickered.

"For what it's worth, you keep up just fine, Jack," said Lucifer. "Better than any human I've encountered."

Jack stood a little taller. "Thanks, Luci."

Lucifer gave him a quick nod. "It'll take me three seconds to defeat you instead of two."

"That extra second must be brutal," Jack said, motioning at Lucifer as his gaze turned to Azrael. "See, Luci here's stuck with me since Talia's squad has disowned me."

"What?" Azrael snapped and glanced at Talia, his eyes narrowing. "Is that true, Talia? Why won't your squad spar with Jack?"

Talia glanced toward the terrace at her squad in a heated drill, and then back at Azrael, a frustrated expression on her face.

"They're feeling a little...betrayed. For the moment," she said finally. "Sorry, Jack. They'll come around like the rest of the lower Heavens."

Lucifer's amusement told him a different story.

"Of course, they will, Jack," said Lucifer with that devilish smile. "Just be patient. They're angels. They'll come around...in a few millennia or so. There's a reason that forgiveness isn't written on the Cloud Chamber walls. Because angels hold grudges."

Dude had a point.

"They'll come around." Azrael insisted with a growl. "After I've had a word with them." The archangel's mood had leveled out, but it was still dark and intense as he turned his gaze to Talia. "Talia, we need to discuss the guard and final preparations for tomorrow's assault." His charcoal grey eyes narrowed again. "Before I have a word with your squad."

"Of course, sir," she said and turned to Jack. "And when I return, we'll have a word with the squad, Jack." She cast a quick glance at Azrael. "So, Azrael doesn't have to."

Jack felt a twinge of guilt as he glanced over at Talia's squad drilling on the terrace without him. They cast occasional probing glances toward the meadow as they focused on blades and footwork. He felt the distance between him and the squad lengthening. All because he'd voted to spare Lucifer. He wasn't wrong. And he'd do it again—in a heartbeat.

Now, after the trial, the guard treated him like he didn't exist. And it hurt. They hadn't even asked him why or let him tell his side of the story. So, he'd just let them be angry for now. But tomorrow, once the guard stormed Hell and battled that douchebag Archangel Samael and his Nephion spawn, Raum, Jack would make them listen. Maybe then they'd set aside their anger and make him part of the squad again? Or maybe they'd still hate him. But either way, if he had to vote again, he'd still vote the same way.

Regardless, Armageddon might continue as scheduled, despite them taking the fight to Samael. And if the world ended—a chilling thought—then none of this mattered anyway.

He glanced at Muriel ignoring him from the terrace. Her cold distance hurt the most. She'd always been one of his favorite angels. She'd always liked him, defended him. She'd always been one of his biggest fans, too, but now, she acted like the rest of the squad. Like she wanted him tossed out of Heaven alongside Lucifer.

Even if Muriel hated him, he stood by his decision. Lucifer had changed. Luci and the Maker needed a heart to heart to discuss what this chance at redemption meant. But it was the first time Jack had ever heard Lucifer say he wanted that chance. Like Berith had asked for it after standing with Lucifer during the Rebellion. She'd been redeemed. So, now, it was time to offer all of the Fallen who wanted forgiveness that chance at redemption, too.

Starting with Luci.

Jack sighed. And Talia's squad needed to forgive him—or at least chill about how he'd voted. The fate of everything hinged on them fighting as bros tomorrow. And they knew it.

"So, what'd the Maker say about Armageddon?" Jack asked again.

"Yes, what *did* Father have to say?" Lucifer asked. "It's not like him to ignore treachery on this level. He took the wings and halos of a third of the angels who defied him last time. Banished them—us—to Hell. I can't imagine him ignoring this situation with Samael and Raum."

Azrael glanced back at the High House spire.

"Seraphina and Lord Kushiel both said that the seventh flight can't be recalled by Heaven," said Azrael in a bleak tone. "And so did the Maker. It will take flight tomorrow. Our only chance to stop Armageddon is to defeat Raum and Samael before the seventh flight touches Earth."

"What happens if we fail?" Talia asked.

Azrael's gaze hardened. "If the seventh flight touches Earth before Raum is defeated, Armageddon can no longer be stopped—even by the Maker. So, we must leave by first light for Hell or we'll never prevent this catastrophe. The Maker asked to see you though, Lucifer. Right away in the Cloud Chamber."

Lucifer's eyes widened. "Now?"

Azrael nodded. "He's with Seraphina and Lord Kushiel who will be taking over Hell once we unseat Samael. Kushiel will be working alongside Abaddon, but they want to talk to you about the fallen angels."

"Right," said Lucifer, tossing the Eterncan blade in the grass. "Must dash, Jack. I'll return to drills shortly."

Lucifer leaped into the air, satiny black wings spread wide, blood red halo bright against the crisp blue skies as he blinked across Eolowen. Toward the High House spire.

Jack's pocket vibrated and he pulled out his phone. A text. From his oldest sister, Meredith. Asking him to call.

"I've gotta make a call, babe," said Jack, almost losing himself for a moment in Talia's sparkling grey eyes.

"Go ahead, Jack," said Talia, moving over to him. She kissed him in a steamy kiss that made him want to forget about the phone call. Hell, forget he even had a phone. "Come to the terrace when you're done. I'll be back shortly."

"Love you, Mrs. Casey," he said.

He turned away from the willow tree, moving away from the terrace, his hand shaking as he tapped Meredith's name. And called Meredith's cell.

It had been so long since they'd spoken. Until this week when they'd texted a few times about Talia's anniversary gift, but he hadn't heard Meredith or Whitney's voice since he got fired from *SanFran Confidential*.

The phone rang twice and then he heard his oldest sister's bright alto voice.

"Jack?" she said.

"Meredith!" he cried. "How are you?"

"Jack!" Her voice was warm and filled with emotion. "It's so good to hear your voice."

"Yours too, Mere," he said as a lifetime of bad memories rushed back to him.

The worst was the night that Dad passed away, leaving Jack alone and scared. He was seventeen. Had no clue what to do that night. Thank God for the hospice nurse, but that first night he'd spent in the dark apartment all alone, with Dad...gone, changed him forever.

Meredith had been out of town, but she got there as soon as she could and took Jack to her place. For the summer until he started college. He had a bed and a dresser there for as long as he needed it and space in their storage shed out back for the few pieces of furniture Dad had left him. And a space in the old barn-turned-garage to park Dad's car, left to him in the will. A 1969 cherry red Pontiac Firebird convertible that Dad called the Firechicken.

A year later, Jack drove it more than three days cross-country from Indiana to L.A. where he kept it in storage after he got cast on *SanFran Confidential*. And when he got fired and lost everything, Meredith let him store the car back in Indiana again. No questions asked.

And he couldn't think of a better anniversary gift for Talia than the Firechicken. That car meant so much to him and because of that, he knew Talia would love it. He smirked. After he taught her how to drive.

"So, about the car…" she said.

"It's okay, isn't it?" he cried, worried that his nephews might have claimed it.

She laughed. "It's fine, Jack."

"Think she'll like it?" he asked. "Should I get her some gold jewelry instead? I know it's not traditional or trendy or modern, but—"

"Jack…she'll love it," said Meredith. He could still hear the smile in her voice. "But I meant what I said. My only caveat is that all four of your sisters get to be there when you give the car to Talia. But not Mom."

Jack burst out laughing. "Oh, thank God. Thought you were going to torture me."

"Thought about it," said Meredith. "But no. Whit and I don't talk to her much these days. We all decided to go around her—all four of us. Jack, we love you and we want to be there for you, famous or not. No conditions."

For a moment, he choked up.

"We let her isolate you for too long." She sighed. "We should have been there for you when everything fell apart. Should have tried to help you with the addiction. Got you into treatment. I'm sorry we weren't there for you."

"Thanks, Mere," he said in a tight voice. "That really means a lot to me. You were more like a mom to me than she ever was. Thank you."

She went quiet for a moment and Jack heard her sniffle.

"Somebody had to make sure you were okay."

A pause that made Jack want to fill it, but he waited it out.

"Listen, Jack, I've talked to Jenna and Tara, too. You tell us what day you want to give Talia the car and where. Whit and I will be taking turns driving it out to Kansas where Jenna and Tara will join us. They'll take over the driving. And don't worry, we've got a flatbed, so we won't put a mile on Dad's car."

All four of them driving the car here—on a truck. For him to give it to Talia. His eyes got glassy.

"You guys are the best!" He smiled. "We're still planning on next Friday for the party. If that changes, I'll let you know right away. You've already got the beach house address. That's where it'll be."

"I can't wait, Jack," said Meredith. "And neither can Whit. Looking forward to meeting Talia and all your friends."

"I can't wait to show off my sisters to them," he said.

"So, call me if anything changes," said Meredith. "Can't wait to celebrate your first anniversary with you."

"Love you guys," said Jack. "I'll call you soon."

"Bye, Jack."

He was grinning when he cleared the call.

"Jack!"

The male voice startled him.

He looked up. Glanced around the meadow.

At first, he didn't see anyone, but as a cloud slid across the sun, the translucent form of Tre Sheridan shimmered at the far end of the meadow. Pale, faded—in soul form. Tre was Zanth's human lover who Jack had helped escape purgatory to be with the archdemoness again.

His stomach dropped. Tre was alone. That wasn't good. Tre and Zanth had always been inseparable. Was Zanth okay?

Jack blinked to the end of the meadow. Tre Sheridan, stone brown hair windblown, dull blue eyes filled with anger and fear, stared at him as he fidgeted, desperation burning in his eyes.

"Tre?" said Jack, squinting. "Dude, what's going on? Where's Zanth?"

Tre's face screwed up into a pained expression, panic rising in his face.

"He's imprisoned her, Jack," he said, holding out his hands. "And he's been doing terrible things to her. Using her to build an army of things like Raum and I can't stop him." His eyes were filled with fury, anger clenching his jaw, teeth gritted as he smashed his hands into fists against his legs. "I can't do a damned thing—especially as a soul."

Zanth was an archdemoness, once one of Lucifer's highest-level assassins. When Lucifer had been trapped in Hell by Talia and Berith's soul tether, Luci sent Zanth after him and Talia. On their honeymoon. She was Lucifer's most powerful demon—and the most difficult fight that Jack had ever fought. Even worse than Abaddon. How had that loser, Samael overpowered an archdemoness like Zanth? Tricked her? Trapped her? Threatened Tre? Douchebag was an archangel, but his fighting skills were on par with the average starlet's purse poodle. No, Zanth would have swiffered Hell's floors with that asshalo. Samuel must have overpowered her somehow—with Raum maybe?

Or maybe Samael had just been the only one left standing in Hell and greedy enough to try and jumpstart Armageddon?

"Zanth is one of the strongest demons I know," said Jack, frowning. "How could a douchebag like Samael overpower her? Take her prisoner?"

Tre rung his hands together and began to pace. "Samael ordered Hell's demons to ambush her. Then Samael imprisoned and immobilized her. And now, for some time, he's been able to control her." He winced. "Assaulting her. Somehow, we've got to rescue her, Jack. Before he destroys her. And the world." Tre's eyes turned glassy. "She's starting to fade, Jack. He's killing her."

After the honeymoon, Jack and Zanth developed an uneasy truce to locate and stop Samael. And release Tre from purgatory. In exchange, Zanth found Jack's father in purgatory and took Jack to see him, a moment he wouldn't trade for anything. He needed to save Zanth. Spring her from her prison and maybe even use her demon powers to help take down Samael once and for all.

But right now, she was in trouble. She needed help.

"Look, we're about to show up on Samael's doorstep with an eviction notice, Tre. And a helluva lot of murder marbles. You have my word that we'll get Zanth away from him."

Tre touched Jack's sleeve and it felt like a rush of wind.

"We have to hurry. She won't hold out much longer." Tre shuddered. "She can't. He's draining her, Jack. Even she can't outlast this."

Jack glanced back at Eolowen and then at Tre. "You need a safe place to crash?"

Tre shook his head. "Samael doesn't know who I am. He thinks I'm just another damned soul. I'm going to go back to her. Stay with her until help comes, but Jack…hurry. She won't last much longer."

"Tell her to hang on, Tre," said Jack. "Help's coming."

Nodding, Tre moved toward the crossroads and vanished into the shadows along the road to Hell.

Jack turned and blinked back toward the willow tree. He needed to update Azrael and Talia about Zanth. And he hoped they would agree to help him rescue her. Otherwise, he'd do it alone.

Jack blinked the rest of the way across the meadow and stopped at the edge of the terrace. He groaned. Just his luck. Right where Talia's squad drilled. They wouldn't even let him on the terrace. And he wasn't in the mood to try and fight his way past them.

He could just fly over them like he'd been doing, but not this time. Dammit, he had a right to be on this terrace. He was walking across it to the round room.

"I'm not asking you to spar with me," said Jack. "But you can damned well let me pass."

They didn't even look up when he paused on the terrace steps, folding his wings at his shoulders. Waiting for them to move and let him walk across the terrace.

Muriel was sparring with Kesien and Anahera practiced with Deemah. None of these dudes even made eye contact with him as they crowded the top of the stairs, not letting him onto the terrace. And it made him feel terrible. Did they really think he betrayed all of them by voting to give Lucifer a chance at redemption?

He shoved his hands into his jeans front pockets and waited as they began to shift to the right.

Maybe he should try talking to them again? Before he told Azrael about Zanth.

He stepped onto the terrace. "Dudes, look—I'm sorry you feel this way. If you'd just let me explain, you'd understand."

But understanding and not wanting to kill him were two different things right now.

Muriel staggered backward from a blow that Kesien delivered and collided with Jack.

Jack fell backward into the grass.

Muriel adjusted her wings and charged Kesien, like she hadn't even seen Jack, and leapt back into the fighting.

The ground was hard and he wasn't wearing armor. He brushed off his Henley, ignored the pain, and got to his feet, the soles of his Vans rasping against the stones.

And stepped back onto the terrace.

"Just give me thirty seconds," he said, raising his voice. "And then I'll leave you dudes alone. I promise."

This time, Kesien pivoted and checked Jack with his right shoulder. Knocking Jack off his feet. Into the grass again.

He pulled himself up on his knees, the dull pain vibrating through his rib cage and his left shoulder. Taking a few breaths, he blocked out the pain and got to his feet. And rushed up the steps to the terrace, but this time Deemah blocked his path.

"Wow, seriously, Deemah?" he said finally. "You dudes won't even give me thirty seconds to explain? Me? After everything we've been through."

He moved left around Deemah, but Anahera was suddenly there, blocking his path.

He stepped around her to the right.

Muriel rushed at him, shield up. An inch from his face. Blocking his path.

"Let it go, Jack."

He moved left, away from her. "No. Not until you listen. This is crazy!"

Deemah's and Kesien's shields landed sharp, upward blows to his chest and chin. Knocking him several feet into the air and halfway across the grass.

The ground slammed against his chest, knocking the air out of his lungs. His head snapped backward, hitting the ground like a sledgehammer. Blowing out all the lights as everything went completely dark.

———

SOMETIME LATER, blackness lightened to a soft grey.

He opened one eye to a slit, his head throbbing.

Eolowen's terrace was still off to his left, stones white and pristine. Clash of swords against shields still thundered across the meadow. Parrish blue skies still flowed around the lower Heavens, accented with ribbons of Constable clouds that scuttled past.

But he still wasn't sure if he was dead or not.

Sounds were muffled, like they'd been gathered into a long, narrow funnel.

No, it was worse than that. Things weren't muffled. They were silent.

He watched two angels spar, one slamming an Eternean sword against a shield. And the blade made no sound when it struck the shield.

He frowned, concentrating on the blade, waiting for it to strike the shield again. When it finally connected, Jack waited for the tinny, sharp clang to reverberate against the metal shield.

But there was no sound.

He swallowed a panicked breath.

No sound at all.

As he turned his throbbing head, gazing around the terrace, he noticed that Talia's squad had finally stopped sparring. They moved down the steps and stood around him in the grass, frowning at him. He groaned.

Were they planning to hang him by his wings from Eolowen's rooftop?

Muriel opened her mouth, shouting at him. Not a sound came out.

He glanced at Kesien standing to Muriel's left. The six-foot-sixish angel of death was also opening and closing his mouth, without a sound. Anahera was on Muriel's right. Deemah on her right. All moving their mouths in the silence.

Where they using those angel notes? So, he couldn't hear them?

A cold chill rolled across his skin. No angel notes. They were speaking words. Soundless. That he couldn't hear.

With fierce, angry expressions, Muriel and Kesien began to pace along the edge of the terrace, swords raised. Moving away from him and then back again.

Jack tried to skitter backward, but every movement made his head throb worse. Wincing, he closed his eyes, waiting for them to hit him again.

For several moments, he waited. But no blows fell. Only when someone shook his shoulder did he open one eye.

He pulled back from whoever had painfully gripped his shoulder.

Muriel. Shouting at him again. But not making a sound.

He stared down at the ground, waiting for her to shield bash him again.

Another shake.

This time, he looked at her.

She yelled at him, her lips moving up and down, but he heard nothing. Just saw her lips moving and her mouth opening and closing.

Someone touched his arm.

He glanced to his right.

Anahera. Kneeling in the grass beside him, lips moving in silence. Then Kesien was beside her, his lips moving up and down, forming words Jack couldn't hear.

He frowned, shrugging as he tried to get to his feet. But everything tilted and he fell back into the grass.

He couldn't hear their voices. None of them.

3

*T*alia hovered in front of the door to Azrael's study that was tucked in a small alcove off Eolowen's main hall. Hints of honeysuckle blossoms floated above the smell of old books as the archangel thrust open the door and drifted through the threshold. He left the door open and Talia followed him inside.

Sunlight poured across the white stones and the antique desk he sometimes hovered behind, reading or meditating. The desk seemed to change with Azrael's moods and today, the desk was a white Louis XVI style, ivory with gold accents along its delicate curves and ivory scrollwork legs. The top of the desk was a smooth walnut, varnished and shiny. And stacked with old books. Along all three walls stood translucent bookshelves filled with human books. Azrael loved books. Collected them.

He floated in front of the desk, turning around to face Talia, looking worried and tense. She hadn't seen him this tense since the day he first informed her about Lucifer's wager.

"Talia, how is Lucifer doing?" he asked, looking concerned. "I know it's only been a day or two since he joined the guard, but a moment ago, I thought he was trying to kill Jack with a sword."

Talia adjusted her wing span wider, allowing her to float in front of Azrael.

"Sir, I confess, I haven't learned to read Lucifer yet. But ever since he's been in Heaven, his moods have shifted like the wind. He is troubled and still struggling with his sudden release from his chains. And this chance at redemption he's been given. But he's made no move to familiarize himself with the guard. And with the situation with Samael going nuclear, we're out of time and don't have the luxury of preparation. He has to become one of us by first light—or at least fight as one of us."

Azrael's wings fluttered, moving around the room. Pacing.

"Agreed, Talia. I'm terrified he's going to decide he's bored with the likes of the lower Heavens. Angels of death." He sighed and restacked the books on his desk. "And that he doesn't need redemption after all, joining forces with Samael and launching a renewed attack on Heaven. Starting with Jack."

Talia shook her head. "I don't think so, sir," she said. "Not this time. I don't know how much, but I do see changes in him. Patient and calm. I even heard him say that he wasn't going to waste his chance at redemption."

Azrael lifted an eyebrow. "Really?"

She nodded. "And he's already pressed Jack for why he voted to spare him."

"Lucifer has always been direct. What did Jack tell him?"

Talia leaned against one of the bookshelves, scent of moldy books tickling her nose.

"Jack told him that he'd seen a lot of moments of good from Lucifer and that he understood his parent issues and feelings of abandonment because of his own past." She nodded toward the door. "That seemed to surprise Lucifer. I think Jack's vote humbled Lucifer in ways he's still processing. In a good way."

"Never dreamed the Maker would spare him," Azrael muttered as he slid away from the desk. "Anything else?"

"Yes, sir," said Talia, continuing. "Jack also told Lucifer that without his pain from feeling betrayed and abandoned, things might have turned out differently. And that Lucifer deserved the chance to find out. Lucifer looked moved by Jack's forgiveness."

Azrael slipped around to the front of the desk and leaned against it, his face scrunched into an intense mask of concentration.

"Lucifer's not the only one. Most of Heaven is reeling over the Maker's decision to spare Lucifer and they're confused by Jack voting to spare him." Azrael pointed over Talia's shoulder toward the terrace. "And your squad is furious at Jack. Did you know that?"

"What? Furious?" Talia felt a chill rush across her wings. "I know they're angry, but furious?"

"Muriel won't even look at Jack," said Azrael, pacing around the chamber again. "Kesien and Deemah look livid every time they see Jack." Azrael held up both hands. "Even Anahera is angry at him."

Talia bristled, but she felt conflicted. Her squad chose not to discuss this with her, yet Azrael and half the guard knew how they felt. It frustrated her. No, it ticked her off.

"I know they've refused to train or even spar with him." She frowned. "And I intend to straighten that out very shortly."

Her squad had always loved and supported Jack. The entire guard. Granted, they had every right to be conflicted by Lucifer's presence in Eolowen. But to blame Jack for it? Poor Jack. He'd be devastated when he realized that the guard—her squad—was shunning him.

And she felt terrible about it.

"I can't order them to ignore their feelings, sir," she said with a sigh. "But I know Jack will be devastated."

Azrael was beside her, arms folded against his chest. "We'll just have to get through this battle and hope, when it matters, the guard will support Jack, too. Then we'll give all of them time to sort through this—after we've stopped Armageddon. And Archangel Samael. And hopefully end this beast of prophecy at the same time." He drifted back toward the desk, his gaze darkening.

Talia nodded. "And keep Armageddon far, far into the future, I hope."

Azrael's eyes narrowed, his gaze distant.

"Although, I don't know what will happen to this prophesied beast if we defeat Samael. Even if Raum dies, another will rise at a future time, I suppose—at the final battle." He shook his head. "Calling this war with Samael the final battle between good and evil is an insult to both good and evil."

Talia nodded. She couldn't agree more. At best, Archangel Samael was a scavenger and an opportunist, surviving by selfishness and cowardly self-preservation. Sending his troops ahead to die for him, so he could run and fight again.

Evil? Yes. Powerful? No.

"We're almost out of time," Talia said, wincing at the thought of her squad's current lack of cohesiveness as they faced Samael tomorrow.

Kesien's wings were not a hundred percent healed yet. Deemah was second-guessing her decisions, blaming herself for Kesien's capture. Anahera's fears over being ambushed again were slowing down her reflexes and limiting her battle prowess. And now that Lucifer was here with the guard, Talia knew that Muriel's hatred for him would keep her watching him and not the battle. Would their anger toward Jack make them act even more recklessly?

She just hoped no one got hurt—especially Jack.

"I know," said Azrael in a worried voice, glancing at the sunlight pooling along the white stone floor. "The lament of the seventh flight is more than most of us can bear right now—a painful reminder of how little time there is to fix this. Much less process everything...like Lucifer's chance at redemption."

Talia nodded, her thoughts drifting back to Jack. He didn't understand (or accept) her squad's anger toward him. He would be shocked and devastated by their shunning him. But he didn't realize that by shunning him, the guard was treating him as an equal. So, in many ways, their reaction was a compliment to him. They weren't treating him like a human. They were treating him like one of their own.

But again, they'd forgotten that Jack was human and his capacity for forgiveness was vast. He lacked millennia of pain and memories to harden his heart and narrow his forgiveness to a tiny pinpoint of light that almost no one—angel, demon, or human—could ever hope to stand in…something her guard should model.

Jack had only lived twenty-seven years, but in ignorant human bliss of the evil forces that angels fought daily. Evil that spanned eons. Evil that had existed from the moment of Creation, hidden in the shadows. Azrael was right though. Everyone needed time to process these events, but right now, they were out of time. They had to act. Assault Samael's growing evil. And set things back onto their intended timetables.

The time for healing had to come later.

"I know we need everyone in the guard fighting together. As one. But right now, Azrael, there are lots of hurt feelings and walls going up."

The archangel grimaced. "I know. That's why I asked Sidriel to send her guard with mine while she stands with Turiel's guard and the cherubim to defend Heaven. Her guard will help stabilize my guard. That will leave Turiel's guard to also cover human soul crossovers until we return."

Talia and the guard had worked with Sidriel's guard before. When they marched on Heaven to rescue Berith and retrieve the Book of Secrets. Their presence would equalize the field and lessen the damage until Talia's guard came to terms with Lucifer's presence—and Jack's vote. But Lucifer's redemption had to be just as personal to Sidriel's guard as it was to hers.

After Raum and those archangels destroyed the angel of death squads protecting Kushiel's couriers, they had to feel the same.

"Archangel!" shouted a voice from the doorway. "Talia! You need to come quick!"

That was Daidrean's voice.

Azrael blinked through the doorway and into the hall and Talia followed him.

Daidrean, dark brown hair windblown, charcoal grey eyes filled with worry, hovered beside them, shield in hand, dove grey wings beating the air, and Eternean armor bright against the shadowed alcove.

"What's wrong, Daidrean?" Azrael asked.

"Talia, your squad just clashed with Jack and—"

"What?" she cried, taking hold of Daidrean's shoulder. "Where's Jack?"

Daidrean squirmed. "I think they were just trying to teach him a lesson, but something happened and Jack…isn't quite right."

A chill burned across her skin. Not quite right? What did that mean?

"What in blazes does that mean, Daidrean?" Azrael demanded.

"Show me!" Talia shouted. "Take me to him. Now."

Nodding, Daidrean blinked down the hallway and up through a portal in the roof.

Talia and Azrael followed.

From the long nave's rooftop, Talia saw her squad huddled around Jack in the grass near the willow tree.

She blinked across the sky twice. Landing in the middle of her squad as they surrounded Jack. Azrael landed behind her, Daidrean to Azrael's left. Daidrean moved beside Deemah who looked shaken.

"Jack, stop this petty refusal to speak and answer me!" Kesien shouted, hands on Jack's arms. "Are you all right?"

"Stop it, Jack!" Muriel shouted. "Answer Kesien."

Jack looked dazed and just stared at Kesien, shaking his head.

"Jack!" Talia cried as she dropped down in front of him and laid her hand against his bruised chin.

He flinched, his pale green eyes watery as he stared at her, looking so sad that it hurt her heart.

"Jack, talk to me," she said, watching him carefully. "Are you all right?"

His eyes narrowed as he pressed his mouth into a taut, worried line, brow furrowed, head shaking.

"Jack?" she repeated, trying her best to remain calm. "Jack, answer me. Please. Are you hurt?" She said it slower this time, but he just didn't respond.

Gently, he reached out his fingers and laid them against her mouth and then shook his head.

What did that mean? But he just kept touching her mouth and then she realized.

She leaned against his left side and sang four angel notes against his ear. The notes were in a pitch that was uncomfortable, but they were notes his human ears could hear. But he didn't even flinch.

He couldn't hear her.

"Jack, touch my face if you can hear me," she cried.

He didn't react, sending worried whispers through her squad.

Quickly, she called up some white Holy fire and with her fingers, drew words in the air in front of him.

Jack, can you hear me?

His expression turned sad as he stared at Talia and slowly shook her head.

"What?" Muriel cried. "Are you saying he's deaf?"

Talia shrugged and gripped Jack's hand. "That's what he's telling me."

The squad got really quiet.

"All right," Talia demanded, gazing around at the guilty looks on her colleagues' faces. "Someone better start telling me what happened. Now."

Muriel sighed. "We were just trying to show Jack we were still angry at him."

"Muriel," she snapped. "What did you do?"

"He wanted to talk to us," said Kesien in a quiet voice. "We were just sending him the message that we didn't want him here. And to stay off the terrace."

Deemah glared. "Yeah, that we weren't going to do anything with him as a squad." She shook her head. "Not after he chose Lucifer instead of the guard."

"We were just trying to scare him a little," said Kesien. "That's all. Make him think about the consequences of his actions for once."

"That's when Deemah's and Kesien's shields connected with Jack, knocking him backward," said Anahera. "Halfway across the grounds. He hit the grass hard."

All four of them bowed their heads, red-faced, looking ashamed.

Talia was furious.

"After everything Jack's done for this squad and you couldn't be bothered to talk to him?" she demanded. "To discuss the situation? All because you disagreed with his vote?"

"Talia," Kesien said with a growl. "He voted to spare that monster!"

"And that monster could have been you, Kesien—make no mistake," said an angry but velvety baritone voice that floated across the meadow, words precise and sounding British.

Lucifer.

"So self-righteous and filled with angelic fury. Murderous. Only wanting vengeance against the archangel who betrayed you and your guard. And you were willing to do anything it took to make him atone, weren't you, Kesien?"

Kesien looked unnerved at Lucifer's sudden presence. He stared at the fallen angel with a mixture of fear and fury.

"Still are, from the looks of you," Lucifer continued, brow furrowed, blue eyes sparking with fire. "And that moment in the Lake of Fire cavern," Lucifer continued, walking toward them. "When your wings had been all but burnt off. Your hair burned almost to your scalp. Who took down the archangels restraining you? Saved your miserable existence. Who was there every time the rest of Heaven told you to solve it yourself?"

Kesien sighed.

"Yes, that's right, my overzealous angel of death friend." He turned toward Muriel and she turned pale. "And you...Muriel. Who put himself in front of killing blows for you? Who stood between you and my army of darkness, my demons. More than once. Who would have taken a killing blow for you again?" He motioned at the entire squad. "For any one of you in this squad—not just Talia."

Her squad looked ashamed now, staring at their feet, at the ground, looking at Jack with painful squints.

"Yes, that's right. Jack Casey would have. So, instead of treating him fairly, you shun him like you're scraping something off your sandals. All because he chose redemption instead of destruction. Damned brave of him to take the long road, wouldn't you say? The one all of Heaven ignored. It certainly wasn't the easiest road. And no, I didn't deserve it either."

Muriel's eyes turned glassy as she glanced at Jack and then down at her boots. Anahera had her arms folded against her breastplate, staring down at the meadow.

"Having someone who has that kind of faith in you," said Lucifer, motioning at Jack. "Just one person who sees the light that you don't. And despite knowing your darkest moments and what you're capable of, they still choose light and redemption...well, that is a rare and fragile thing. Especially in a human. Don't lose that."

Lucifer, hands behind his back, walked around the squad, the silence heavy and uncomfortable as he studied each of Talia's squad. Judging them? No, he was warning them. To not be like him. Explaining why Jack did what he did.

"And know this," said Lucifer, behind them.

Talia turned to face him.

"Jack Casey would be that one light in your corner as well. The one lone voice demanding that one last chance at redemption for you. Come Hell or high water and he's stood in both. So, whatever anger you're carrying for him, please...direct it at me, not him. Because he doesn't deserve it. He's damned brave to be the one voice following the last flicker of someone's light, believing it will turn into a beacon."

Talia helped Jack to his feet. "Come on, Jack," she said, knowing he couldn't hear her. "Let's get you to Berith. Hopefully, she can heal this."

Jack held onto her arm as she led him inside Eolowen. She shouted for Berith until the redeemed angel appeared in the round room.

"Talia, what's happened?" she asked as Talia sat Jack down on the bed.

"Jack's hearing seems to have left him after a hard fall," said Talia. "Can you heal him?"

Berith slid a yellow, palm-sized gem out of her charcoal grey robe pocket. "I still have the gem infused with seraphim healing I used on Kesien. That should do the trick."

Talia slipped out of the round room and blinked back toward the willow tree, where Azrael's angry voice rose on the wind.

"And if we don't assault Samael as one voice," Azrael shouted. "As one force…he and his beast will destroy us. All of Creation. Do you all understand that?"

Her squad members nodded and assured Azrael that they were all well aware of that fact.

"And like it or not, that now includes Lucifer," said Azrael. "I understand your anger and your mistrust. At this moment, you have no reason to trust Lucifer. Find one. Before first light."

"First light?" Muriel replied, casting an uncertain look at Talia and then Azrael. "Are you serious, sir?"

"As serious as that eerie requiem from the seventh flight circling the Heavens," said Azrael. "We leave for Hell at first light. To end this Nephion beast and bring back Samael in chains before the seventh flight touches down on Earth. And Lucifer will be at the front of our assault, so I suggest you locate some trust. Fast."

In a moment or two, Berith walked out onto the terrace, steering Jack into the meadow. Jack looked…vulnerable. Upset. When Berith reached the willow tree with him, he stopped in front of Azrael, wings flat against his back, halo a little crooked. Jack refused to look at Muriel or Kesien. But not out of anger, she realized.

It was shame. He didn't want to face her squad.

"Jack!" Talia cried, wanting to rush to him and wrap her arms around him, but his demeanor made her stop.

She knew he had to work this out with the squad himself. Not through her. She just wished that he'd heard Lucifer defend him.

"Jack, can you hear me?" Berith replied.

He glanced back at her and finally, he nodded. "Yeah."

His voice was devoid of emotion or momentum. It was deadpan and flat.

At hearing him speak and confirm he'd heard Berith, the squad seemed to relax a little, the tension dissipating.

"Jack," said Muriel in a sheepish tone. "Look, I'm sorry. I didn't mean to hit you with my shield so hard like that."

Kesien didn't say a word. He walked up to Jack and laid his hand on Jack's arm, squeezing.

Jack bit his lip.

"I'm sorry, Kesien," Jack said in a quiet voice. "Deemah. Anahera. I should have just stayed out of the way."

"Forget it, Jack," said Deemah. "We should have trusted you."

He looked surprised now.

Kesien nodded. "You turned out to be more of an optimist than any of us expected."

Muriel moved over to Jack and ruffled his hair. "I'm really sorry. Forgive me?"

At last, his eyes brightened. "You know I do." He pulled Muriel into a hug.

"We still squad mates?" Kesien asked, extending his hand to Jack.

"If you let me back into the squad," said Jack, shaking Kesien's hand.

"Back in?" said Deemah and patted Jack on the back. "Jack, you've never left."

"You're our vanguard," said Muriel."

At Deemah's and Muriel's remarks, he smiled at her and emerged from the silence and shame and uncertainty he'd been feeling since he'd cast his vote at the tribunal.

When Jack saw Azrael, his gaze darkened. He needed to tell the archangel about Zanth. "Uh, Azrael, there's something you need to know."

Azrael frowned. "What is it, Jack?"

Jack's gaze shot toward the end of the meadow. And the crossroads.

"While I was on a call with my sister," said Jack, his gaze still hanging at the edge of Eolowen's meadow. "I saw someone."

And that worried Talia. A lot.

Azrael raised an eyebrow. "Someone? At the crossroads?"

He nodded. "Tre Sheridan. The soul of Zanth's lover who was in purgatory."

The squad went quiet, faces scrunching, gazes growing distant. Except for Talia and Azrael. Lucifer looked intrigued.

"This can't be good," said Muriel.

"Jack, you saw Tre Sheridan?" said Talia, laying her hand against his cheek.

He nodded.

Azrael frowned. "The archdemoness' lover?"

Jack nodded again. "Tre committed suicide to help Samael get the Book of Secrets out of purgatory."

"Yes! I remember now." Azrael. "What is an escaped purgatory soul doing here? And where's the archdemoness?"

"Good questions," said Jack. "He was begging me to help Zanth."

"My archdemoness?" Lucifer replied, hands on his hips as his gaze shot toward the crossroads. "Whatever for?"

"Yeah, your Zanth, Lucifer," said Jack. "And according to Tre, Samael is using her to create a Nephion army."

"That's monstrous!" Talia cried.

It made Talia ill to think about that. Was Archangel Samael forcing himself on Zanth? Forcing her to birth those half demon half angel hybrids? And not just demons...they would be archdemons. And not just angels. Archangels. These Nephions would be tough to fight. And no one had any idea how many already inhabited Hell. No one except Archangel Samael. How had an archangel managed to become so twisted and filled with hate?

Somehow, the guard had to stop Samael.

Sure, Zanth was a demon and tried to kill her and Jack on their honeymoon. But later, she helped them go after Archangel Samael. And the Book of Secrets. She'd even reunited Jack with his father in purgatory for a little while. And now, she was being violated in ways that made Talia sick all over. For that alone, she wanted to strike down Archangel Samael...along with all the other harm Samael had done to her guard. And Azrael.

Was Raum her son? The firstborn Nephion, half archdemon, half archangel. The beast of prophecy. Archangel Samael's secret weapon. She glanced at Lucifer.

The former King of Hell looked murderous, his blue eyes turning red, narrowing, teeth gritted as he smashed his hands into fists.

"I will make Samael pay for his avarice. And for every assault on Zanth. I don't know how he was able to subdue an archdemoness of her power, but these Nephions are unlike anything you've fought before."

Lucifer clenched his hands into fists and began to pace, his red eyes darkening as fury tightened his features. Talia expected horns to sprout from his forehead and his feet to turn cloven, but that part of Lucifer seemed to have disappeared. But his rage was electric and she felt it from here.

"Azrael," he snapped, whirling around. "We must end this unrepentant monster before he creates an unstoppable army. With archangel and archdemon-level powers. You know the devastation they're capable of...and the longer we wait, the more we will have to fight."

Azrael's charcoal grey eyes narrowed, his expression pinched. "We leave at first light, Lucifer."

"What horrific things he must have already done to poor Zanth?" Lucifer winced, bowing his head, the remorse haunting his angry red eyes. "This is my fault."

"No, Luci, it's Samael's fault," said Jack. "And I'll help you take him down."

Lucifer studied Jack for a moment and then smiled. "Much appreciated, Jack."

Talia knew that with so many angelic losses during the apocalypse —especially the loss of two seraph—Heaven had a fight on its hands. Even with Lucifer leading the charge. Most of the losses were Lucifer's fault, so it was only fitting that he fix this. But it wasn't going to be easy.

"All right, squads!" Azrael shouted across the meadow and the terrace. "Gather around."

All of the guard, including Sidriel's angels of death, fluttered across the sky and hovered above the willow tree. Angels on the terrace paused their drills and moved into the meadow. They crowded together and huddled close to the archangel, giving Azrael their full attention.

"Finish your drills. Ready your armor and weapons. We leave at first light, following the road to perdition. To Hell. Where Archangel Samael has assumed Lucifer's vacant throne and will be sending an army of demons and Nephions against us, including one that prophecy calls the beast. With these Nephions who carry the power of an archdemon and an archangel, Samael intends to force the battle of Armageddon to begin. To stop this battle from starting and ending the world, we must defeat Samael and Raum, the being from prophecy. Or take them prisoner...before the seventh flight touches down on the Earth. Now, go and prepare. Time is short."

Talia reached out and pulled Jack close, wrapping her arms around him. He slid his arms around her and she laid her head against his shoulder.

"Ready to take down this archangel douchebag, Mrs. Casey?" he asked in a subdued voice.

Talia nodded. "From the very first time that Samael and his guard appeared in the skies above Eolowen with swords drawn," she said. "From his very first betrayal. It's long overdue."

"Couldn't agree more, Talia," said Kesien, sheathing his sword.

"We have to take him down," said Jack. "Otherwise, Earth ceases to exist. And then how would we celebrate our first anniversary at our beach house, Mrs. Casey?"

She smiled, kissing him.

Jack pulled her tighter against him, his hand stroking her hair. "Besides, if that happens, Heaven gets stuck with me. And nobody wants that."

Muriel and Kesien smiled, Muriel ruffling his blond hair before following Kesien and the rest of the squad back to the terrace.

If they didn't take Samael down, once and for all, Talia knew it was the end of everything. And maybe having Lucifer at the forefront of this battle would make all the difference?

4

Just before dawn in the watercolor twilight, Jack stood at the edge of Azrael's dais, dressed in the guard's gold Eternean armor, including the short grey robe/dress he hated, gold greaves, sabatons, bracers, and pauldrons. Wind blew through his silver-grey wings that were loosely folded at his shoulders, feathers rippling as he tensed them. Worried about the battle in Hell.

His Eternean sword bobbed in a sheath at his left side as he watched the crossroads for movement. Sniffed the air for any trace of sulfur. Listened for the shuffling rustle of those leathery black demon wings or the soft padding of shadow panthers.

But everything was quiet. Even the seventh flight's lament was absent, but he knew it wouldn't be long before they cycled back around over Eolowen in their ghostly, terrifying holding pattern. Waiting to end his world. He swallowed hard and gripped the hilt of his sword.

It felt awkward in his fist. He preferred using his seraphim and rare angel powers over a sword, but it came with the armor, so he carried it just in case. Besides, it made him better blend into the guard. So, he'd have less chance of being singled out and attacked. The guard needed his seraphim powers today. Powers that would keep the love of his life safe, too.

He heard Azrael behind him, ascending his dais. In a moment, another voice joined his in the quiet. Lucifer's warm, bright voice sounded serious this morning, so Jack listened carefully when a third voice joined them. Pravuil. The Maker's Scribe. And his tone was as dire as his words.

Talia's musical soprano voice lilted above the rumble of Pravuil's gruff tone.

Last minute huddle. They were tenth and goal, fourth quarter. Two-minute warning. And they refused to punt. But the sound of her voice was intoxicating and Jack drank it in...listening.

"You have to take that putz's spawn down fast." Pravuil said, grumbling.

"And the putz. We cannot let that traitorous winged prat escape again." Lucifer.

Jack groaned. Like he hadn't heard all of this before. What he needed to hear was how. How did they take these monsters down fast?

He hoped his hearing stayed sharp. Berith told him that the sudden, hard blow to his head caused his temporary deafness. It probably would have cleared up on its own in a few hours, but she used the seraphim healing just in case he'd ruptured an eardrum. Regardless, he needed all his senses when the guard entered the depths of Hell. She warned him to wear a helmet because it could happen again.

Jack turned toward the dais, pretending like he was checking his gear, but he needed to hear what Pravuil was saying.

Azrael's face was taut, his eyes steely, mouth pressed into a flat line. He looked so worried and tense—like he had at the tribunal. Lucifer stood tall and intimidating, appearing stoic but deadly. But Jack saw the glint of fire in those pale blue eyes. He was angry. Pravuil looked crankier than usual, eyebrows pressed down over his hawkish gold eyes, nose wrinkled, and upper lip curled. And Talia's grey eyes were owl-big, waxing like full moons, her face pale, fingers tangled into a clenched knot as she quietly discussed the plan.

Bring down Samael and Raum. Fast. First two objectives set in stone. But beyond that, Jack had his own agenda. At the top of it was saving Earth then Zanth. He had to get her out of there before Abaddon and Kushiel entered behind them, completely shifting the punishment of damned souls. And addressing the issue of the fallen angels who fell with Lucifer.

Zanth had proven her loyalty and Jack wouldn't leave her for Kushiel to eternally punish when she wanted to redeem herself.

"I regret that we must divide into two forces," said Azrael.

Jack swallowed a breath.

"What?" Talia cried. "No, Azrael, that's too dangerous!"

"Talia, we have no choice," said Azrael in a forlorn tone. "Samael and Raum won't be together down there. Intentionally. To try to divide and conqueror us."

"But splitting up is so dangerous when we don't know how many Nephions are down there." Talia replied, looking worried as she folded her arms against her breastplate. "Is that wise, Azrael?"

He sighed, looking conflicted as he shifted his wings against his shoulders. "Can't be helped, Talia. Even with Sidriel's guard along, we're outnumbered. One force must challenge and defeat Raum. Quickly. While the second force breaks into offense and flank, with the goal of surrounding and capturing Samael."

Lucifer nodded. "Agreed. We can't risk one of them escaping. Fighting them in two theatres is the only option."

"In two angel days, at sunset California time," said Pravuil, his eyes narrowing, "the seventh flight will touch down on Earth." Pravuil's gold, eagle-eyed gaze got sharper and more intense. "You must have Samael off Hell's throne by then—dead or in chains—and Raum dead or in chains. If not, the battle of Armageddon will play out and the Creation—all of it—will expire. I know you've heard it a million times, but I have to make sure you understand what's at stake and when we've crossed the point of no return."

Azrael closed his eyes and nodded. Lucifer sighed, glaring as he glanced toward the crossroads. Talia's entire focus was on Pravuil's words.

Jack knew that Talia and the guard had the most to lose if they failed in Hell. Most immediate at any rate. He, on the hand, would lose everything. Gianni and Izzy, Banks and Morgan, his sisters—the planet. Literally everything.

"We get it, Pravuil," said Lucifer finally, his gaze shifting from the Scribe to Azrael. "All right, Azrael ol' boy, how do you want to play this?"

Azrael laid his hand against his chin and stared into the distance, deep in thought. Jack could almost see the thoughts passing across his eyes.

It was so surreal watching Azrael and Lucifer planning an assault together.

"Raum must be brought down first...and fast," said Azrael. "Stopping Armageddon. He hasn't achieved his full power yet and despite his parents, he isn't as powerful as he thinks. Not yet anyway. My guard with Talia's squad leading it, Jack as vanguard, will have the best chance of defeating him quickly. Do you agree?"

Talia nodded. Lucifer thought for a moment and then nodded.

"My worry is Samael escaping," said Azrael. "Again. Lucifer, you and I are the best chance of capturing Samael, ensuring he does not get away this time. I will lead Sidriel's squads. Lucifer, you will flank Samael with my remaining guard. He won't expect you. Talia, when you and the other squads have brought down Raum, you and the guard will join Lucifer's flank. And we will make sure that Samael does not escape this time. Questions? Concerns?"

Lucifer chewed his bottom lip. "A sound plan, Azrael. But I recommend adding Kushiel to your offensive when you attack Samael."

Azrael frowned. "Kushiel? Why?"

Lucifer smiled. "Because Samael is terrified of Lord Kushiel. When he sees Kushiel, free of Raum's control, he'll know that his reign of annoyance is over. And he'll fear Kushiel's punishment. And start making mistakes—more of them, that is."

Azrael paced back and forth along the dais, finally nodding his head.

"I like that," he said, hand still on his chin. "Setting him off guard will only work in our favor." He turned to Pravuil. "Will you brief Kushiel, Scribe?"

Pravuil chuckled. "Trust me, Azrael, Kushiel will be thrilled. He hasn't forgiven Samael's forced control over him at the tribunal. And he intends to fully punish the transgressor who caused it. Raum may have been causing it, but Samael was pulling the strings."

Satisfied, Azrael returned to the dais. He glanced past Pravuil, smiling.

Berith stood behind Pravuil.

"I'll leave you a few moments with Berith before you depart," said Pravuil as he spread his wings wide and blinked away from the dais, headed toward High House.

Probably to inform the Maker after he'd tapped Kushiel into this fight. Jack knew Kushiel would jump at the chance to help bring down Samael. Jack doubted that there was an angel in Heaven who didn't look forward to that moment. The most annoying archangel ever. He hoped Kesien wouldn't go ballistic and become a loose cannon when he found himself a last minute add to flanking Samael.

Lucifer stepped away from the dais, gathering up his weapons and putting on Heaven's armor. Would he wear his sleek black ebony armor or the guard's gold Eternean armor? Lucifer hefted a breastplate off a terrace bench and Jack saw the shiny black glistening in the dawn.

Wearing the Devil's armor. He wanted Samael to know who was coming for him. And why. He wanted that annoying little douchebag to cower before him when he saw the might of Heaven and Hell on his doorstep. Shackles ready.

Couldn't happen to a bigger asshalo than Archangel Samael.

Jack still needed to find Zanth in Hell and find a way to release her. He owed her that. After Samael was in chains. And one more little errand.

In a blur, Talia blinked across the grass to him, wrapping her arms around his neck.

"Everything okay, Jack?"

He nodded. "Tal, you know I have to help Zanth, right? Get her out of there?"

"No," she snapped. "*We* have to help her. Because helping her is doing the right thing. After we stop Armageddon."

Smiling, he pulled her into a kiss. "I knew I married the right woman."

"Yes, you did, Mr. Casey," she said, stroking his clean-shaven face. "And I can't wait to celebrate our first anniversary together."

Jack glanced across the terrace at the guard assembling, wondering how many of them still wanted to tear off his wings and then his limbs for voting to save Lucifer. It made him sad, knowing that angels who'd been like family to him now had no use for him. He sighed. Like his mother had disowned him.

"Think Muriel and Kesien will ever speak to me again?" he asked, the smile fading from his face.

Talia stroked his cheek. "Jack...they've already apologized. Just be patient and give them time to adjust. If it hadn't been for you, they'd all be in a standoff, refusing to work with Lucifer. They love you."

He shrugged. "With an apple in my mouth maybe. I've never seen Muriel that cold before." His gaze fell to his feet. "That hurt. A lot. And seeing Kesien glare at me like I was a demon he needed to crush...hit me right in the feels. Miss those guys."

Talia kissed his lips. "It'll be all right, Jack. They'll make their peace with Lucifer. They already realize that you did the right thing."

Did she think he did the right thing?

"What do you think, Tal?" he asked.

She stroked his cheek again. "I think you did the right thing, Jack. And we're about to prove it when we descend into Hell."

Jack glanced around. "So, what are we waiting for?"

Talia glanced toward the crossroads, but her intense gaze snapped toward the sky as that creepy, dark chant hung above the clouds, the seventh flight making another ghostly rotation above the lower Heavens.

Finally, her gaze zeroed in on something in the distance toward the edge of the meadow that reached almost to the crossroads. It was little more than a shadow beneath the clouds and Jack couldn't tell if it was a bird or his imagination until finally, the grey-on-grey shadow emerged near the white stone pergola, dipping low. And two Watchers landed near Azrael's dais.

Talia's face turned pale, her eyes widening. "That," she said with a nod.

"Watchers?" he replied, frowning.

"Not just any Watchers, Jack," she said as Azrael stepped off the dais toward them.

Talia tugged Jack alongside her, blinking toward the Watchers.

"Watchers covertly assigned to Raum and Archangel Samael," she said, her expression brightening.

The guard, made up of both Sidriel's and Azrael's death angels, already filled the terrace and the grass surrounding Eolowen's grand hall, over two hundred strong, as Azrael stepped off his dais in front of the two tall, slender Watcher angels. One Watcher had black hair and dark skin and the other had grey hair and brown skin, both wearing grey robes. Already, their bluish white wings began to shift to a greenish grey cast, allowing them to blend in with the grass and shadows. Jack had never noticed that their wings changed color to fade into their surroundings.

"Watchers, report," said Azrael, wings twitching, hands on his hips as he stared at them.

"Both targets are currently present in Hell, making war preparations," said the Watcher with black hair.

Lucifer stood beside Azrael now, his pale blue eyes animated as he listened to the Watchers' reports.

"How far along?" Lucifer asked, looking surprised. "Are the preparations just within Hell?"

Azrael looked intrigued when the grey-haired Watcher spoke.

"Not far along," said the second Watcher. "They seem to think that they are meeting Heaven on a distant battlefield and not in Hell."

"Why in blazes would they think that?" said Azrael. "We assured them we were coming for them."

Lucifer was grinning now. "Simple, Azrael," he said. "Hubris. That I took advantage of."

Unnerved, Azrael turned to the former King of Hell, brows furrowed.

"Lucifer…" he said in a chastising tone. "What did you do?"

Lucifer shrugged, looking pleased with himself.

Jack squirmed, his gaze falling on Talia who looked frightened. Azrael looked terrified.

"Lucifer!" Azrael shouted. "What. Did you. Do?"

Lucifer glanced at the sky. "I love clouds, don't you?" he said, hands behind his back as he rocked back onto the heels of his shiny black sabatons, extending his black wings to their full length. "Always so mystical and majestic, covering Heaven in a mysterious cloak of mist."

Azrael shouted his name again as Lucifer lifted about twenty feet into the air and beat his wings hard. The clouds scattered. Revealing translucent, shimmery fabric that draped across the meadow, the pergola, and the entirety of Eolowen. And projected across that fabric were images of war preparations that included cherubim carrying vast containers of supplies between them. Toward Earth. Toward some distant battlefield.

"Lucifer, did you do this?" Azrael asked, eyes wide, voice filled with surprise and wonder.

"Yes. In a moment of brilliance. For Hell's demonic watchers, who have been encircling Heaven since my trial." His smile became a grin. "So, I just showed them what they wanted to see. A bit of a smokescreen. And they reported it all back to Samael. Just as I'd hoped."

"That's…brilliant," said Azrael.

"Dude, well-played," said Jack as he watched the images scroll beneath the clouds.

"I wanted to be sure that Samael and Raum were at home to

receive us," said Lucifer as he landed and tucked his wings back against his shoulders again. "There's no excuse for poor hospitality."

"Especially after they invited us to the party," said Jack. "I'm bringing the chips." He smirked. "And by chips, I mean murder marbles."

Lucifer chuckled, but Azrael still looked like he was in shock, still staring up at the clouds.

"How did you—"

"Archangel Zephana and her forge, some Watchers, bits of Eternean, and some angel powers," said Lucifer. "It was quite economical, really."

At last, Azrael smiled. "Lucifer, I'm impressed. Great work. Keep me in the loop next time."

Lucifer nodded. "I apologize for that oversight. I know you keep confidences. I should have told you."

"No matter," said Azrael. "Great work, Lucifer. We now have everything. Let's depart beneath the cover of this...projection fabric before the sun fills the sky.

"Samael will never see us coming now," said Lucifer.

"Why's that?" Jack asked.

Lucifer's smile didn't fade. "Because I also had the Watchers place the fabric above the road to Hell. It will reflect back quiet roads to any demons flying above it. Until we reveal ourselves to Samael and his spawn."

Azrael's smile lifted into a grin. "Then let's not keep Samael waiting."

"It'll be like the in-laws dropping in unannounced for dinner," said Jack, armor creaking as he unfurled his wings. "Can't wait to see the look on Samael's face."

Lucifer lifted his fist, teeth gritted. "Especially when he realizes, much too late, that he is a trapped rat with no way out. Not even a flight path."

Azrael blinked back to the dais.

"All right, angels! Fall into formation and prepare to blink on my mark."

Jack followed Talia across the meadow and into the lead block formation alongside Kesien, Deemah, Anahera, and Muriel. Daidrean's squad was behind them, with Deemah and Daidrean almost side by side. They had already moved closer to each other, whispering and smiling like teenagers on a first date.

Talia took her place, front and center of the five-angel block in the guard's formation, but Jack stayed behind the others, his gut clenching.

There wasn't a place in her squad's formation for him. Only room for five angels in the pentagram formation.

He winced. Talia's squad was still all kinds of pissed at him. Guess it would take more than an apology to get back into their good graces. Maybe someday, they'd understand why he'd voted to save Lucifer?

"Hey, where's the vanguard?" Muriel called to Talia.

"Talia, we're missing our vanguard," said Kesien.

Anahera spoke in a quiet voice to Talia, but Jack couldn't hear her.

Talia turned around. "He was just here," she said. "Right beside me."

She glanced around, her gaze quickly connecting with his when she saw him hanging back between the formation's many squad blocks. A sad look touched her eyes as she crossed her arms.

"Jack," she said in an empathetic tone.

The rest of the squad turned around, staring at him and he wanted to blink out of the guard, hit Hell on his own. So, he wouldn't disappoint any more angels.

He shrugged. "I didn't want to assume..."

Muriel sighed and blinked out of formation, appearing right in front of him.

"Jack," she said, a hand on his shoulder. "You will always be part of this squad, no matter how pissed at you we get."

"And our vanguard," Kesien called to him, a smile on his face.

Finally, he gave in and followed Muriel into formation, unable to hold onto his actor's mask of ambivalence. It slid away with the hint of a smile.

Kesien reached over and poked his shoulder with his fist as Anahera ruffled his hair.

Deemah laid her hand on his gold spaulders. "Can't tell you how many times they've tossed me and Kesien out of this squad, Jack."

Jack's eyes widened. "What? Are you serious?"

Kesien nodded. "A lot," he said. "Until the next fight."

Their comments made Jack's smile widen.

"Talia throws me out of the squad every few months or so, Jack," said Muriel with a chuckle. "I'd think she was mad at me if she didn't boot me out once and a while."

"That's how you know you're a full member, Jack," said Anahera, her short red hair tousled by the breeze. "Can't throw you out if we don't think you're part of the squad to begin with."

Jack laughed.

"Well, you guys taught me a valuable lesson that I won't forget for a long time," he said.

"What's that, Jack?" Talia asked.

"Make sure your squad knows how much you care about them, so when you go off and do something hell-for-leather, they won't kick your ass all the way back to Burbank for it."

"Just to the crossroads," said Talia and the squad broke into laughter.

He was glad to hear them laugh. Meant they were all on the same page again—and in this thing together. Regardless of whether Lucifer was at Azrael's left hand.

Suddenly, like a flock of seagulls diving for a dropped French fry, the entire guard of angels of death took to the air, flying low beneath the clouds. Away from...what'd Azrael call it...Lucifer's projection fabric.

Dammit! Azrael gave an angel note as the signal and he couldn't hear it. Not because of any injury. Because he was human.

Jack spread his wings wide and shot into the air, making sure he blinked across the sky well south of Lucifer's magic perdition picture show to catch up with Talia and the squad as they shot across the meadow and through the crossroads. Turning right onto the road to ruin.

Banking right, Jack followed, a beat behind the squad as Azrael lead the force away from the comfort of sunny skies, the scent of jasmine, and thick green grass. Toward the sickly brown grasslands, rocky cliffs, and stark rock formations ahead that trembled with thunder and lightning from growing thunderheads and darkening skies. Wind whipped across the road, scraping the rocks and the dirt, wild with electric energy, and smelling like ozone and sulfur.

The farther they traveled away from the crossroads, the darker and stormier the skies got, bringing back all kinds of bad memories of the first time they assaulted Hell. Lightning split the dark skies, thunder a ubiquitous rumble.

Jack shuddered, remembering the fear and uncertainty he'd felt after Lucifer abducted Berith and taunted him to come after her. In Hell.

Or worse, when Lucifer tethered Jack's soul and dragged him off to Hell that first time. Along this very same road.

Jack remembered his panic. The surrealness of it. The terror he'd felt being surrounded by a massive force of squirming, frenetic demons crawling all over him as the yawning cavern of Hell burned ahead, the overpowering stench of sulfur making him hurl as they descended into the oppressive well of heat and dark, only the glow of lava and demon eyes to light the way. And the whole time, he knew he couldn't escape. That he'd never see his world—his home—again.

He jumped, pulse racing as someone grabbed his arm. He jerked his head up, gulping air.

Talia. Flying beside him. She seemed to know how much this was freaking him out, even though Lucifer was only ten feet in front of him, on guard and wary as he flew beside Azrael. Fighting for Heaven. Was this really happening?

"Doing okay, husband?" Talia asked.

He nodded, but the unconvinced look on her face bore right through his chest.

"Actually, no," he said with a sigh. "I'm not."

She flew closer, sliding her arm around his waist, pulling him near enough to kiss. He struggled not to tangle his wings with hers, but Talia extended her wings and deftly kept them separated. Her mouth was warm and anxious as she pressed another soothing kiss against his dry lips. He kissed her back, hoping she wouldn't notice his lips trembling or the goosebumps prickling his skin.

Why was he reliving all this now? And letting his worry over what could happen in there overwhelm him?

Samael was a raging narcissistic douchebag, but he always had a way of causing a lot of damage and a lot of pain. Always slipping away from capture. Jack feared that more angels would get erased today. How many would be lost here? He needed to keep Talia close, but he'd never forgive himself if something happened to Azrael or Muriel or the squad.

Somehow, he had to keep them all safe.

Talia held him tight until he felt his shaking dissipate and his uncertainty ebb. Only when he saw the pale gold light did he realize that Talia was healing him.

He squeezed her hand. "Thanks, Tal."

She leaned over and kissed him again and finally, let him go, blinking back to front of the squad's block formation.

And like a mirage, the entire formation entered the winding tunnel that bore through basalt and dirt and descended into the dark, gaping maw of Hell that had been torn into the broken earth, lightning flashing around them as the tunnel tilted into an almost vertical descent. Ending in a long, wide tunnel bordered by bright red lava on the right, stalactites dripping with sulfurous water as steam roiled through the passage. Brimstone burned his nose and rasped across his lips as the stink of sulfur nearly overpowered him.

He pulled in a hot, steamy breath, trying to fill his lungs, but already, the oxygen felt thin and he felt lightheaded. He gulped air and tried to control his breathing, to psych his body into believing he wasn't about to asphyxiate.

Ahead, as the steam clouds cleared, the tall, black, forbidding Gates of Hell cast long, terrifying shadows through the tunnel that roiled with heat. He groaned. Both sides of the gates hung open about six inches or so, blown open when Lucifer broke the last of the seals. It would take work to slip through that opening, but Jack knew that too many demons had already slithered through it. At least it kept the larger more terrifying demonic creatures in Hell. Like Devourers and Eaters of Hearts. Must have kept the Nephions inside, too, or the angels would have already been fighting them.

And they would have known what they were up against instead of flying blind into Hell, hoping they had enough power to end the Nephions like the any other demon. But they knew almost nothing about Raum and his growing sibling army. Were there ten? Or a hundred? Or were they outnumbered by thousands...about to be swallowed up by a force they never had a chance at opposing?

The thought terrified Jack.

When Heaven's forces were within sight of the busted gate, Azrael halted everyone. Talia listened intently and Jack tried, but it was all angel notes.

He frowned. Shut out again.

In a heartbeat, in the unnerving silence, Lucifer disappeared into the shadows with part of Azrael's guard at his back. Taking a side tunnel that only he would have known. To get him into position to flank Samael, using the Watchers' information as his guide.

Talia's head jerked toward Azrael and Jack knew he was calling the squad into position to go after Raum. Into the abyss. Opening night with flickering stage lights, no understudy, and a full house.

Guess it was showtime. He just hoped a stage light didn't fall on his head and crush him.

In a heartbeat, Talia was beside him. Wrapping her arm in his, Talia blinked the two of them forward. In front of Azrael.

Azrael motioned ahead, past the gates.

"To the right, where the souls reside beneath the first bone bridge," said Azrael. "There is a—"

"Black tower," said Jack.

Azrael nodded. "Yes, a black tower. Forgot you spent time down here, Jack."

"Wish I could forget it," he replied. "So, Samael's spawn is holed up in Luci's penthouse," he said with a growl. "Isn't he?"

"Afraid so, Jack," said Azrael. "Watchers say he's alone. Hit him fast and hard until he's dust. And a warning. You can't come back through the Gates of Hell."

"What?" Talia replied, frowning. "Why? The gates are open enough to squeeze through."

Azrael shook his head. "True, but now, leaving Hell that way will shred your wings. It's Abaddon's latest attempt to secure Hell. Bad timing and a long story. Just take tunnels back to the vertical gallery and circle back around to my forces."

"What about Raum's powers?" Talia asked. "Do we have enough to counter it?"

"That's the beauty of our timing, Talia," said Azrael. "Raum's powers aren't at full strength yet. And they won't be until he stands on Armageddon's battlefield. You and Jack can defeat him with your combined powers." Azrael's face turned pale. "Talia, we can't fail here." His voice was quiet and dark. Dire. "We can't."

The trepidation in his voice made Jack shake all over.

"We won't lose everything, Azrael," said Talia in a reassuring tone. "Not now. Not today."

"I pray to the Maker you're right," said the archangel, motioning toward the gate. "Now, go. Let's finish this."

Talia opened her mouth and Jack only heard silence. But he knew she was singing a series of angel notes he couldn't hear until four squads of angels hovered around her. She stayed close to Jack as she motioned upward with her hand and they all rose above the tunnel floor.

He stayed right beside his beautiful angel of death wife as they passed over a river of lava that encircled the Gates of Hell, a lava moat that kept anything without wings behind those gates. But he, Talia, and five angels of death squads flew right over top of the Gates of Hell and veered right through a familiar winding corridor. Where Berith's private quarters had been. But he had no idea what Azrael meant about Abaddon's protective measures and chewing up wings trying to fly back across through the gates.

They banked through a corkscrew tunnel that twisted into three, tight curves, coming out into a cavernous space filled with the stench of sulfur as tall, old brick buildings arose out of the steam and haze. Where ravenous souls (more like animals) awaited the arrival of new, freshly damned souls to attack them. He shuddered, remembering being swarmed by them in these burned-out buildings filled with beige floors, beige walls, and beige tiles. Dirty mattresses, nightmares, and constant carnage.

All dipped in beige. Definitely a vision of hell.

Talia hugged the walls on the right, flying over the bright, bubbling stream of lava, leaving it behind as another tube fanned out into another cavernous space. Where Luci's tall, forbidding black tower rose in the distant shadows and flickering lava light. The tower cast its menacing shadow across three bone bridges that stretched high above the dusty red ground once dotted with demons, soul-filled torture frames, and metal fight cages bloody and surrounded by screaming souls and demons. All those awful memories flooded back to Jack as they flew over.

Hell had once swelled with souls and demons, but now, it looked like a creepy playground after school had let out for winter break. Or forever. The constant wail of souls had softened to raspy, distant moans and whispers that echoed above the hiss and bubble of steam rolling off the lava rivers. The brimstone smell was as thick as sulfurous clouds rose from the lava.

Ahead, in the dark and heat and flickering red flames that gave the cavern a deep ruddy glow, the black tower was dark except for a row of warm white lights gleaming across the top floor. Where Lucifer had lived for millennia. It probably still had its white leather and chrome modern furniture, priceless paintings, statues, and other priceless works of art on display. And a huge wraparound balcony that overlooked the torture posts and tall metal cage where fights once raged and demons teemed through the spaces.

Now, all the cages were empty, doors hanging open in the eerie quiet. Not a single demon lurked in this entire section of Hell. Samael's demon army had to be huge and gathered in the main caverns. It made Jack a little queasy. How many hid in the shadows, protecting Raum? And Samael? Ready to ambush the guard.

Jack stared up at the tall, ominous tower.

Luci's old place could hold a shit-ton of demons.

Were they all hiding in there? Ready to ambush them? Overwhelm them? He sighed. Make them an easy takedown for this prophecy beast that was half archangel and half archdemon.

Talia leaned against Jack as they flew low around the black tower, staying in the shadows.

"Raum's up there," said Talia. "Doesn't know we're here."

Good. At least they hadn't alerted the hybrid—and who knew how many demons—that he had company coming. Maybe no one would die fighting Samael's spoiled little hell spawn? Still, that archangel-archdemon half and half mixture meant all trouble, even if this Nephion wasn't at his full power yet.

"Be ready for anything," Talia whispered. "Especially my signal."

Talia sent two squads around the tower to the stairwell, one to the rooftop where Watchers had confirmed that the flight portal into Lucifer's old penthouse was still there. That left the rest to approach the front.

She directed Jack and the rest of the squad around the back of the tower.

To the balcony that faced the cages and torture poles.

Jack, Talia, and the other squads all approached their targets from the shadows as Talia used omnificence to scan for Raum's exact position. Jack was glad she was using hers. He could barely stand and use his at the same time. Flying and omnificence didn't mix for him. It hadn't been meant for humans to use anyway. It required an angel's intense concentration, something he lacked even on his best day. Besides, it wouldn't drain her powers—just his.

Suddenly, Talia gasped and pressed him into the shadows, her body against him as they hovered together. He smiled, taking in her jasmine and new-fallen rain scent that washed over him like a hot shower and made him ache all over to kiss her. He nestled his face against her neck, breathing in another tease of jasmine and rain, wanting to lose himself in it.

Something zipped off the balcony almost in front of them. Forcing Jack's attention away from Talia.

He gritted his teeth as Lare Dumont's bright red eyes and shaggy dark hair rose between beats of those leathery black bat wings he'd acquired. Jack fought down the urge to blink across the cavern and smash his fist into that coward's narcissistic, plastic face.

Talia held Jack in a tight embrace as they hovered together and watched Lare fly into a group of three other winged demons that appeared nearby. Talia cursed under her breath.

No, they weren't demons. Their wings were black and feathered and they had no halos. They were fallen angels...and some douchebag archangel had used his angel powers to somehow bring back their angel wings.

"Lare Dumont," said Talia, eyes narrowing. "With Reptev, Pharzus, and Lix—the traitors from Deemah's and Kesien's old squad."

"Lare—that bastard," said Jack with a snarl. "That's trouble. They'll try to flank Azrael." He sighed. "And Luci."

Talia nodded. "If we surprise Raum and defeat him quickly, we'll be there to flank Lare and Reptev. Before they flank Lucifer."

"Good," said Jack as Talia pulled him closer to the balcony. "Let's do this."

The squads hovered in the shadows until wide-eyed, Talia pointed.

"There," she whispered, motioning past the railing as the rest of her squad floated around them. "Raum is on the top floor. In the main room. Drinking wine."

"Luci's wine cellar is epic, Tal," said Jack, remembering all the luxuries he'd acquired.

Lucifer had tons of wine bottles and aged spirits from some incredible moments in human history. French Champagne from the Civil War. Bordeaux corked as the first bombs of World War I fell on Belgium and France. Eighty-year-old brandy bottled the year that the

Titanic sank. German lagers preserved in bogs for centuries. And those were just some highlights from Lucifer's stash.

"I've heard," said Talia in a flat tone, unimpressed.

"At least it's grabbing the Nephion's attention. He still seems unaware that a force of angels is about to show up for a housewarming party." He smirked. "And by housewarming, I mean murder marbles and Holy fire."

"Lots of Holy fire," said Kesien with a nod. "There aren't any panicked demons rushing toward the tower, trying to warn Raum. And I haven't heard any sounds of fighting. Or a peep out of Samael."

"Well, they're about to find out we're here," said Jack. "Just wish we could keep this asshalo from warning Samael."

"Me, too, Jack," said Talia. "So, we hit him hard and fast."

"A few shield bashes on top of that Holy fire should do the trick," said Muriel.

"Don't think we can get it done with just shield bashes and Holy fire," said Jack. "This dude is supposed to be the beast. Hard to kill."

Muriel smiled. "At Armageddon. Right now, he's just a credible poser."

"I like how you think, Muriel," said Jack.

Talia hovered a moment, closing her eyes, only feet from the balcony. Her mouth puckered and she pulled in a deep breath for the angel note of instruction to the other squads positioned around the black tower.

"Tal, no," Jack whispered, blinking to her, putting his hand over her mouth.

Her eyes were a mixture of murder and shock. He'd better talk fast.

"Tal," he whispered. "Raum's half archangel. You start tossing out angel song and he'll hear it, too. And know we're coming for him."

Her face went pale, fear burning in her eyes. Only then did Jack pull back his hand.

"Sorry, babe," he said. "I didn't—"

"Jack!" she whispered, gasping. She laid her hand against his face and gently kissed his lips as they hovered in Hell's thick, humid darkness beside the black tower balcony. "Thank you...I forgot that Samael's his father. How can I signal all the squads now? If I can't sing out commands."

He couldn't stop the smirk from curling at the corners of his mouth.

"I've got a good idea how to do that," Jack said, flexing his wings. "Just be ready to hit him with everything you've got."

Her gaze narrowed and she stared at him with suspicion now. She wasn't wrong. She knew him too well.

"Jack...what are you about to do?"

"Something that works every time," he said.

"Jack, be careful," Muriel snapped.

"Just back me up," he whispered and blinked across the darkness, hovering four feet from the balcony railing.

He landed without a sound on the balcony, keeping his Eternean sabatons on some sort of black cloth mat that covered the balcony floor, and called up murder marbles in each hand.

Waiting a moment or two, he made sure he hadn't alerted Raum, and then blinked between the translucent white curtains fluttering in the sulfury hot breeze that constantly blew off the rocky cavern. Into the main room filled with Lucifer's familiar white leather and chrome furniture, stone statues, and brightly painted masterpieces in yellows, reds, turquoise, and greens that hung on the walls. Stolen by Nazis in World War II and taken from them by Lucifer.

"Internal Revenue Service!" Jack shouted. "About that extension you requested..."

Raum whirled around, a shocked look on his face, glass of red wine sloshing. His face turned red as anger twisted his features. Even from the edge of the balcony, Talia saw the half-moon scar encircling his right eye. It was Raum. His thick sandy brown was disheveled, blue-grey eyes fully of anger.

"You!"

Raum let the glass vanish from his hand as Jack chucked the first handful of murder marbles across the floor at him.

They exploded in a burst of flame and smoke. Knocking Raum to the floor. And everything off the walls.

But the Nephion blinked up from the floor, wings spread wide. Headed for the balcony. What the hell? Raum wasn't trying to fight. Dude was running.

Jack flung the second handful of murder marbles at him.

Raum's wings crumpled when they exploded and Jack tackled him to the shiny maple floors.

By then, angels of death poured into the room from the stairwell, from the rooftop, and over the balcony. Restraining the big, scary beast of prophecy. Who thankfully hadn't achieved his full power yet.

They'd gotten to him in time. He smiled. He'd take the win. But it made him queasy. Bringing down Raum had been too easy.

The smile quickly slid off Jack's face as an unseen force threw him and the entire squad off Raum. The Nephion snapped up from the floor, black flames roiling in his hands.

Grinning as he aimed those flames at Jack.

5

*T*alia flung herself onto the balcony a heartbeat after Raum tossed Jack and her entire squad off him like ragdolls and rose to his feet.

Raum looked hungry, black wings stretching wide, red eyes glowing as he held up both hands, writhing black flames in both palms as he turned toward Jack.

"You are an unpredictable loose cannon, human," said Raum. "And black fire will trump oblivion spheres every time. You've already lost."

Talia blinked forward a few steps behind Raum until she was within an arm's reach of him, but he was so focused on Jack that he didn't sense her presence behind him.

"You say that like it's a bad thing, Raum," said Jack, smirking as he leaned against the white leather and chrome sofa arm and called up murder marbles in each hand. "And let's find out if murder marbles outgun black fire."

The whisper of wings echoed from the black tower's rooftop and from somewhere below the penthouse. Her other squads. They made no other sounds as they approached.

Inside the penthouse, Kesien was the first angel of death back in the air, hovering near Raum's back as the Nephion moved toward Jack who backed further into the room. Her wings were a soft rasp as Kesien moved toward Raum. Anahera scrambled to her feet, wings whispering as she advanced cautiously. Quietly.

"I know you're still there, angels," Raum snapped, not turning around as he continued to advance on Jack. "If you don't want to be obliterated, you'll stay away from me." He chuckled. "While I take his seraphim powers."

Talia bristled. Raum could sense her squad behind him, but he hadn't thought beyond this room. Couldn't he sense the rest of the angels moving toward him?

Maybe he was too arrogant to even consider that he could be taken down by mere angels of death…or a human? As the beast of prophecy, he must think he was untouchable. Samael probably filled his head with all those lies.

And she would use that arrogance against him.

Deemah's and Muriel's wings one floor below were a silent flutter, ascending the stairwell behind Jack in silent motion.

In seconds, all of the squads would converge on Raum, but he didn't seem to care. He was too focused on Jack. And his seraphim powers.

She had to be faster. To make sure this monster didn't kill Jack in the microseconds before their arrival.

Holy fire roiled at her fingertips, her eyes beginning to burn with white heat as she matched Raum's movements, crouching behind his wings, shielding herself in shadows. Even Jack wouldn't see her until she struck. She had to move fast. Before she got two handfuls of murder marbles in the face.

"Trust me, it's no compliment, human," said Raum, the black flames coiling between ribbons of smoke that trailed toward the ceiling. "No matter. By the time the angels are on their feet, you'll be a stain on my rug. And I'll have all your sweet, juicy seraph abilities."

Talia felt the first hum of a seraphim ward thrumming through the room.

Raum laughed.

"An angel ward? Against me? You must be joking." His raucous laugh filled the penthouse as another whisper of wings drew closer, rising on the hot updrafts through the stairwell.

In a breath, more angels had slipped through the roof portal into the next room.

Behind her, Kesien and Anahera shadowed Talia's movements, fanning out left and right with shields raised.

She smiled, making the curtains billow with a turn of her index finger. Drawing Raum's peripheral attention away from Jack. To the room.

But Jack took it back.

"The only stain on Luci's rug is the priceless Bordeaux you just spilled. Dude, that bottle was over a hundred year's old. You're a monster!"

"Typical human," Raum spat, launching a tendril of black fire at Jack with his left hand.

Jack lurched out of its path.

"Humans only care about things," the beast continued. "Missing the big picture. Having no clue about that big picture." He flexed his wings, looking bored now. "You have something I want, human." A leering smile curved across his face. "And I'm going to take it."

Another coil of black flame already burned in Raum's palm, replacing the one he'd launched at Jack.

Jack waved him off. "Sorry, no autographs and absolutely no selfies for arrogant little douchebags. Especially since I've met your loser dad."

Talia's heart fluttered as the white light of Jack's seraphim ward began to flicker.

"My father, Samael is smarter and wiser than a hundred of you humans," Raum fired back as he lifted his right hand.

And those deadly black tendrils of energy darkened.

"Is that why all of Heaven's got him backed into a dumpster, about to set it on fire?" Jack replied. "Dude, his halo definitely spins slower than the other angels—much slower. Dude's just smart enough to get himself erased by the Maker."

Raum threw the black flames from both hands at the ward.

The flames crackled and buzzed, dimming the ward's white light a moment, and then dissipating.

"Not sure how you're keeping that pathetic little ward lit," said Raum. "No matter. I'll burn it down quick enough. And then I'll tear you apart and take those seraphim powers."

Jack laughed. "Too bad you'll be in timeout while the grownups have a talk with Hell's latest wannabe king. And by talk, I mean Holy fire blasts. Lots of Holy fire."

Raum screamed and lunged at Jack, flinging burst after burst of black flames at Jack's seraphim ward. But the ward held fast in the face of this prophesied beast who wasn't as powerful yet as he thought. Thank the Heavens.

Talia closed the distance between them.

"How are you doing that?" Raum demanded, pointing at Jack as the whisper of wings slipped into the room from the stairwell.

Muriel and Deemah, another squad at their back, crested the top of the stairs, shields lifted high.

Above Talia, angels of death dropped down from the ceiling along the periphery of the room.

"Seraphim powers, bitch," said Jack, tapping the ward with his index finger.

With both hands, Talia launched a massive burst of Holy fire. Past Raum's wings. Into his back.

Raum screeched, flailing against the Holy fire wrapping around him like fabric.

Talia knew what was coming next.

She dropped to the floor and rolled left, out of the path of murder marbles as Jack flung two handfuls at Raum.

They exploded, one by one, knocking him to the floor with a cascade of concussive bursts.

When the last one went off, Deemah shield-bashed Raum in the face.

Muriel hit him from the other side. As Kesien and Anahera shield-bashed him, front and back.

Until he didn't get up again.

The remaining squads pounced on the Nephion, immobilizing him with shackles. Securing him in restraints not even Lucifer could escape.

Talia blinked to Jack, throwing her arms around him as he got to his feet, looking horrified.

"Tal, I had no idea you were behind him!" he shouted, hands against her face. "I could have killed you. Talia…I could have killed you!"

She pulled him into a long, steamy kiss and held him at arm's length.

"I waited until the last moment and then blinked sideways, rolling out of the murder marbles' path." She ran her hands through his light blond hair, but he still looked upset. "Jack, I knew the murder marbles were coming and I moved accordingly."

"You sure?" he said.

"Completely, Jack," she said and tweaked his sexy sculpted nose—like Michelangelo had shaped it. "I was counting on the murder marbles after I blasted him with my rare Holy fire."

At last, his expression lightened, the corners of his luscious mouth curving into that sexy smirk.

"You saying I'm predictable?" he asked, wrapping her in his arms, holding her close.

"Dependable," she countered, returning his smile with a quick kiss. "In the wildest, sexiest way."

"I'll take it," he said with a shrug and glanced at Raum. "Think we can get Zanth's location out of him?"

Talia nodded as she walked over to Raum who had been completely immobilized, hands and feet shackled, wings battened down tight against his back.

Inhaling, she pressed her hands together and closed her eyes. Summoning the barrage of images that was omnificence. As the flood of places and things deluged her mind, she reached out and pressed her hand against Raum's temple.

"What are you doing?" Raum demanded. "Stop. Stop!"

Talia exhaled in a long, slow breath, pushing Zanth's name and image along through the stream of things and places, using her left hand to narrow down the time stream, pushing it into an ever-narrowing focus. Until a dark room below on the first floor of the tower appeared in her head. Dark. Smoky. Filled with cages, some with dead or dying Nephions, most of them hybrid failures. Their bodies were shadowed and dark, impossible to make out their features.

But she knew that these two or three deadly amalgams of archdemon and archangel had survived at early stages. Making them prototypes. And they were being replicated to create a growing army of Nephions. How many, she had no idea.

The thought was chilling.

And then, in the flurry of images, she saw Zanth struggling against her bonds in a dark, dirty cell beside the Nephions, groggy, confused, and injured. Tre's ghostly soul form hovered beside her, looking frustrated and helpless.

"Found her," said Talia. "Zanth's being held on the first floor. Let's go release her." She turned her gaze to the squads holding Raum.

"Restrain him completely," she said. "And don't let him out of your sight."

Muriel blew a handful of small, glowing, downy white feathers into Raum's face. He sputtered and gasped and then collapsed, sagging in his bonds.

"Keep him out and motionless until he's in a High House cell," Talia ordered.

One of the squads wrapped Raum in a blue ward of light. They hefted him between the five squad members and blinked off the balcony, into the dark edges of Hell. Talia sent a second squad that formed on their wings to make sure this beast reached High House safely.

That left her squad and two others. Fifteen angels of death and Jack.

All three squads crowded around her, awaiting orders as Jack shifted toward the balcony.

"We're really going to spring Zanth—as a squad?" Jack asked, a pleading look in those pale green eyes, their sizzle and heat melting her heart.

She nodded and reached out to him, running her fingers through his light blond hair. "It's the right thing to do." She turned to the angels crowded into Lucifer's former penthouse.

"Are we really about to free an archdemoness from Hell, Talia?" asked one of the other squads, her black hair short and thick around her angular face and bright grey eyes.

Talia nodded. "She was once the deadliest assassin in Lucifer's command. Nearly killed Jack and I on more than one occasion."

The angel of death looked confused. "And we're rescuing her?"

Talia nodded.

"Why?" the angel of death asked.

"Because, over time, we've recruited her to Heaven's cause," said Talia. "And now, she seeks redemption."

The angel of death looked surprised. "A demon seeking redemption? Never thought I'd see that."

Talia smiled at her. "Bet you never thought you'd see Lucifer in the death angel guard either."

The angel of death chuckled, shaking her head. "Never a dull moment in the guard."

Everyone laughed as the angel of death stood ready with her squad.

"Let's go free Zanth, squads," said Talia. "She's locked in a cage below us. First floor."

Grinning, Jack held out his hand and motioned toward the balcony. "Lead the way, Mrs. Casey."

She pulled him onto the balcony, the other angels of death following. Together, she and Jack leaped into the air, wings spread wide, and veered left around the tower, sliding into the shadows as they followed the darkness around the tower. Down the side to the first floor.

It took several moments to quietly locate the door into the bottom of the tower. The door was narrow and featureless, dull black, almost hidden in the curve of the tower wall.

Kesien and Muriel jiggered the handle and pressed on the door until the latch released and clicked open. Muriel swung the door open, into the tower room.

And into complete darkness.

Kesien called up a small blue orb and tossed it into the space where it floated and gently cast a dim blue glow. Just enough to see outlines of the room and its furnishings.

Talia shuddered at the distant clang of metal against metal that echoing across the cavern and through Hell's depths.

The battle had begun.

Jack snapped his head toward the sound, looking pale and concerned. "They've found Samael."

"Sounds like it," said Talia as dread turned her fingers icy.

"Or they ran into my old squad and the Nephions," said Kesien, his tone bitter.

"With Lare Dumont in a guest starring role as traitor number one," Jack replied, his tone bitter. "That little bitch."

Talia felt worry creep along her spine and shudder through her wing feathers. The noise was too dense to be a squad fight. Unless there were hundreds of Nephions, a thought that chilled her wing feathers. No, most likely, the fight with Samael had begun.

Regardless, she and the squads had to hurry and outflank Kesien's and Deemah's old squad. And then cut off all avenues of escape for the traitorous archangel. Now that Raum was in custody and winging his way to Lord Kushiel.

"We need to hurry," said Talia as she entered the first-floor space, following the sphere's light through the expanse.

But darkness swallowed the light in this horrible, cavernous space, requiring more orbs.

She didn't need the orbs. Her omnificence lit the way inside her head, but her squad needed the light.

The others tossed out more blue orbs as she zigzagged around metal tables, cages, and crates that littered the sticky floor, feet floating two inches above it, her wings quiet as they held her aloft.

The oppressive space seemed almost deserted, not even demons guarding it now.

The rest of the squads followed, trailing her lead.

Jack was right beside her and she felt his heart racing as his sabatons ticked softly against the stone floor. The rest of her squad and the two remaining squads floated just above the floor, closer now, armor and wings not making a sound. It was hot and sulfury, the smell of fresh-tilled earth hanging in the air.

Jack and the others bumped their way around tables and crates until enough blue orbs lit the space. She let her omnificence lead her as she kept her arm firmly wrapped in Jack's and tried to steer him around the furniture and obstacles. Ahead, against the far wall stood two large cages with heavy metal doors. In the one on the right, a dull greyish glow flickered in the darkness.

Tre Sheridan's soul.

"Tre?" Jack called. "Zanth? You in here?"

"Jack Casey?" Zanth's smoky alto voice was weak, her heavy French accent ragged, sending chills across Talia's wing tips. "Is that really you?"

She'd never heard Zanth sound like that before.

Jack rushed over to the cell door, shook it hard. Locked.

"Let us, Jack," said Kesien.

Jack stepped back as Kesien and two other angels of death grabbed hold of the bars. Deemah moved beside him and also grabbed hold.

"On three," said Kesien. "One, two, three, pull!"

They yanked hard on the cell door until they ripped it out of the wall. They stumbled back with the heavy door and laid it on the floor to the right.

Jack rushed into the cell, Talia behind him as Tre stumbled to his feet.

"Jack! Talia! You came!"

"With the cavalry, dude," said Jack, motioning to the angels of death that crowded around the door, keeping watch.

Jack dropped down on his knees beside Zanth who lay on the grimy floor, curled into a fetal position. The smell of dirt and brimstone was cloying. Her ashen skin had darkened, red eyes weak, face cut and bruised. She looked thin, broken, folded like a paper doll on the floor, a filthy, long-sleeved black sheath of a dress hanging on her scarecrowish frame. Her once-shiny, black bobbed hair was flat and tangled, her normally full red lips ashen pale. Her long blood-red nails were broken and brittle, feet bare.

The thought of what Samael had done to her infuriated Talia. Sure, Zanth was a demon, but it still made Talia sick. And furious. At Samael. Enough to tear his wings off, feather by feather.

"I knew you and Talia would come for me, Jack Casey," Zanth said in a shaky, tired voice as she laid her hand against Jack's face, fingers brushing across his cheek. "For me and Tre."

Jack gave her his best actor's smile, but Talia felt his anxiousness—and fury—as he stared at the smoky black chains around Zanth's wrists and ankles. Talia felt her anger spark. There was archangel power in those black, demonic chains and she wondered how twisted and corrupted Samael's angelic core had become to create those chains. To turn an archdemoness into a Nephion factory. It sickened her.

Jack gently rubbed Zanth's shoulder. "Just lay your head back and rest, Zanth, while Tal and I try to break these chains."

"Jack," said Talia, still staring at those chains, the rage rising in her chest. "These are archangel shackles—corrupted now. Meant to bind an archangel. I don't know how Samael managed to cast them, much less bind Zanth with them."

Raum's powers perhaps? She'd ask Azrael after all of this was over.

"So, none of your squads can break them?" said Jack, wide-eyed as he glanced from the roiling smoky chains to her, looking for a solution.

Talia shook her head. "Your seraphim powers can break them though. But you'll need to ward Zanth and Tre from the blast first. With a seraphim ward."

Jack nodded and turned his attention back to Zanth.

"Hear that, Zanth?" he asked in his best, everything's okay, no worries voice. "Gotta use some seraphim fire to break these chains and then you'll be free. I'll need to ward you and Tre first though."

Zanth grabbed his arm and held it tight, her red eyes filled with tears.

"Stop him, Jack," Zanth pleaded. "He will never let me go with you. He wants to watch Heaven, Hell, and the Creation burn…so he can rule what survives."

Jack looked stricken, shaking his head in confusion as he glanced at Talia.

"To do that, he needs me to build his army." Zanth's voice trembled with fear and pain, tears dripping down her cheeks as the sound fell to a desperate whisper. "Hurry, Jack, Talia. Save me from him. Save it all from this horrible army."

Talia was stunned. She'd never seen a demon cry before.

"Close your eyes," Jack said in a quiet, comforting voice and Talia knew he'd been moved by Zanth's emotional state, too. "It's all gonna be okay, Zanth."

Demons didn't cry. Whatever Archangel Samael put Zanth through was as incomprehensible as it was reprehensible.

Jack's gaze narrowed as he held out his hand and summoned a white seraphim ward. White light roiled around his fingertips. He pressed the light gently against Zanth's arm. The ward light rolled across Zanth and onto Tre and then exploded in a burst of bright white light.

As the ward buzzed in the darkness, Anahera dropped down beside Talia.

"They're coming," she said.

"Who's coming?" Talia asked.

"Demons," she said, breathless, wings unfurling. "Lots of them."

"Squads," Talia called out in a steady, controlled voice, standing up and extending her wings to shield Jack while he summoned enough seraphim Holy fire to burn away Zanth's chains. "Demons are about to swarm us. Defend this cell. And Jack."

Deemah grinned and lifted her shield as she took up a position to Talia's right.

"Time to dance," said Deemah.

Kesien had a greedy smile on his face as he drew his sword and shifted his shield into his left hand.

"Looking forward to this rave."

Muriel and Anahera took up positions beside Kesien, swords and shields raised.

"Then let's get this party started," said Muriel as the other squads positioned themselves around the cell. "Supremes formation, angels. Shields to the sun. Let's rock their worlds."

Talia smiled. Jack's influence would never fade from her squad.

Jack chuckled as the first flame of seraphim Holy fire lit his fingers. "Cue up some AC/DC for me, Muriel."

In a single burst, all of the blue orbs shattered into shards of light, the room going dark.

"You got it, Jack," said Muriel as the buzz of bat wings—lots of wings—vibrated around them. "Starting the drum solo."

The first shield bash rang out like an alarm bell as a flurry of bat wings overtook them, demon screeches filling the silence, the red of their eyes lighting up the dark and strobing through the room.

Talia slammed her shield hard, uppercutting a winged demon, knocking it backward. As two more leaped at her.

The gong-like tones reverberated through the room in flashes of electric red as Jack set Zanth's chains alight with seraphim Holy fire. They ignited like a fuse, crackling and sizzling with white light as the Holy fire burned through them, turning them brittle until they shattered and floated away like ash.

When the Holy fire reached the ward, the shadowy cuff and remaining lengths of smoky chain blew away as wings beat the air. Freeing Zanth's hands and feet.

Zanth tried to rise from the floor but collapsed against the wall, her chest heaving from the effort. She was too weak.

Slowly, Jack lifted Zanth up from the floor and into his arms, Tre beside him.

Talia bashed two more demons and turned to Jack.

"Jack, I'll call for Watchers to carry Zanth and Tre back to

Eolowen. As a human, you can't fly and carry her, not even a short distance."

He nodded. "You're right."

Talia sang out a string of angel notes and shield-bashed another demon. In moments, two of Azrael's Watchers appeared beside her. In Enochian, she instructed them to quickly take Zanth and Tre to Eolowen. To Berith for healing. And not to stop. Not for anything.

Nodding, a sandy-haired Watcher gathered Zanth from Jack's arms and another one with long black hair picked up Tre.

Zanth reached out and gripped Talia's shoulder.

"Merci, Talia," she said in almost a whisper, looking exhausted. "I understand Jack coming to rescue me, but you? Why would an angel rescue me?"

Talia laid her hand on Zanth's arm. "Because you seek redemption, Zanth," she said. "For you and Tre. Your actions have proven that. And…to quote a certain smokin' hot blond actor, love frees all."

Zanth offered her a brief smile. "I am beginning to believe that now."

The Watchers lifted Tre and Zanth into the air.

"Guard, surround the Watchers!"

Jack and the three squads blinked into the air, shield-bashing demons out of the Watchers' paths as they blinked out the door and into Hell's cavern.

Talia and Jack flew alongside the Watchers, the squads forming a circular formation around them, closing the gaps with their shields. The tight formation kept the flurry of demons back as they escorted Zanth and Tre into the corkscrew tunnel beyond the Gates of Hell. Talia made sure they stuck right with the Watchers all the way to the vertical gallery. She let the Watchers through and watched them ascend the vertical shaft to the top.

"Guard, close the gap!"

Together, she, Jack, and the guard capped the gallery from below, preventing the demons from following the Watchers out. Together, the squads shield-bashed demons over and over, knocking them out of the air, to the ground, and back into the tunnels. Over and over until the Watchers were too far away to overtake. Only then did she give the order to clear the gallery.

By then, the demons had fled. Returning to the main battle.

"All right, guard," Talia ordered. "To Lucifer. Let's close off Samael's escape route and keep the demons off Lucifer's flank."

She doubted Lucifer needed help with demons, but closing off Samael's escape route was a different story.

"Lead the way, Tal," said Jack, motioning her out of the gallery and into the main lava tunnel.

Back into the corkscrew tunnel.

Smiling, she gripped Jack's hand and blinked with him and the squads along the tunnel's turns until she located a narrow tunnel on the right. The one that Lucifer had taken. Together, she and Jack blinked into the tunnel, darker now that they had turned away from the river of lava flowing beside the main tunnel. The sulfur stench was strong, the ozone thick as the crack of swords against shields was a constant drone through the tunnels. Intensifying.

She focused on Lucifer and let her omnificence drift to Archangel Samael, gathering his location and an image of the raging battle as she, Jack, and the three squads surged down the narrow tunnel.

It seemed to take forever, battle sounds echoing, growing louder as they came out, approaching the Gates of Hell. Where they'd first entered. Somewhere above the tight, narrow cavern where Archangel Samael, surrounded by hordes of demons, tossed Holy fire at Azrael and his forces. Samael's forces fought at the cavern's edge. Where the lava moat ringed the plateau where the Gates of Hell stood. If they had crossed from the plateau side, they would have hit Abaddon's wing-burning escape prevention attempt.

Behind Archangel Samael were five Devourer of Angels, their massive corpulent bodies dwarfing the red-skinned greater demons. In front of the force, where Azrael and his guard had engaged the army of demons, shadows appeared and disappeared in shadowy bursts.

Assassin demons! In shadow panther forms. And mixed in with the army of demons were the tall, stringy-bodied Eaters of Hearts whose wild-eyed, dead stares and skin-crawling screeches raked against the panther pules. And mixed in with all of those forces, Talia saw a dozen Hell Princes fighting with flaming swords and black flames. Samael was throwing everything Hell had against Azrael.

Until Lucifer and his forces popped up on Samael's flank, forcing Samael to attack Heaven on two fronts. Weakening him. Leaving the corrupt and dangerous archangel only one way out: the cavern portals. Flight tunnels. For quick travel…and escape.

Half a dozen portals tunneled high through the rocky walls, leading up through the main cavern where the Gates of Hell loomed below…and the river of lava that encircled it. The only way out of this fierce battle against the army of death angels was through those flight tunnels.

If Samael got through one of those portals, he'd have a whole vertical gallery to flee through. There weren't enough angels to fight demons and block all the egresses leading out of Hell. So, they had to cut him off from those portals.

Azrael's commanding voice filled the cavern.

"Keep those tunnels blocked!" he shouted. "And don't let him blink past us into the main cavern!"

At the other main tunnel entrance, Lucifer and his squads had battled their way through hordes of demons to get behind Samael. Now on the archangel's flank, they clogged the tunnel opening, closing the other major escape route. They had also blocked three overhead flight tunnels. Hordes of flying demons kept trying to pull them away. Giving Samael time and space to blink out. And escape. But Lucifer and his forces had become an immoveable force. Blocking all the remaining escape routes.

Trapping Samael.

Talia clenched her hands into fists and cheered. *No escape this time, Samael!*

"All squads!" Talia shouted. "Reinforce those portals! My squads, reinforce Lucifer's position!"

They all blinked at once, covering portals, standing with Lucifer's forces.

She and Jack shot past a major force of demons and took up positions flush against the rock. Bashing demons. Helping Lucifer's forces hold that tunnel.

"Hello, Talia and Jack," Lucifer shouted as he fried a demon with a fiery burst of Holy fire. "How nice of you to assist. And I assure you, your timing is impeccable."

"How's Azrael doing?" she asked, bashing a demon out of her path as Jack tossed a handful of murder marbles at them, disintegrating more than a dozen demons.

"Well done, Jack!" said Lucifer. "Appreciate the moment's break." Lucifer turned to her, that smile still present. "Azrael and I are managing to hold Samael and his forces away from the flight portals—and mostly contain the Devourers. Shadow panthers have been a bit of a problem, the Hell Princes an annoyance, but we're managing. Samael's been unable to even approach one of the portals since we engaged him from his flank. With reinforcements, we should be able to hit him with more firepower. Take the offensive." He flashed a grin at Jack. "Add more murder marbles, since he's sent the totality of Hell against us. Won't kill him. Just piss him off, but still worth the effort."

Talia wondered how the Hell Princes had reacted to Lucifer showing up alive. Fighting for the other side. Probably not well.

"Glad to do my part," Jack said with a smirk and tossed another handful of murder marbles as another horde of demons descended.

The blast obliterated them. Parts of smoking leathery wings rained down as Jack called up another handful.

"What do you need from me and my squads?" Talia asked.

Lucifer pointed across the chasm at the massive demons causing havoc with the guard. "First, we need to bring down those Devourers and the Eaters of Hearts. That should level things off quite nicely."

"Squad two and three, focus your air attacks on the Devourers and Eaters of Hearts," she ordered. "Go. Take them down."

She watched ten angels of death blink into the air, swords raised, and take on the closest Devourer of Angels. Teasing it into pursuing them. They worked as a team, confusing it as they shield-bashed and sliced at it with their swords.

Lucifer turned to her, his blue gaze intense against his tangle of blond curls.

"But Talia, I need you to keep that pathetic miscreant in your sights with omnificence," said Lucifer, motioning toward Samael who remained in the center of an almost endless and impenetrable procession of flying demons...and a ring of Hell Princes. "The moment he sees any light in one of these portals, he'll try and escape. We can't let that happen or it's the end of everything."

Lucifer was right. She had to keep eyes on Samael the entire time.

"I'll tag him with my omnificence," she replied. "That will make him visible to every angel in the vicinity."

"Perfect, Talia!" Lucifer exclaimed and burned down four demons with his angel powers. "Now, let's take him down. And those ignorant Hell Princes supporting him."

"Why would they support Samael?" she asked.

Lucifer rolled his eyes. "Because they're stupid enough to believe that Samael will preserve their current affluent lifestyles. Samael will have them all destroyed if he wins this battle. They're smarter than the average demon—much more powerful too—but greedy enough to overthrow him. I should know. I created them."

"We'll have to go through them to get to Samael anyway," said Talia. "Consider them targeted."

"Perfect, Talia," said Lucifer as he moved to one of the squads under his command and directed them to target the Hell Princes once the Devourers were down.

Talia closed her eyes, hands pressed together as she cycled through every life force in the chasm, stopping when she located the corrupted, muddied dim light of Archangel Samael. She slashed a white-hot symbol across his angel light that burned bright white.

"Well done, Talia!" Lucifer cried. "I can now see him from across the cavern."

She opened her eyes.

There, in the center of all the demons, Hell Princes, Devourers, and shadow panthers, a bright slash of white light burned through Samael's rusty, dim halo. Making him easy to spot now.

"Nice work, Mrs. Casey!" Jack shouted and shield-bashed a demon that flew at him.

She smiled, leaning against Jack a moment to steal a quick kiss that made his pale green eyes sparkle.

Cheers erupted through the cavern, two squads of angels circling as a Devourer of Angels collapsed into a black and red puddle of demon goo.

Four left.

The shadowy flash of black startled her. A shadow on shadow.

Talia turned.

A shadow panther leaped at her, knocking her to the cavern floor, claws clamping onto her wings as they tumbled off the rocks onto a narrow ledge below. Below that, only darkness.

Jack's frantic voice screaming her name echoed as she and the assassin demon plunged into the darkness.

6

"*T*ALIA!"

Jack's scream reverberated through the cavern as he threw down the shield and spread his wings. He leaped over the edge of the rocks. Into thick, oily darkness and scalding air that reeked of sulfur.

Below, the muffled pules of a shadow panther drew him down deeper into the vertical well of darkness, only the thrum of his heart and the beating of his wings throbbing in his ears as he descended at breakneck speed.

"Talia!"

The sound of scuffling drew his attention, hot smoke and ash roiling as he blinked right. Into one of the blackened cavern walls.

Dazed, he dropped through the darkness, disoriented, unable to tell up from down.

Still tumbling, he beat his wings hard and fast until he hit a pocket of scorched air that created an updraft and slowed his descent. His wings moved faster as he began to level out and rise on the warm air currents.

Looking up, he saw how far he'd been in a free fall. Lucifer and the angels of death squads were only bright specks against the black rocks far above him.

"Talia! Where are you?"

He was too far down.

His heart pounded his rib cage as he blinked upward through choking tangles of sulfur and smoke, the air so hot and thick it took his breath.

Rising.

Rising.

Until a flash of dove grey to his left caught his attention in the swirling blackness.

Above him, distant voices calling out to him reached his ears, but he tuned them out, focusing on Talia.

The growl of a panther drew him toward the cavern wall just below Lucifer's position beneath the blackened rocks.

He listened for more sounds until the panther's throaty yowl pulled him toward the wall. Against it.

He fumbled until his feet found solid ground in the darkness. A narrow ledge about a hundred or so feet below Lucifer and the angel squads.

Jack beat his wings hard against the dense smoke, scattering enough darkness and smolder to see the muscular, fluid outline of a shadow panther. He winced. Pinning Talia against the ground, her wings trapped beneath its sharp claws and heavy paws.

The image fluttered.

The demon was about to shift out of panther form and into its demon form.

Moving as quietly as he could, Jack slipped through the smoke and ash until he hovered above the shadow panther as its red demon skin began to fade through the dissolving shadow panther form.

He held his breath a moment. Folded his wings against his back.

And dropped like a stone on top of the assassin demon in mid-shift. When it was at its most vulnerable.

He snapped his arm around its neck, blinking right for only a breath. Knocking the shifting demon off Talia and at least ten feet away.

The murder marble throbbed in his right hand as he wrestled the screeching demon to the ground, its sharp, pointy teeth snapping at his arms, but unable to slash at him with its still-shifting paws.

It tried to shift back, the muscular body lengthening, darkening, and growing in strength. Jack couldn't hold it much longer.

He shoved the murder marble in its mouth. And blinked upward, out of the detonation path, as the murder marble exploded. Spraying the wall and the rocks with black and red demon goo.

He glanced left. Talia lay motionless, out of range on the rocky ledge as the battle against Samael raged above.

"No, no, no! Talia!"

Jack blinked back to her side.

He slid his arms underneath her shoulders and gently lifted her into his arms, clasping her against his chest.

"Tal! Wake up!" He held her close to his heart, cradling her. "I'm here now. Tal…please…wake up."

He rocked her gently, panic rising as he gazed up through the darkness. As four pairs of grey wings descended through the floating ash and swirling darkness. Blinking onto the ledge.

"Jack!" Muriel dropped down beside him. "What happened?"

"Shadow panther…" It was all he could get out, his chest so tight that the air barely escaped his voice box.

Kesien knelt beside Muriel and gently slid Talia out of Jack's grasp.

Jack studied her wings, her armor—her face, checking for injuries. There wasn't a mark on her—not even a claw mark.

Kesien touched her forehead, engulfing her in light as gently, Muriel laid her hands against Talia's breastplate and lightly pressed down.

Once. Twice.

Light and air flooded into Talia's body as she pulled in a deep, anxious breath, her eyes snapping open. She sat up, staring at everyone surrounding her.

"What happened?" she asked.

Jack threw his arms around her and held her tighter than he had in the longest time.

"You're okay," he said, his voice breaking as he sucked in a breath of overheated air.

Muriel patted his shoulder. "Angels are creatures of light and air, Jack," said Muriel. "Sometimes, we get the air knocked out of us like humans. She and that assassin demon must have hit the ledge hard, knocking her out. A little air and light and back to normal again."

Finally, Jack let Talia go and helped her to her feet.

"That ledge rising out of the smoke is the last thing I remember," said Talia, brushing the dust off her armor. "But I do remember falling over the cavern's edge, tangled up with that shadow panther."

Shaking all over, Jack laid his hand against his heart. "I think I just aged fifty years," he said and held out his hand to her, his way of telling her he loved her.

Talia smiled and laid her hand on top of his, gripping it, accepting his heart. Pressing her closed fist against her chest. Her way of telling him she loved him back.

"Good thing you've stopped aging," she teased, leaning toward him and kissing him.

He pulled her into his arms again and drew in a deep steadying breath.

"Everything all right down there?" Lucifer shouted, leaning over the precipice, that devilish smile on his face.

Jack gave him the thumbs up.

"All right then," said Lucifer. "Could use a bit of help with these Devourers."

With his arm still around Talia's waist, Jack flew beside her, back up to the cavern rim where the battle had heated up, the space above the cavern filled with black, leathery-winged demons clashing with angels of death, dove grey wings bright against the dark rocks, smoke, and ash drifting around them like snow.

Talia gazed around the cavern, looking tense until her wings stopped twitching.

"Samael's still in that protected space in the center of his army," she announced. "But we've already cut through half his forces."

"But he's ringed by greater demons and Hell Princes," said Lucifer. "The worst is yet to come." Lucifer's brows furrowed. "Did you and your squad end his beast spawn? Please say yes."

"No," Talia replied and Lucifer winced. "We took him prisoner instead. He's now in a High House holding cell—a present for Lord Kushiel." She closed her eyes a moment. Using omnificence, Jack knew. "I can see Raum's life force there right now...through my omnificence. In a cell."

"Good," Lucifer snapped. "Let Father and Kushiel deal with him then." He motioned across the chasm. "Looks like three Devourers remaining. And all the Hell Princes. Jack, think you could throw some murder marbles at the problem?"

Jack grinned. "Can't let Azrael's guard have all the fun."

Talia grabbed hold of his hand. "Not without me, you don't, Mr. Casey. I'll never speak to you again if you get eaten."

"But Tal," said Jack, holding out his arms. "Devourers hate the taste of humans. They spit me out like burnt Thanksgiving Brussel sprouts."

"We'll ride shotgun, Talia," said Muriel, nudging Anahera who unfurled her wings. "To make sure the vanguard doesn't get eaten."

"Shields to the sun, angels," Deemah said, lifting her Eternean shield. "Time for more demon-bashing."

"Squad, form around the vanguard," Talia announced. "Supremes formation."

Jack grinned.

"All right, guard!" Lucifer shouted. "Form on me and keep this tunnel blocked! We're targeting Hell Princes now."

Jack smirked as Talia and her squad encircled him. "Let's get this party started then," he said. "And...blink!"

Lucifer's forces closed rank, tightening their blockade of the tunnel with two of Talia's squads as Jack, Talia, and her squad blinked across the chasm. Toward one of the Devourers tearing through Azrael's front lines.

Tossing angels like tables, the ten-foot-tall, fleshy, jelly-like demon screeched and knocked everything out of its wake as it lumbered toward anything with feathered wings. Hangry for an angel sandwich.

Jack called up a handful of murder marbles as he, Talia, and the squad buzzed the Devourer's head.

Angry, it clawed at them, trying to snatch an angel snack out of the air, but Jack and the squad were too fast for it.

Deemah shield-bashed it, forcing it to turn in her direction. She blinked back as Kesien shield-bashed it and then blinked away. Muriel hit it next and then Talia, confusing the hell out of it.

Leaving it open for Jack to swoop close and smash his fist into its gaping mouth, releasing the murder marbles.

"Blink!" he shouted.

He and the squad blinked away as Jack counted down three seconds.

An explosion thundered through the cavern, shaking the ground, tossing plumes of ash and demon goo high into the air as red jelly bits of Devourer demon splattered the chasm walls.

Angel cheers rose through the massive chamber as Azrael's forces brought down the third Devourer.

That left two.

Cheers erupted from Samael's flank as Lucifer brought down a Hell Prince with Holy fire.

Talia flew next to Jack, sliding her arm around his waist and giving him a quick kiss as they hovered a moment.

"Next target, squad!" she shouted. "Blink!"

They blinked as a unit, Jack letting Talia's blink transport them to the next Devourer.

As a squad, they hovered over it. It was further back from Azrael's forces at the front lines. A sizeable force of Azrael's guard had surrounded this Devourer, keeping it engaged at a distance.

Muriel and Deemah started their bash and dash runs, Muriel and Talia buzzing the Devourer's head.

So, where was that jackass Samael in all this chaos that he'd caused?

Jack glanced around the cavern until he located the bright slash of Holy fire marring Samael's halo. Still surrounded by a huge force of demons and Hell Princes.

Dude probably thought Azrael and Lucifer would get tired—or bored—and just quit, leaving him with Hell's throne. Did that narcissistic douchebag even know that Zanth was free and his spawn was in chains in High House? Jack hoped so. He wanted Samael to know all of those updates as the angels choked off every one of his escape routes, leaving him trapped to face long overdue consequences.

Turning back to the Devourer, Jack bashed and dashed, the shield he'd picked up from the cavern floor shuddering as he blinked and shot out of the demon's reach. And he waited for the right moment to feed it some seraphim skittles it would never forget.

When the angry Devourer began stomping and staggering around in a circle, clawing at the squad, Jack flew at its face, tossing some murder marbles into his gaping mouth.

"Blink!" he shouted.

They shot away from the doomed Devourer.

"Three, two, one...confetti!"

The Devourer exploded into demon goo and demon jelly, spraying the huge terror of demons flying toward them.

He and Talia worked in tandem beside Muriel and Anahera as Kesien and Deemah shield-bashed the massive force of demons that had arrived.

One by one, the demons fell out of the air, disappearing into the chasm's smoky darkness below.

Behind them, cheers erupted as the last Devourer fell to Azrael's guard.

"To the flank, angels!" Talia shouted.

Jack followed her and the squad across the cavern. Back to Lucifer's position.

The former King of Hell and his forces were inundated with demons.

Fighting as one, Jack and the squad swooped low over the horde of flying demons, shield-bashing them until Lucifer hit the force of demons with an expanding burst of Holy fire that burned off their wings. Every last one of them.

The entire force of demons plummeted into the chasm's darkness.

Jack landed beside Talia as squads two and three returned, too.

"All right, angels!" Talia shouted. "Wedge formation. Block this tunnel!"

Falling into positions in front of the tunnel, Jack took his place in formation as angels of death positioned themselves in a V formation in front of the tunnel, swords out, and shields raised.

Lucifer's forces held the front line ahead of them, flanking Samael, the Hell Princes, and his attack forces. Trapping the traitor between Lucifer's and Azrael's forces.

Again, Jack searched the cavern for Samael's bright white slash of Holy fire where Talia had marked him. The mark still burned in the center of the cavernous abyss. But his demon forces had dwindled drastically.

Azrael's booming voice filled the cavern. "Angels! Swords out. Shields to the sun. Charge!"

Azrael and the entire guard rushed Samael's front line.

A dozen shadow panthers leaped from the shadows, but Azrael's guard quickly cut through them like weeds, engaging the handful of Eaters of Hearts that stood between Samael and a still sizeable force of demons that encircled the cowardly traitor.

"Squads one, two, and three, you heard the archangel!" Lucifer shouted. "Swords out. Shields to the sun. Engage!"

Lucifer advanced with three of his five squads and slammed the wide outer ring of demons protecting Samael with swords and shields.

Jack glanced up at the cavern's ceiling. All of the portals were still blocked and being held by squads of angels of death. The closest escape route now for Samael was this one. The one behind him.

Talia slid closer to Jack.

"Be on guard, Jack," she said. "In case Samael makes a break for this tunnel."

Jack nodded. "It's the closest escape tunnel to his position."

"Exactly," she said. "That's why Lucifer's trying to force Samael's hand by attacking the flank. I think he's hoping to catch Samael between his forces and ours."

"Let's take this prick down then," said Jack as he set himself, keeping one hand free for murder marbles and the other on his shield.

Nodding, Talia held up her right hand and summoned a long, flaming sword.

"Squads, be ready. If Samael bolts, it'll be toward this tunnel."

Azrael's forces rolled over three of the Eaters of Hearts and put down the last of the assassin demons.

Turning, Lucifer and his forces spread out and then closed ranks on the two remaining Eaters of Hearts. Pressing close to the innermost ring of demonic forces protecting Samael. Almost to the final push. To take that douchebag down once and for all.

Behind Samael, Lucifer and his forces chewed through demons as Lucifer slammed them with his angelic powers. The demons fell in droves as Lucifer's forces cut a sharp line through that innermost ring. Shaving off demons right and left. So close to Samael's position now.

Another Eater of Hearts fell.

"Forward, angels! Charge!" Azrael.

Panicked chatter rose from the last ring of Samael's demons and Hell Princes as angels of death poured into their final circle.

Lucifer charged with his squads, pointing them at the remaining Hell Princes like a spearhead. Cleaving the ring apart.

"Take him!" Lucifer shouted.

As the final circle collapsed around Samael, the last Eater of Hearts falling, Archangel Samael blinked into the air with a contingent of demons and Hell Princes surrounding him. A dozen maybe.

Jack swallowed a breath, his mouth going dry as angels surrounded the remaining demon forces that began falling all around them. And Azrael.

"Flank them!" Lucifer shouted, blinking into the air after Samael, his squads following.

Samael sent some of his forces at Azrael. And another handful at Lucifer. As he swiveled around and blinked toward the tunnel.

"Ready swords and shields!" Talia shouted. "Prepare to defend the tunnel. Do not let Samael through."

"Don't let him get away!" Azrael shouted as he blinked into the air after Samael, two squads of angels at his side.

Azrael and Lucifer surrounded Samael high above the chasm as he tried to reach the tunnel, but the douchebag's remaining demons were no match for Azrael and Lucifer.

One by one, Azrael and Lucifer brought down the demons defending Samael, peeling them away until Lucifer lunged past the remaining demons and grabbed Samael by the wings. Lucifer glared at the archangel, his eyes glowing red as he held him aloft.

"You dare to try and take my throne!" Lucifer shouted. "You're not worthy."

Samael shrank back from Lucifer, looking terrified as he struggled to free himself from the former King of Hell.

Lucifer held him tighter, his shiny black wings furiously beating the air as Samael struggled harder.

Azrael shot toward them and threw rings of Holy fire around Samael, binding his arms, wrists, and feet. And then his wings.

Out of the smoke and ash, Lucifer summoned archangel shackles. He snapped them on Samael's wrists and ankles as a chain of half-light and half-smoke materialized in his hand. Lucifer attached the chain to the shackles and wrapped it around his fist, shoving Samael forward in front of him as he moved toward Azrael.

The cavern erupted in a cacophony of cheers as Lucifer and Azrael dragged Samael across the chasm to solid ground. Azrael bound in him in more chains—chains of light.

"It's over," Talia cried as she joined in the cheers. "Samael's in custody."

Kesien let out a whoop as Deemah whistled and cheered, banging her shield with her fist. The rest of the squads holding the tunnel joined them, including Jack who pumped the air with his fist.

"One archangel douchebag down!" he shouted. "GOOOOAAAL!"

He turned to Talia, his wife of almost exactly one year. "Babe, we did it! Armageddon's been rescheduled."

She slid her arms around his waist and pulled him close as he smashed his mouth against hers and then let her go.

Talia reached out and brushed a lock of hair out of his eyes.

"Deferred, Jack," she corrected him. "To a later date. To be decided by the Maker."

He nodded. "Rained out. That works for me."

"Let's round up the last of these demons," she said, giving him another quick kiss that sizzled against his lips.

"Lead the way, Mrs. Casey."

She floated above the ground, turning toward the angels of death. "Guard, break into your squads and let's clean up this place."

The other two squads took to the air and traversed the cavern, hunting for demons. Muriel and the others in Talia's squad hovered in formation, waiting for her to address them.

"Squad," she said, holding Jack's hand. "Form on the vanguard. Let's sweep for stragglers."

As a unit, they blinked away from the tunnel entrance and flew low over the cavern as they watched Azrael's guard take possession of Archangel Samael and make their way toward the main tunnel. Jack snickered. Samael was wrapped so tightly in Holy fire that his grey eyes bulged.

Jack looked forward to this douchebag's trial, doubting that ol' Samael had even a hint of remorse or had ever felt a single pang of redemption. But that would be up to Heaven to figure out. He just hoped that he wouldn't have to testify. He sighed. Or vote.

The loud screech made everyone halt as Lord Kushiel appeared in the cavern. He blinked across the chasm and landed in front of Samael who was trussed up like a box store Christmas tree ready to load on the car's rooftop. Jack followed Talia as she and the squad landed near the scene.

Kushiel was all shadow and fire, eyes burning with flames as he landed in front of Samael who tried to pull away when Kushiel approached him.

"No!" Samael smashed his eyes closed and screeched again. "No! Don't let him take me! NO!"

Kushiel looked laser-focused and menacing in his dark robes of justice as he loomed over Samael who looked small and pathetic now.

"Azrael," said Kushiel, hands on his hips, those red-tipped white wings spread wide. "Do me the pleasure of escorting this—archangel to a High House cell." Kushiel's eyes sparked. "Just near enough to your Nephion-spawn to see that he's in custody, too."

"You have Raum?" Samael said with a gasp.

Kushiel nodded. "Courtesy of Talia's squad. And Jack Casey."

Grinning, Jack hovered nearby, Talia beside him. "This is better than that episode of Crossing Paths when Gianni's doctor character got turned into a vampire and got cured by a passing alien ship that landed nearby. He recovered just in time to deliver this woman's baby whose car ran out of gas on the way to the hospital. On Halloween night. In an ice storm."

Talia frowned. "That's awful, Jack. You're making that up."

Jack shook his head. "No, truth. Ask Gianni about it when you see him. Whoever guesses the correct number of shades of red he turns gets to cook dinner."

"Betting, Jack? Really?"

Jack glanced up to see Lucifer standing beside them, arms crossed.

Lucifer shook his head. "Haven't you learned anything about making wagers by now?"

The sparkle in Lucifer's eyes told him that the former King of Hell was joking. Even poking fun at himself.

"Best thing that ever happened to me, Luci," Jack said as Talia put her arms around him, holding him close. "Without that wager, I wouldn't have met the love of my life."

Talia pulled him into a kiss. She turned toward Lucifer. "The worst day of my life became the best because of that wager. When I met Jack underneath those hot stage lights."

Jack kissed her again as her wings wrapped around him.

Kushiel turned to Azrael, his face an unreadable mask of retribution.

"Azrael, could you send a squad to escort us to High House." Lord Kushiel cast a dark glance at Samael. "I want to make sure the archangel gets to a cell."

Azrael glared at the immobilized archangel who squirmed against his bonds, still trying to escape Kushiel.

"With pleasure, Lord Kushiel."

Azrael assigned a five-angel squad to the archangel of punishment and his entourage of two cherubim. The cherubim took possession of Samael and then called the squad into formation as Kushiel blinked to the back of the line. Together, they surrounded Samael and blinked as one out of the cavern, into Hell's main tunnel.

"Great work, everyone," said Azrael. "Especially you, Talia and Lucifer. You made this operation a success." He turned his gaze to Jack. "And to Talia's squad and Jack and his murder marbles. Together, you took down those Devourers like they were dried brush. And ensured that Raum was captured."

"Thank you, sir," said Talia.

Lucifer gave Azrael a sharp nod. "Believe me, Azrael, nothing pleases me more than having Archangel Samael in custody at last."

"Lucifer," said Jack, glancing at the fallen angel. "We also rescued Zanth and her ghost bae, Tre Sheridan."

Azrael raised an eyebrow. "Talia, report."

Talia turned toward the archangel of death. "Sir, we located Zanth in the black tower and freed her from some corrupted archangel shackles. She was in bad shape, so we sent her and Tre with two Watchers back to Eolowen. She's going to need a lot of healing."

Azrael nodded. "Good work...I think. We'll check in with Berith when we get back to Eolowen. Make sure everything's all right."

"Azrael, if it's all the same to you," said Lucifer. "There's one last thing I need to do while we're here in Hell."

Azrael looked apprehensive. "And what's that?"

"The fallen angels," he said in a quiet voice. "The angels who fell with me during...the Rebellion. They are still trapped here in Hell and can't just walk through its open gates." Lucifer sighed and ran his hand through his blond curls and Jack saw pain in his eyes. "Thanks to my unbridled arrogance and rage, I dragged them down with me. If you notice, none of them fought at that hack, Samael's side."

Azrael nodded for him to continue.

"I've been given a chance at redemption that I didn't deserve," he said, his gaze falling to his black sabatons. "Regardless, they're trapped here and I intend to do everything within my power to help them get a chance at redemption, too—if they're willing. Lift them up and out of this darkness. Give them the same chance to return home that I got."

Jack couldn't help but smile. Seeing Lucifer show remorse and already trying to make amends was comforting. He knew he'd made the right decision, even if all of Heaven didn't agree.

For a moment, Azrael was quiet, studying Lucifer and the hot, smoky cavern.

"What do you plan to do today?" Azrael asked finally.

"I want to talk to them," said Lucifer and sighed. "Tell them what's happened and that they have not been forgotten. They need to hear that from me."

"Uh, Luci," said Jack, stepping forward. "If you need any help with that, I'll go with you to talk to them."

Lucifer turned toward him, a surprised look on his face. "Jack... you'd help me speak to them?"

He nodded. "I'm little more than a testimonial, but yeah, I'll help."

Lucifer was quiet for several, long moments. "All right, Jack. Thank you. I appreciate and accept your help."

"Jack," said Talia, her voice sounding wary. "This place isn't safe. There are still lots of demons loose in here with orders to kill any and all angels on sight."

Before Jack could counter with a poor excuse for why he'd be fine, Talia turned to Azrael.

"Sir, permission for me and my squad to provide support and protection to Lucifer and Jack," she said. "I think Lucifer's mission is important and he should speak to the fallen angels."

"I think that's wise, Talia," said Azrael as he unfurled his wings. "You, Jack, and the squad accompany Lucifer to make contact with the fallen angels while the guard and I finish securing the tunnels and sweep for demons. And any Nephions." He frowned. "I'm surprised we didn't encounter any other than Raum. Abaddon is on his way to Hell to try and secure the Gate again. Sing out if you need backup."

Azrael had a point. Outside of the black tower, Jack and the squad hadn't seen another Nephion. Would they even know what one looked like? None of the guard—including Azrael—had ever seen a Nephion except Raum. None of them knew what one looked like. Raum looked like an angel of death with moon pale skin and muted blue-grey eyes. Did the others look like him? Or more like Zanth with ashen skin and red eyes? And with only a handful of dead Nephions in those cages, Jack wondered if this secret Nephion army of Samael's even existed.

Maybe this Armageddon army was all vaporware and not as far along as Raum and Samael claimed?

"Thank you, sir," said Talia who called her squad into formation behind Lucifer.

"Report back to the cavern when you're done," said Azrael.

"Will do, Azrael," said Talia as she dragged Jack into formation beside her.

Jack squirmed at the squad's presence and Talia noticed as Lucifer spread his wings and moved toward the tunnel they had been guarding.

"What's the matter, Jack?" she asked.

He sighed. "Didn't need protection," he said. "Just to speak to Lucifer's fallen fam."

She squinted at him and then gave him that probing stare of hers. Checking to see if he was lying. And he was—sort of.

"Jack Casey!" she cried, crossing her arms. "You're not telling me everything. Are you?"

"Okay, okay!" he shouted.

Lucifer and the squad halted. "Jack, are you lying to angels?" he asked with a chuckle. "You know how that always ends up."

"Look, I left out one little detail, that's all," he said, holding up both hands.

"Oh, I can't wait to hear this," said Lucifer crossing his arms and grinning at Talia. "I love to watch a good smite!"

She glared at Jack. "Spill it," she snapped.

"Okay," said Jack, groaning, and he began to pace as Muriel chuckled. "On our way back to the cavern, I was…"

Talia blinked in front of him, hands on her hips. "You were what?"

"I was…planning to rescue Cerby and Orthy, okay? Happy now?"

Lucifer laughed as Talia's fierce expression softened.

"Tal, they're good boys! They don't deserve to be stuck down here guarding an open gate and souls who refuse to redeem themselves."

Lucifer laid his hand on the back of Jack's neck and roughly patted him on the back.

"And you were expecting something nefarious, Talia?" said Lucifer. "From Jack Casey? The poster boy of Do Gooding? Who's part golden retriever?" He let go of Jack. "Honestly, I can't fault him for trying to rescue Cerberus and Orthrus. I confess, I wanted to smuggle them out myself."

"See, Tal, Luci's in!" said Jack.

Muriel leaned forward. "Jack, where you gonna put them? Azrael will blow a gasket if he finds hellhounds in Eolowen."

His gaze fell on Talia. "I thought that maybe…if Mrs. Casey said yes…we could…um, keep them at…the uh, beach house."

"Jack!" Talia cried. "You want to keep the guardians to the Gates of Hell at our Pacific Palisades beach house?"

"I'll fence in the yard."

Lucifer laughed. "Better seraphim ward it, too, Jack and add Holy fire chains to their collars. They'll escape and cause havoc along the coast. Besides, they're bred to go home if they stray too far."

Jack bowed his head. That sucked. Orthy and Cerby didn't deserve this.

"They saved my life when demons burned down my trailer," he said in a sad voice. "They deserve better."

Lucifer put his arm around Jack's shoulders. "Oh, Jack, so humanly naïve…and quite endearing. I'll talk to Father, okay? See what can be done to give them a good life since their guardian days are behind them."

Jack's head snapped up and he stared at Lucifer. "You'd do that?"

"Of course," said Lucifer. "Frankly, I'm a bit moved by your concern for them. And here your angel pals all thought you were up to something wicked."

At last, Talia smiled and wrapped her arms around Jack's neck. "There isn't a wicked bone in Jack's body, Lucifer. I have to keep reminding myself of that though."

"Agreed," said Lucifer. "Still want to help with the fallen angels, Jack?"

Talia let him go. He unfurled his wings. "Hell yes. Let's do this."

"Like your spirit, Jack," said Lucifer. "You have a good heart. Let's go see if we can redeem more of the fallen."

7

*T*alia kept Jack close as she and her squad followed Lucifer through the maze of dark, curved, and corkscrewed tunnels, back to the black tower. The wailing of souls was barely a distant moan as ash drifted like snow flurries through the vaulted chamber, the shadowy tower rising up toward the dark, rocky ceiling. Bright white lights still gleamed along the top level, the sulfury stench of the lava river heavy as its red and yellow glow illuminated the empty torture racks and abandoned metal cages dotting the cavern floor.

The bone bridges cast rough, prickly shadows across the basalt rocks, the moan of a mournful, sweltering wind the only sound as they approached the tower.

Lucifer halted and stared up at the tower floors, looking lost in thought. Jack stood beside him, the former King of Hell a head taller than Jack, his shiny black wing feathers glinting red in the wash of his blood red halo. He was silent for several moments until finally, he turned around, fixing Jack with his gaze.

Talia wondered what was going through Lucifer's mind right now.

"I've spent millennia right here in this smoky furnace, scurrying through these tunnels like a troll hunting prey with only fury and indignation for company. And lots of demons." He glanced past Jack, staring at the hollow expanse, a dark expression burning on his handsome face. "That entire time, I had only myself to blame for being trapped down here."

"Maybe so," said Jack in a soft, understanding voice. "But pain can drive us to do things we'd never do without it. Not an excuse, dude. Just a damned good reason why you deserved the chance to change."

He turned to Jack, looking surprised. "But why, Jack? Why do you insist that I deserve this chance after everything I've done?"

"Because you regret those things," said Jack, pointing at Lucifer's face. "I see pain and remorse, not bragging, in your eyes every time you talk about it. You don't shout about being the victim. You say it was your own fault. The old Luci would be blaming everyone but himself."

A strange look that Talia couldn't read washed across Lucifer's face. Part surprise. Part realization.

"Your main focus since the trial ended has been to earn your dad's forgiveness," said Jack. "Dude, you want him to love you like us, humans. Because that's how much you love him. How long has it been since you felt love, Luci? For anyone? Or anything?"

Talia was surprised when Lucifer's eyes turned glassy and he bowed his head a moment, staring at his feet. And for the first time ever, she saw pain in Lucifer's face.

"The reason those things still cause you pain is remorse, dude. Love and remorse…proof that you want and can be redeemed."

Anger rose in Lucifer's face as he turned around, teeth gritted, and glared at the tower, the cages, even the river of lava. All of it seemed to disgust him now.

"I hate everything about this place," he said, hands clenched into fists.

Talia almost expected to see horns bud out on his forehead and his feet turn into cloven hooves.

"How could anyone ever want to live in this horrible place!" Lucifer raged as he paced in front of the tower. "And I lived here for eons and eons. Exiled. Alone. Deluding myself into believing that I could turn it into my own paradise. When all I ever wanted was to go home. To Heaven. Under cool breezes, blue skies, and golden sunlight warming green meadows. And in my hubris, I dragged a third of Heaven's angels down with me into this flaming pit of misery and despair. How could I do that?"

His face pinched into a mixture of anguish and rage.

No one spoke, including Jack. Lucifer needed to work through his rage as much as he needed to work through his anguish. Both made him into the most dangerous being in the Creation. But his chance at redemption had changed him.

Lucifer whirled around toward Jack and gripped his forearms like they were life preservers, pain sharp in his pale blue eyes that were turning red.

"Jack…they trusted me! They believed me when I said, *humans will replace angels on Father's pedestals and inherit Heaven while Father's angels are cast out into the abyss.*" He sighed. "And trust me, this is the abyss."

He winced, letting go of Jack's arms as he turned back toward the black tower.

Jack remained quiet, letting Lucifer work through the guilt that was now boring its way through him. Talia felt it like nausea in the pit of her stomach, knowing how it was eating at Lucifer. And Jack seemed to recognize that this was part of Lucifer's journey to redemption. The unpleasant part.

"Join me, I said!" Lucifer laughed bitterly. "Let's stop this. Let's take back our home. And all of us were swept from the Heavens like bugs off the carpet. Forgotten and left to rot in this abyss. And now, I've been forgiven and they continue to rot down here. Alone. Ignored. In pain and in silence. Because of me."

"Luci," said Jack, a hand against Lucifer's sleeve. "You're here now to make it right. You didn't forget them. And that speaks volumes about you."

"Yes, it does."

Talia turned. Procel the Fallen stood behind them.

He wore torn and tattered angel robes. Once white, they were threadbare, grimy, and grey now. His ghostly skin was gritty with ash, dull hazel eyes sunk back in his head, giving his thin face an almost skeletal look. His wheaten hair was wild, scraggily—like dead sagebrush as a hot wind blew through the cavern.

Lucifer smashed his eyes closed as he slowly turned to face the angel that had helped him open the Gates of Hell and start the apocalypse.

Behind Procel, dozens and dozens of fallen angels gathered outside the tower, their faces stern and smudged with ash, robes blackened and worn.

Finally, Lucifer turned around to face his flock, his face flushed, mouth taut, and eyes still glassy and sharp with pain.

"Procel," Lucifer said with a hiss. "How I have wronged you." He took a step toward them and held out his arms. "How I have wronged all of you."

Talia heard the deep regret trembling in Lucifer's voice, in his words.

Procel didn't react. He stood motionless in front of the gathering procession of fallen angels studying Lucifer.

Talia bit her lip as she stared at their broken, dazed expressions. They had no hope. No purpose. No wings at their back or even halos to light their paths.

"We thought you'd abandoned us down here," said a black-haired angel of death with putty-colored grey eyes. "After you got your sparkly white ticket back through Heaven's Gates."

Lucifer seemed to wilt at her comment. What could he say? To these fallen and forgotten, it probably did look like he'd just been handed a golden ticket. And left them to rot.

To Talia's surprise, Lucifer moved toward them and spread his arms wide.

"And now, I am sharing this…sparkly white ticket with all of you."

Murmurs echoed through the group of fallen angels.

"What does that mean, Lucifer?" Procel asked. "Come to gloat and dangle it in front of our faces, knowing it can never be ours?"

"No. No! That's what I'm trying to tell you. I've been given a chance at redemption and I am bringing that same chance down to all of you. A chance to go home again."

The murmurs grew louder until the crowd was abuzz with voices as the tiniest glimmer of hope lit their tired, broken faces.

"How?" Procel demanded.

"Do you regret what we did?" Lucifer asked as he paced through the group. "Do you understand that what we did was misguided? And wrong?" More voices rose, the dull thrum getting louder. "That I led you to ruin."

"Yes," said a tiny voice in the back of the group.

A fair-haired, dark-skinned Watcher with amber eyes and pain in her face.

"Lucifer, I want to go home."

Smiling, Lucifer rushed to her and laid his hands on her shoulders. "Irinis," he said. "To come home, you need to stand before your Maker and ask to come home. To tell them that what you did was wrong and you want to fix it. And you must mean it."

The Watcher's eyes brimmed with tears. "What we did was so wrong, Lucifer. I live with that ache every moment down here." A tear threaded its way down her cheek. "And I would give the last drop of light from my angelic existence to change it."

Lucifer laid his hand against Irinis' shoulder and closed his eyes. Talia knew he was conversing with the Maker.

As something wondrous began to happen.

The palest hint of tarnished gold light encircled Irini's head and floated above it.

The Watcher cried out and reached her hand over her left shoulder. When she pulled her hand back, it was smeared with a pale streak of goldish light.

"What's happening to me?" Irinis asked with a gasp as her gaze shot back to Lucifer.

"It's called forgiveness," Lucifer said in a quiet voice. "That light is from the first tiny buds of your wings growing back."

Lucifer sang out a series of angel notes in his warm baritone voice and two Watchers flew down through the chamber and landed beside him.

"Take her home," he said. "The Maker is waiting to see her."

He turned to Irinis again. "By the time you reach Heaven and stand before your Maker, you'll have your wings back. If you show him that you have changed."

She grinned and hugged Lucifer. "Lucifer...thank you!" she cried, tears rolling down her ash-smeared face.

"This has nothing to do with me," he said. "This is all your doing, Irinis." He turned his gaze to the Watchers and lifted his hand into the air. "Now, rise."

The Watchers lifted her between them and blinked across the cavern.

"You see?" said Lucifer as excitement burned through the fallen angels. "Contrite, honest. Willing to change—that's your ticket home again. If I sense those things in you, I can bring you home again. Just like Irinis. And Berith."

Procel looked surprised. "But Lucifer, how did you convince the Maker that you were sincere and contrite?"

Jack stepped forward. "Luci here didn't convince anyone," he said. "His actions did. That's what made the Maker give him that chance at redemption. And that's what you have to do. Show the change."

Procel squinted. "I know you," he said. "You're that meatsack Lucifer dragged down to Hell. The one who conned him into a trap in the Garden. And later, you stopped him from killing the Maker in the Throne room. Why would we believe anything you say?"

"Because I'm the reason Luci here got that chance at redemption."

Procel's angry gaze shot back to Lucifer, his brow furrowed, his lips curled into a snarl.

"Is this true, Lucifer?" Procel demanded.

Lucifer looked pissed. Talia hoped it wasn't at Jack.

"Yes, Procel, you impossible dolt, it is. Every angel in Heaven voted to burn me up in the Lake of Fire. Jack Casey's was the only voice who spoke up and voted to spare me. And Jack was right. I did want redemption, but I knew I didn't deserve that chance. My Father agreed with Jack and gave me the chance to prove it."

Procel looked shocked. He moved toward Jack, standing there with crossed arms as he studied Jack like a museum specimen.

"You really voted to spare Lucifer? Without coercion? Against all of Heaven?"

"No one forced me to vote that way," Jack snapped, bristling at Procel's accusation.

The hint of a smile lit Procel's sallow face. "Well, someone bribed you then!"

Jack glared at the tall, lanky fallen angel with disdain. Talia knew that he didn't like anyone questioning his honesty. Least of all an angel who had turned on Heaven and tried to destroy it, falling from Heaven for his crimes.

"I have seen the changes in Lucifer. If one of Heaven's tenets is Love Frees All, then it has to free Luci here, too." He motioned toward the fallen angels. "And all of you…if you can show the Maker that you want to change. Damn, people! You just saw Luci here transform one of your Hell bros and fly them out of here. When was the last time that happened?" He smirked. "Oh, wait…never."

"The human has a point," said a female fallen angel of death. "Why shouldn't we trust Lucifer? Yes, he led us to the greatest fall from Heaven ever, but he never lied to us. Or abandoned us. Even now, he didn't have to return here. He could have left us to our own misery and forgotten we existed, but he didn't."

More voices joined hers and it became obvious that Procel's hesitation was his alone. The others had found hope again and Talia felt their changes of heart as they stopped hiding their remorse from each other. In an instant, the heavy, oppressive pall they'd carried for millennia had begun to lift.

"Lucifer, tell us," said a once-archangel as he stepped forward, long white hair flat against his back. "What do we need to do?"

"I have already spoken to Father twice about your redemption," said Lucifer, looking relieved. "He has agreed to see each of you. So, prepare yourselves to stand before Heaven. Your Maker will see and sense all, so you can't hide anything from him. You'll each get one chance to earn that redemption. And if you revert to old ways or Father senses them in you, you'll find yourself back here for eternity."

Lucifer let them discuss his proposition for a few moments.

"As soon as it can be arranged, I will return here with a flurry of Watchers who will bring you before your Maker. The rest is up to you. But know, that in Heaven, I will be there to help you once you are home again."

Talia felt hints of light begin to radiate through the dirty-faced fallen angels. Lucifer had negotiated one chance for each of them with the Maker.

"Thank you for not forgetting us, Lucifer," said the archangel.

Procel remained silent and Talia wondered if he would be one of the fallen who refused to change. There would be some. She'd expected Lucifer to be one of them. He had surprised her in ways she was just beginning to process.

"Well, you can shove your redemption, Lucifer you traitor!" a voice from the air shouted. "I don't want it and I'll see you back in Hell or thrown in the Lake of Fire!"

Talia's gaze shot toward the vaguely familiar voice. It came back to her from a dark, lonely rainswept Oregon road where she'd crossed over two souls after they died in a car crash. Where squads of angels of death stood around watching the car slam into the guardrail, not doing their jobs. They stood there unaffected and watched both humans gurgle their last breaths. And they stood there, stoic and useless while the two souls panicked and clung to the crash site because it was the only thing still familiar to them.

Even then, Talia remembered him spouting drivel about being on strike and refusing to crossover any human souls until Azrael was brought before the Maker in chains for allowing her and Jack to be together.

Reptev. Kesien's former squad mate. Samael's right hand.

"Reptev!" Kesien shouted, blinking into the air. "I can't wait to watch you burn!"

Talia shot into the air and grabbed hold of Kesien before he could launch himself at Reptev. And Lix and Pharzus, his other two squad members who hung back in the shadows. Ready to ambush anyone who went after Reptev.

"The traitor's pet parrot speaks!" Lucifer replied, looking amused and unimpressed by Reptev's outburst. "That the best you can do, Reptev? Now that your puppet master is in chains and on his way to High House?" Lucifer smiled. "Jealous, little angel of death? Don't want redemption because you know you'd never get it? Just like your pathetic coward-of-a-leader, Samael?"

"You've gone soft, Lucifer," Lix shouted.

Lix, another traitor angel of death from Kesien's former squad, hovered defiantly. His dark brown hair was short and wavy, eyes a dark, waxy grey, like a melted crayon. His ragged wings were faded black, wingtips shredded, feathers missing.

"Soft, Lix?" Lucifer said with a quizzical look. "Because I can see the monster I was and I now have the desire to change who I've become? You're about as self-aware as a bowl of Fruit Loops, you miserable prat. Do not lecture me on…on, well, anything, you pitiable nob."

Pharzus joined his squad mates, hovering above the fallen angels when a fourth flyer joined them, his leathery black bat wings in hummingbird-like motion.

"Speaking of douchebags," said Jack, his gaze narrowing. "It's Lare Dumont, climbing onto the railing of the Titanic for his big bromance moment with his demon dudes. That how you got those wings, Lare?"

"Shut up, Jack!" Lare fired back at him, wings in frenzied motion. "You may have grabbed Samael, but you're not getting out of Hell alive this time. That's a promise."

Terror filled Talia's eyes as dozens and dozens of demons popped up from behind the black tower and from the smaller tunnels around it. But they weren't the red leathery skinned minions. They had ashen skin. Their eyes were an intense orange or red and they moved like shadows. Quiet. Quick. And deadly. Like arachnids.

Unlike any demons she had ever seen.

Lucifer's gaze turned dark and angry, wings unfurling as he moved close to Jack.

"Meet the first division of Samael's Nephion army," said Lare as a grin curved across Reptev's face.

That's why the cages surrounding Zanth had been empty. They weren't failed experiments. They were in training. And they'd been hidden until now.

Samael's secret weapon.

"And since Samael won't be using them, we will. To get some old-fashioned demon justice." He pointed at Jack. "You're dead, Casey."

8

 ack unfurled his wings in a wide span as he stared at the army of Nephions surrounding them. Tall, gangly, ashen-skinned, their eyes glowed. Some had red eyes, others gold, and others a bright copper color, no hair on their smooth heads. These dudes moved like big cats, deft and quiet, not the clumsy plodding of demons. No, they moved like predators. Hunters. Deadly. Like Zanth.

He swallowed his breath. Damn. These dudes were terrifying.

Lucifer moved closer to Jack and Talia in a protective gesture, he realized. Talia's squad formed a tight circle around them, facing the Nephions, but even Jack saw the fear shining in the squad's grey eyes.

"Procel," said Lucifer in a calm, precise voice as he maintained his poise, his gaze fixed on Samael's douchesquad. "Take the fallen into the tower and barricade yourselves in my library. Now, please. And don't come out until you hear only the bubbling of the lava rivers."

"But Lucifer—"

"Procel." Lucifer gritted his teeth as he tossed down wards that led behind him to the black tower. "They will kill you all like mortals. Erase you. They're Nephions born of archangels and archdemons. Go. Now."

Nodding, Procel motioned the fallen angels toward the tower. They huddled together and rushed into the ward lights, following them behind Lucifer and Jack, and then Talia and the squad. Back inside the tower.

"Come now, Reptev," said Lucifer, distracting them, Jack realized. "I'm sure Samael was quite displeased when he discovered his new army missing, wasn't he?"

Reptev smiled. "He's probably just begun to figure out that his former squad has double-crossed him."

Jack knew Lucifer was buying the fallen angels time to barricade themselves into his library. Jack just hoped he, Talia, and her squad didn't run out of time either. They couldn't even call for Azrael. Any angel notes would be heard by these douchebags.

He shuddered. And the Nephions.

Talia landed beside Jack, Kesien behind her as Deemah, Muriel, and Anahera surrounded him and Lucifer. Her squad looked terrified.

Jack hated to see angels unnerved. If they were unnerved, then he should be hella scared right now. Not of Lare Dumont or those douchebags from Samael's guard. From these Nephions surrounding them. Raum was only one Nephion and even at low power, he'd been difficult to take down. With three squads of angels. But those glowing eyes told Jack that these Nephion bastards were probably fully charged.

"You were counting on Samael to lose that battle, weren't you, Reptev?" Lucifer asked, still smiling.

"He would have been dead weight at Armageddon," said Pharzus with a sneer. "Even Raum said so."

Their best shot at escape was to get to the main cavern. And Azrael's guard. Before these things erased all of them. Even Lucifer.

"Jack," Talia whispered against his ear. "Don't make any sudden moves."

He nodded, her proximity comforting as he gazed around the space, looking for the best way out of this mess. Any way out of it.

"Well, then," said Lucifer. "I look forward to seeing you three on

Armageddon's battlefield. Can't wait to see what you'll do with this Nephion army. When I crush it and all of you."

Reptev chuckled. "You're finished, too, Lucifer. You're just another angel lackey."

Lucifer's smile was deadly. "Am I now? I can't wait to meet you on the battlefield. And crush you into dust." He glared at Reptev, those wild blue eyes darkening to red. "You do know that I have all my powers back, Reptev? All of them."

"Luci, how do we get out of here fast?" Jack whispered. "Back to Azrael and the guard?"

Lucifer's gaze ambled around the chamber, not drawing attention. If anyone could get them out fast it was Lucifer.

"There's a tunnel behind the tower," Lucifer whispered. "Leads right to the gates. From there, we take a tunnel bypassing the gates and meet Azrael and the guard below. To fight these things as one."

"I knew you'd have an escape route close to your penthouse," Jack whispered.

"You know me well, Jack," said Lucifer as his bored gaze returned to the traitor angels of death and Lare Dumont.

"Oh, I'm far from finished, my arrogant little angel of death." His smile widened into a deadly grin. "I'm just getting started."

"We'll see. Oh, and Kesien!" Reptev shouted. "This is payback for all that self-righteous bullshit you and Deemah put our squad through when you refused to obey Samael's orders. Over and over."

Kesien slammed his fist against his shield. "I don't follow traitorous orders any more than I follow traitors. And I can't wait to smash you like the cockroaches you are."

"Reptev," Deemah said with a charming smile. "Heaven's crest on my shield will be the last thing that goes through your mind after I shove those wings right through your chest and out your prayer hole."

"Lovely image, Deemah," said Lucifer, nodding at her. "I like this one. But let's all hold onto that image for when we destroy these insects." Lucifer lowered his voice to a whisper. "Hold onto my armor. When I insult Reptev's manhood, we all blink as one behind the tower. Into the tunnel. Look up at these bellends and laugh if you understand."

Jack glanced up at Lare Dumont as Talia and the squad lifted their gazes to Reptev, Lix, and Pharzus. Jack laughed along with Lucifer and the squad.

Which incensed the traitors.

"I always thought you were an idiot, Reptev," said Lucifer. "But I'm certain now that you've spoken."

Jack snickered and grabbed hold of Lucifer's breastplate as Talia took hold of his pauldrons, the others gripping the shiny black armor.

"Nephions, attack!" Reptev shouted, motioning toward the tower.

Lucifer lifted his arm and he and the squad blinked backward. Behind the tower. Thirty feet away from the tunnel. Lucifer pointed his hand at the tunnel and blinked again, launching all of them into the dark, narrow tunnel.

They flew along it in darkness, bunched together, wings almost touching. Only the glow of halos lit the rocky corkscrew tunnel that rose and fell through the rocky walls. It seemed to go on forever.

Jack's heartbeat was a runaway train pounding his rib cage and making his whole body shake as he took the turns like a Prohibition bootlegger. They'd need wards and Holy fire just to keep these things off them. But they needed a miracle to escape them.

They needed Azrael and the guard.

The tunnel went on forever until the faint red glow of lava became a glowing speck in the distance.

And then they hit the cave-in.

Scorched walls, some still burning, had crumbled, sealing off the tunnel ahead. Deliberately blocking their escape.

Only one tunnel was open ahead. A narrow one that snaked off to the right.

"Bollocks!" Lucifer snarled.

"It's blocked," Jack said with a groan.

"Worse," said Lucifer. "They've collapsed the bloody tunnel that bypasses the Gates of Hell." He punched the wall. "They're herding us to the gates! Hoping to slow us down. Overwhelm us before we can reach Azrael and the guard." Lucifer sighed. "Or burn up our wings crossing the lava river. Making us sitting ducks."

Talia nodded toward the only open tunnel. "Then let's beat them at their own game and get to Azrael and the guard."

"Faster, angels!" Lucifer shouted. "Don't let them close the gap."

"Wait!" Jack shouted. "Grab hold of my armor! I'll seraphim blink us ahead."

He felt several pairs of hands latch onto his breastplate, pauldrons, and sabatons.

Lucifer reached back and grabbed hold of Jack's breastplate, moving in close with the squad as Talia wrapped her arms around Jack's waist.

"Everyone aboard?"

"Yes!" Muriel cried.

"Go, Jack!" Kesien shouted.

Jack closed his eyes, concentrating on the distant red glow at the end of the tunnel. And blinked for all he was worth.

All seven of them shot forward like a rocket launch through the tunnel and tumbled out through the opening. Right beside the Gates of Hell.

Jack rolled, wings over feet through the air and managed to right himself as the rest of the squad and Lucifer spun around and shifted through the darkness, wings outstretched, halos rocking, until they banked around the tall, black metal gates and hovered beside them.

Below the windswept rise roiling with ash and heat, the Gates of Hell stood on a peninsula that overlooked a river of lava encircling it. Across the river was the cavern where they'd just fought and defeated Archangel Samael. That was the distance they had to cross now to reach Azrael and the guard. And survive Abaddon's wing-burning gauntlet.

"Talia," said Lucifer. "Angel notes to Azrael. Hurry. Before the Nephions arrive and overrun us."

Talia opened her mouth and sang out notes that Jack couldn't hear. He held his breath until she turned back to him and held his gaze in a searching glance that scared him.

They were in trouble.

He pulled in a breath as the first set of glowing red eyes appeared near the mouth of the tunnel.

His heart sank. The Nephions were already gathering at that opening. With the douchesquad right behind them. When they had the numbers, they'd attack.

Jack sighed. They knew herding us to the gates bought them time because of the burning wing thing. Abaddon's latest attempt to hold those gates closed. And it just might be his, Talia's, and the squad's demise. And that included Lucifer.

Past Hell's tall, heavy iron gates was a down-sloping, ramp-like hill that towered above the lava river separating the main cavern from the Gates of Hell. Their only escape route.

"Listen carefully," Lucifer said, motioning past the gates and down the hill. "We've got to blink down that slope. You must hit the air above the river with as much speed as your wings will grant you to get across before the Nephions overtake us. And to survive Abaddon's escape-proofing. Is that clear? We've got one shot at this. Otherwise, we'll never reach Azrael in time."

Jack felt the fear churning through his body now. If Lucifer was afraid, then he was terrified.

But barking whines drew Jack's attention. His gaze shot toward the hill.

Sitting at the bottom of the slope were Cerberus and Orthrus, tails and tongues wagging. His heart broke. They were trying to find a way across.

"Look! It's Orthy and Cerby!"

Lucifer looked sad. "Jack…we can't get them in time."

"But the Nephions will chew right through them," he said in a pained voice. "I can't let them die."

Talia laid her hand against his face. "Jack, it's us or them right now. I'm sorry."

The skittering sound drew his gaze back to the tunnel. Where the first Nephion stepped out of the tunnel's mouth, but hung back, still waiting for the others.

"Blast it, the first group has already caught up to us," said Lucifer. "We're out of time."

Muriel grabbed hold of Talia's shoulder. "Talia, we have to go. Now."

"Do we go in one group or one at a time?" Kesien asked.

"All at once or we're leaving dead angels in our wake." Lucifer.

Jack winced, his eyes getting glassy as he looked over at Cerby and Orthy waiting so patiently. Not knowing they were about to be torn apart by these bastards.

"Jack?" Talia said, shaking him. "Did you hear Lucifer?"

"What?" he said, his gaze flicking back to her.

"Jack, listen carefully to me," said Lucifer, his voice steady but dire. "When I give the signal, we all go at once. Do you hear me?"

He nodded, his head whirling as another group of shadows with glowing orange and gold eyes emerged from the tunnel.

"Squad, wings wide," Talia said.

Jack extended his wings as far as he could stretch them.

"We can use the updrafts around the gates to grab some momentum," said Muriel.

"Good observation, Muriel," said Lucifer. "Position yourselves now with your leading wing touching an updraft. Hurry!"

Quickly, Jack shifted back and forth around the gates until he found an updraft. He let his right wing dangle in its path as he turned his body toward the slope.

He had seraphim powers. He could do this.

"The lava river is constantly releasing heat that's picked up by winds throughout the cavern," Lucifer explained. "At regular bursts. The downside is that the heat now prevents anything with wings from crossing the river unscathed. Blame Abaddon. It's his latest defense against demons escaping Hell."

"What does that mean?" Jack asked.

"Jack, it means that it will literally burn the edges of your wings," said Lucifer. "Slowing you down and making it difficult to fly further than the other side. If it doesn't completely damage them, rendering them useless...dropping you into the lava river."

Jack's eyes got wide. "So, you're saying that once we touch those rocks over there—if we make it—we're grounded?"

Lucifer nodded. "Unfortunately. Unless there are squads of healers over there. Can't be helped. There's no other way out from here because we're cut off from the tunnels bypassing the gates. Regardless, those gates will soon be teeming with Nephions. Everyone, wait for the second burst of heat and then the updraft…and go!"

Lucifer spread his wings wide and held one wing steady, like he'd found his updraft.

Jack's heart was pounding so fast he thought it would explode, his breaths coming in overheated gasps as he waited for the first updraft. Sweat poured off his face and beaded across his neck.

More Nephions crowded around the mouth of the tunnel, gathering numbers into a hazy ashen presence. Jack swallowed hard. As they began shifting into the shadows. Moving toward the Gates of Hell.

Time was up.

"One," Lucifer whispered, counting off the first heat burst.

Talia and the other angels tensed, muscles tightening, deep breaths taken.

Jack took a deep breath, his body trembling, wings quivering as he glanced at the downward slope ahead. Like a slalom run. He had one shot at this.

"Go!" Lucifer whispered.

Jack shot into the air with the other angels and barreled down the slope as fast as he could fly.

Behind them, Nephions shouted, shadows shifting, the heat stifling. As they rushed toward the gates. Toward Jack and the angels.

Jack dropped low and banked downward, gathering speed. Rushing toward the end of the slope—toward Orthy and Cerby—at light speed.

Spreading his arms as wide as his wings, he grabbed both hellhounds by their collars. And blinked.

His seraphim blink shot him over the river, into a crosswind, and then some drag. Slowing his trajectory as he began to feel the hellhounds' crushing weight. Pulling him downward toward the lava.

As his wings began to burn.

Flames ignited at the tips, chewing through feathers.

Gritting his teeth, he blinked again. Lifting a little. Surging across the chasm.

He hit the rocky ground hard, bouncing, tumbling over and over, tangling with the two hellhounds. Until he faceplanted into the ashes.

Dazed, he struggled to get up, but five wet hellhound tongues were licking his face, bringing him back to total awareness.

He sat up. Grinning. He did it! He got Cerby and Orthy over safely. Too bad Talia was going to kill him for it.

"Run, boys!" he shouted, motioning them into the cavern. "Go find Azrael. Go!"

They loped away from the rocks and into the cavern.

Talia grabbed his arm, fury in her eyes, about to burn with white fire as she dragged him backward, into the middle of the squad.

"Shield screen! Now!"

Jack grabbed the shield hanging at his side and thrust it over his head as Talia, Lucifer, and the squad put theirs up.

A heartbeat later, four Nephions bounced off their shields. The first wave was just beginning.

Lucifer tossed a ward over them, distancing the shadowy creatures that had begun to swarm.

"There's too many of them!" Muriel shouted.

Jack dropped to one knee, calling up a wave of Holy fire. He slammed his palms against the ground and launched the wave of Holy fire at the landing Nephions, wings still burning and smoldering.

The wave of Holy fire hit the hybrids like a semi-truck, bowling them over. Some fell into the lava river chasm. But there were more behind them.

Jack glared as Lare Dumont and the death angel traitors appeared above the lava river. Headed across. As their wings began to smoke.

Dammit! Where was Azrael?

"Hit them again, Jack! Harder!" Lucifer shouted as his ward began to waver.

Again, Jack launched a wave of Holy fire at the Nephions. Disintegrating some. Knocking a few others into the lava river below. But there were more behind them.

And still they poured out of the shadows. Swarming the wards.

Sweat beaded across Jack's brow, dripping into his eyes as he tossed a seraphim ward on top of Lucifer's, stabilizing it.

Nephions bounced off again as Talia and her squad kept their shields in position.

"Lucifer, there's too many of them!" Talia shouted as she threw murder marbles out of the ward at the Nephions.

"Did you hear that?" Anahera cried.

Angel notes. Jack frowned. That he couldn't hear.

Muriel began to laugh. "Azrael's almost here! Talia, he heard you."

"Then let's keep these bastards busy until the cavalry gets here," Jack said with a grin and unleashed a third wave of Holy fire rolling across the ground.

Slowly, they began to wear down the shadowy force of Nephions, but Jack's seraphim powers were quickly draining. He tossed up another seraphim ward when the other one collapsed and held his Eternean shield aloft, trying to conserve his powers for the douchesquad that had just landed.

They were using one of Samael's tactics. Wear down their opponents with impossible foes and then when they were too exhausted and drained to fight back, attack.

Jack wouldn't let that happen. Without the Nephions, they outnumbered Reptev and Lare two to one. And he aimed to keep it that way.

Jack's ward began to dim, flickering.

Lucifer put up another one, but Jack saw the strain beginning in Lucifer's face. The swarming Nephions were draining his powers, too.

"Swords out, angels!" Talia shouted, calling up a fiery archangel's sword.

Without a word of protest, the squad drew their weapons. Lucifer summoned a long, flaming red archangel's sword, too as the ward began to fail.

Jack threw another ward around them as the cavern began to spin. Talia caught him before he stumbled.

"Jack, there's too many," she said. "You can't protect all of us. Just be ready with the murder marbles, okay?"

He nodded. He sucked with swords, but he was damned good with the murder marbles.

Reptev approached, six Nephions shifting around him, Lix, and Pharzus at his flank as Lare crowded in beside him on the right. Their eyes glowed orange, red, and gold.

"Nice try, angels," Reptev said with a chuckle, "but it's the end of the road for you."

"Only for you, traitor," Kesien shouted, shield-bashing Reptev in the face.

Dazed, the angel of death staggered backward, holding his face as Deemah rushed Lix and Pharzus. Muriel launched herself at Pharzus, slamming him with her shield as Deemah repeatedly shield-bashed Lix in the face.

Kesien and Lucifer joined them, cutting down Nephions as Anahera and Talia lunged at Lare Dumont.

Jack called up a handful of murder marbles as Cerby and Orthy leaped into the fight, both of them grabbing hold of a Nephion. He grinned. They'd come back to fight!

"Incoming!" Jack shouted.

Lucifer, Talia, and the squad blinked backward, dragging the hellhounds along with them as Jack threw down a big handful of murder marbles. Taking out six Nephions. Staggering Lix and Reptev.

Lucifer engaged Reptev, flaming sword guttering as it caught Reptev's breastplate in the sternum. Knocking the traitor backward. He rushed after the traitor, sword raised as Cerby and Orthy took down two Nephions.

Six left.

Anahera and Talia closed ranks as the two remaining Nephions shifted closer to Lare and attacked. Deemah, Muriel, and Kesien had Lix and Pharzus on the ground, shield-bashing them into oblivion.

Behind him, Jack heard the distant clang of Eternean armor and the beat of dozens of wings.

Azrael!

He just hoped Azrael got here before another horde of Nephions crossed the lava river. They couldn't handle another wave of those things without Azrael and the guard.

"Cavalry's almost here!" Jack shouted. "Hold on a little longer."

9

*T*alia slid around Anahera and swung her flaming sword in a wide arc. Knocking two Nephions and Lare Dumont backward.

Anahera pivoted left and plunged her Eternean blade into one of the Nephions' chests.

Staggering it.

It shuddered, spinning and flailing, head tilted toward the cavern's ceiling. With an ear-splitting screech, it fell to the ground and didn't get up again. It stared straight ahead, its glowing gold eyes going dark.

As four more Nephions lunged toward Talia and the squad.

Turning, Talia swung her blade in a tight arc, catching two of them, severing their heads from their ashen bodies. She wheeled around, searching for the other two Nephions. And the one with Lare Dumont.

But they were gone. All three of the hybrids had faded into the shadows. Disappearing. And so had Lare Dumont.

Where was that coward hiding?

Frantically, she glanced around the cavern, trying to keep all of the Nephions in front of her. In range of her blades.

Jack snatched a dropped shield from the ash and bashed the nearest Nephion's vicious sword swings. It rounded on him, slamming the sword against his shield.

The first blow staggered Jack, but he bashed the Nephion over and over, driving it backward.

But there were just too many. Where was Azrael?

Her heart sank. And Lare Dumont. She jerked her head back and forth, trying to see past the shadows and the smoke, but that coward had vanished.

She had to locate him. Quickly. Before he attacked when she—or Jack—had their backs turned. Lare was too much of a coward to directly assault her or the other angels—or even Jack. No, he'd ambush them. Come at their backs.

She had to be ready.

A sword singsonged through the air.

She turned as Jack swung the shield upward, clocking the Nephion in the face. Staggering it.

It recovered quickly, its orange eyes so burning bright against its ashen skin.

It leaped at Jack and driving that sword with both hands against Jack's shield. Driving the shield and Jack backward.

Jack stumbled, the shield hitting him in the face as he fell, his head thumping the hard ground.

"Jack!"

She started toward him, but he waved her off as a murder marble exploded beneath the Nephion's feet. Launching it over the cavern's edge. Into the lava river below as Jack got to his feet.

Talia turned, searching the cavern again for Lare Dumont, the actor-turned-demon, but the cavern was too dark. Too many celestials and Nephions. And too much chaos.

Quickly, she held out her left hand, sword poised in her right, and unleashed omnificence. Trying to locate Lare's demonic life force among the growing tangle of so many hybrid Nephions.

To her right, Lucifer and Kesien battled Reptev and Pharzus in a frenzied sword battle.

The traitorous angels of death were losing ground quickly. They were no match for Kesien—much less the former King of Hell. Reptev kept blinking the two of them backward. Lucifer and Kesien followed, backing them toward the cavern's edge. And the bubbling lava river below.

Talia glanced over at Muriel and Deemah who had Lix and two more Nephions on the ground, bashing them down with shields and swords until Anahera launched herself at Lix, flanking him.

Orthy had one Nephion pinned to the ground, gnawing and tearing until the gold-eyed hybrid didn't get up. Cerby had two more cornered, shredding them with his three mouths full of sharp dagger-like teeth.

One left. Until the next wave crossed the lava river.

She glanced around the edges of the cavern, omnificence burning in her head, showing every detail of the terrain. And the position of every angel, demon, Nephion, and human.

She stared into the omnificence images and kept scanning for Lare Dumont. But froze.

According to omnificence, a Nephion stood right behind where she and Jack had just fought those other Nephions. To the right of Lucifer and the squad.

Something crunched. Footsteps whispered across the ash.

Out the corner of her eye, a shadow dropped out of the cavern's fluid darkness beside her, the last Nephion on her like smoke. The next wave still struggled to fly across the lava river, wings burning in the blackness.

"Jack!" she shouted over her left shoulder at her exhausted husband as the Nephion knocked her to the ground.

"Tal!" Jack shouted, holding his head. "Look out!"

He rushed toward her.

"Murder marbles, Jack!" Talia shouted, barely blocking a smoky sword blade slicing toward her throat. "Now!"

Talia slammed her flaming blade against the Nephion's shadow blade. The swords cracked against each other and rang out a shrill, piercing note that reverberated through Hell's caverns.

Talia shoved the Nephion back from her and held up her flaming archangel's blade.

Grinning, Jack tossed a handful of murder marbles across the rocky, ashen ground.

The gold spheres kicked up a small plume of ash and rolled right underneath the last Nephion.

Talia blinked left a heartbeat before the murder marbles exploded. Taking the Nephion with it!

"Talia!" came the distant call.

Smiling, Talia pulled herself up from the ground. Azrael! That was the archangel's voice ringing across the cavern. Bringing squads of reinforcements.

"Over here, Azrael!" she sang out in angel notes.

Reptev, Lix, and Pharzus closed ranks, slipping closer to the edge of the cavern as Lucifer and her squad surrounded them. The next wave of Nephions were still struggling to land on the edge of the cavern near Reptev.

She turned left toward Jack.

"Jack, over here!" she called. "Hit them with more murder marbles!"

Enough to put the arriving Nephions and Kesien's traitorous former squad over the chasm's rim. Into the river of lava.

Suddenly, Jack had a funny look on his face as he held his right ear.

She shouted at him again, but he didn't even look up. She rushed toward him, waving her arms until, finally, he looked up, an anxious look on his face. He pointed to his right ear and shook his head. Blood dripped from his ear down his neck.

He couldn't hear her!

She'd better stick close to him until Berith could heal him again. Talia started toward him when she saw the shadow. Sliding up behind Jack.

Lare Dumont stepped out of those shadows, clutching a knife, its blade glowing a faint, eerie red as a Nephion slid out of the shadows beside him.

Behind Jack!

Another Nephion! Hidden. Shielding Dumont from her and Jack.

"Jack, look out!"

Jack shook his head, still holding right ear.

Her stomach dropped. She blinked toward Jack, sword raised. Plunging the blade deep into the Nephion's gut. Dropping it to the cavern floor.

She whirled around to face Lare Dumont.

Lare was right behind Jack as he started toward her. He couldn't hear Lare behind him!

"Behind you, Jack!"

Knife blade gleamed at Jack's back. And he couldn't hear Lare behind him!

"No!" Talia lunged for Lare Dumont. "Jack!"

A heartbeat too slow.

Lare plunged the glowing blade deep into Jack's lower back, between the seams of his armor. And twisted it hard.

Jack shouted, falling to his knees as Dumont twisted the blade again. Harder and deeper.

Talia's blade arced toward Lare Dumont's neck.

Stumbling backward, Lare dropped the knife, and fled toward the last Nephion that called up the shadows that churned around it. Both of them disappeared into the roiling darkness. With wings spread, the Nephion rose into the air and shot toward the Gates of Hell, carrying Lare Dumont out of her reach.

Talia flung her sword of Holy fire at the fleeing Nephion, slicing off its right arm at the shoulder.

Lare Dumont screamed and plummeted through the darkness. Into the lava river below.

The remaining traitors, once part of Kesien's and Deemah's squad, stumbled toward the chasm's edge as a rush of shadows swept over them from the remaining wave of Nephions that materialized in the blocked tunnel's mouth that was suddenly open into the cavern. Bypassing Abaddon's deadly flight trap. As one force they scooped up Reptev, Pharzus, and Lix from the heated air and carried them back across the cavern. Back toward Hell's Gates.

Retreating.

"No! NO!" Kesien shouted as Lucifer, furious, threw down his flaming sword. "They're getting away!"

The three traitors had escaped back across the lava river. Toward Hell's Gates. And none of them could follow with damaged wings.

Talia rushed toward Jack.

Gasping for air, Jack thrust his right hand against his back and staggered to his feet, confused and in terrible pain.

"Jack, are you all right?"

Blood dripped from his hand onto the rocky floor as he pulled it away. Talia gasped, her mouth quivering as the shock set in. Lara's blade found a path underneath Jack's breastplate.

Jack looked at her in confusion, those pale green eyes weak as trails of blood ran down his arm to his elbow and pooled on the cavern floor.

"Jack?" Talia cried as he fell to his knees. "JACK!"

She caught him as he fell forward, his face almost bone white.

"Jack, no…" Her voice trembled as she fumbled with the clasps on his breastplate, snapping each one open until she got it off him. His grey robe was already wet with blood and dripping down his back. Into the dirt.

"Tal…" he said in a ragged, confused voice. "I can't—hear you. Why's it so dark? Where's—Nephions?" He struggled to speak, unable to hear himself or her.

"You've been injured," she said, trying to remain calm as she sent the image of Lare stabbing him through omnificence, into his head. And then an image of Berith with a healing stone.

"We'll get you back to Berith. You'll be okay. Just stay with me, okay?" She knew she was reassuring herself because he didn't hear a word she'd said.

He winced, eyes closing to slits as she pressed her hands against the wound, trying to staunch the bleeding.

Lucifer and the squad turned away from the cavern's edge. Lucifer was still furious, but his anger melted when he saw Jack on the ground and in Talia's arms. Bleeding profusely.

"Bollocks! Jack!"

Lucifer rushed over and dropped down beside Jack, examining the wound. His gaze met Talia's and she saw the panic hovering there. Knots twisted her stomach.

Lucifer didn't panic, but the look on his face told Talia everything. It was really bad.

The rest of the squad hurried over, forming a protective circle around her and Jack, shields up as they watched for Nephions.

"Need some healing light, do you, Jack?" said Lucifer, forcing a lighthearted tone into his voice as his hands shook.

"He can't hear you," said Talia. "Ears got injured in the fight."

Lucifer's right hand glowed with golden white light as he turned Jack's head to the left and then right. Both ears bled down the side of his face as Lucifer laid his hand over the knife wound.

"Looks like he's ruptured both eardrums, Talia," said Lucifer. "You can heal that."

Talia laid her shaking hands against Jack's ears and summoned her gold healing light. She bathed his ears in the healing light until the bleeding disappeared.

"Jack, can you hear me?" She asked.

Surprised, he turned toward her. "Some. Thanks, Tal."

She'd get Berith to heal it completely.

"I should yell at you about those hellhounds, Jack," said Lucifer. "But you got them across without killing yourself, so I won't."

When the light faded from Lucifer's fingertips, they were covered in blood. His eyes widened as he summoned more healing light and laid his hand against Jack's wound again.

This time, the bleeding began to slow a little.

"Talia!" Azrael.

Azrael blinked beside her.

"We got here as fast as we could." Then he saw Jack. "Oh, no—Jack! Talia, what's happened?"

She tried to keep her voice steady, her bottom lip from trembling as she held Jack tighter. But couldn't.

"Lare Dumont stabbed him in the back."

Alarmed, she felt fear spike through Azrael as he called up his archangel's healing light and laid his hand beside Lucifer's.

"We need to get him to Berith fast," said Azrael.

"Unfortunately, none of us can fly," said Lucifer. "Escaping across the lava river damaged our wings. Abaddon's latest escape trap—don't ask."

"Then I'll get him there," said Azrael. "Fast." Azrael turned to the rest of the guard that had gathered around them. At least fifty angels of death fresh from the fight.

"And I need five angels to blink my best squad back to Eolowen in a hurry." Azrael.

Five angels stepped out of the group as Azrael picked Jack up in his arms, his hand still pressed against the wound.

Azrael glanced over at the blade that Lare Dumont had dropped. "Kesien, bring that blade and any others those traitors dropped."

"Yes sir," Kesien answered.

Azrael made a sour face and pointed at Cerberus and Orthrus who sat obediently beside Lucifer and Jack. "And I need two more angels to bring the hellhounds. Can't leave them here for the Nephions to kill." He glanced at Talia. "Let me guess…Jack's doing?"

She nodded, a tear tracking down her face. She quickly swiped it away.

Angels of death didn't cry. At least not in front of their squad and their commander.

"See you in Eolowen, Talia," said Azrael, fear shining in his charcoal grey eyes.

She nodded, holding in her emotions as Azrael blinked across the chasm with Jack in his arms and disappeared into the tunnel.

Only then did she let the first sob tremble free. Muriel put her arms around her and hugged her.

"He'll be okay, Talia," said Muriel. "Azrael will get him to Berith fast."

"I hope you're right," said Talia as one of Sidriel's guard approached her to fly her back to Eolowen.

This angel of death was as tall as Kesien, his hair long and black, skin a warm brown, eyes a bright grey. She didn't know his name. She grabbed hold of his armor.

"Hurry," she said.

With a nod, the angel of death blinked her across the cavern and shot down the main tunnel and lifted them into the vertical gallery.

*T*alia was the first of her squad to arrive at Eolowen. Sidriel's angel of death set her down on the terrace and flew off toward the crossroads as Talia blinked along the terrace. And into the round room.

Into chaos!

Jack lay sprawled on his stomach on the round, white bed, his blood already staining it red as Berith hung over him frantically trying to heal him. She pressed a gleaming yellow stone against the wound in his lower back, a panicked look on her face.

"Azrael, it's not stopping. Azrael!"

"Getting Pravuil," said the archangel as he blinked through the rooftop portals and shot across the sky toward the Archive.

Talia fell down beside the bed, calling up her healing light. She pressed her hand against Jack's back, next to the bloodied wound.

"Talia!" Berith cried as gold healing light lit up her hands while she held the seraphim healing stone steady. "What happened to him?"

"Lare Dumont stabbed him in the back," she said, her voice quivering as tears welled in her eyes. She winced, the tears tracking down her cheeks. "Because I was a moment too slow, Berith."

He was so still and pale. And there was so much blood.

"Every time I think I've gotten the bleeding stopped, it starts up again," Berith cried. "What is this wound?"

Talia frowned. "I don't know! It was just a knife, but it had strange markings on it."

Berith shook her head. "Then it wasn't just a knife. I need to see those markings because it had to be cursed or touched with some kind of dark power."

"What? Cursed!"

She hadn't even considered that! Was that why Lare Dumont hid in the shadows so long, waiting for just the right moment to ambush Jack with a cursed knife. Get his revenge at last.

"No matter what I do, the bleeding starts back again," said Berith. "Hopefully, Pravuil will have something."

Pravuil had a lot of powers. Maybe he could heal Jack?

A rush of air swept through the room as Lucifer flew through a roof portal and landed in the room. He rushed over to the bed.

"Jack Casey," he said as he dropped down on one knee beside Berith. "Accept the healing light and heal, so we can go after that insufferable meatsack, Lare Dumont who has just earned the entirety of my wrath."

"He's dead, Lucifer," said Talia in a quiet voice.

"What?" Lucifer cried. "Dumont's dead?"

She nodded. "I severed the Nephion's arm carrying him across the river. Lare Dumont fell into the lava."

Lucifer looked shocked. "Well done, Talia. I'll let Kushiel punish him—after I'm through with him."

"Lucifer!" Berith cried. "Help me heal Jack."

"Of course." Lucifer called up the pale gold healing light he carried and joined it with Berith's and Talia's healing light.

Every time they hit Jack's wound with a round of healing light, all three of them in tandem, the wound stopped bleeding.

"Well, that seems to be working," said Lucifer, the tension leaving his face.

Berith let out the breath she'd been holding as she slid the seraphim healing gem away from Jack's wound.

"Thank the Heavens."

Lucifer started to stand up when the blood began to bubble up against the gold healing light and seep through the wound again.

"What the bloody hell?" he cried, eyes wide as he cast an incredulous look at Berith.

"Not again." Berith moaned and pressed the stone back against Jack's back.

"Lucifer, could those monsters have done something to the knife that stabbed Jack?" Talia asked.

She'd never seen a wound do this before.

"Done something to the blade?" Lucifer repeated, raising an eyebrow as he called up more healing light and added it to Berith's and Talia's healing lights again. "What do you mean?"

Talia glanced from Jack's wound to Lucifer. "We all know that this wound isn't behaving like a normal wound," she said. "It slows down the bleeding, almost stops, and then the bleeding returns full force again. We all know that Lare Dumont's hated Jack since they met on Jack's old show. He's been trying to get revenge on Jack for a long time."

Lucifer's brows furrowed and he gritted his teeth. "Wait…you said that knife had markings, right?"

Talia nodded.

His eyes narrowed. "What did those monsters do?"

"What do you mean, Lucifer?" Talia asked as she called up more healing light.

His reaction frightened her.

Jack groaned and shifted in the bed.

"Hold on, Jack," she said.

"We need to examine that blade," said Lucifer, eyes narrowing. "Quickly."

"Azrael ordered that any weapons left behind be brought back here," said Talia. "Kesien should have it."

The rest of her squad hurried into the round room from the terrace, wings folded against their backs as they stared helplessly at Jack, looking frightened.

"At last," said Lucifer, exhaling sharply.

"Talia," said Muriel in a timid voice as she stood behind her. "How's Jack?"

Talia glanced up at Muriel and shook her head. "We can't stop the bleeding."

"Kesien, the weapon, please," Lucifer commanded.

Kesien stepped toward the bed and laid a bundle wrapped in soot-covered cloth.

"This is the weapon that Lare Dumont dropped," he said in a quiet voice. "There weren't any others left behind."

Lucifer looked murderous as he stepped back from the bed, the healing light fading from his hands, and unwrapped the bundle that Kesien set down.

Inside, the eight-inch knife blade's hilt was roughly wrapped in weathered black leather, tied in place with a thin red leather cord. The serrated blade glowed with four, angry red symbols. Talia gasped.

They looked Enochian…but—altered somehow. Corrupted. The symbols looked familiar, but changed enough that she couldn't read them.

"Lucifer, what is that?"

"It's Demonaic," he said with a growl. "A bastardized version of Enochian. My first demons spoke Enochian, but over time, it changed to suit the demons. Like angels, they speak all languages, but they altered their *native* language to suit their needs."

"What does that say?" Talia demanded, trying to hold in her fear.

He sighed, bowing his head. "Fire. Shortened from *Of Hellfire*." His eyes hollowed, the fear rising and she couldn't rein hers in now. "Talia, it means that they've tempered this blade with Hellfire."

"What does that do?" Talia cried as she laid her other hand against Jack's forearm, stroking it gently. "Lucifer, I've never heard of demons tempering any sort of weapon with Hellfire. Or placing curses like this on humans."

The rest of her squad shook their heads, looking surprised. They'd never seen it before either.

Lucifer's blue eyes began to darken, the red gleam of anger brightening as he gritted his teeth.

"That was before Hell's throne was empty. Before that jackass, Samael cowered there with the pathetic remains of his army. Before that monster decided to force a captive archdemoness to create Nephion-spawn. Fathered by him. Before that coward Lare Dumont went to Hell and joined forces with Samael again."

"But what does that mean for Jack?" she asked, her voice quivering now, her heart aching.

"By design, Hellfire consumes all human flesh, leaving only the damned soul behind. It's what they were designed to do." Lucifer's eyes turned glassy, anguish winning out over his fury. "So, every time the healing light stops enveloping Jack's wound, the Hellfire corrupting this blade curse his wound again, consuming the flesh that it has touched." He bared his teeth. "Slowly killing him."

"By the Maker!" Berith gasped. "But we're angels! Can't someone counter this Hellfire?" Her face pinched with anguish. "Lucifer...I can't heal this wound."

The chilling finality of Berith's words tore through Talia's heart like a bullet.

"You can't heal Jack?" she said, unable to quite parse those words with the pain that radiated through her human soul. "What do you mean, you can't heal him? Berith! You have a seraph's healing stone in your hands! And rare angel healing powers!"

Lucifer shook his head. "It will take more than a mere angel, dear Berith, to heal Jack." he said as he laid his hand against Jack's wound again, drenching it in more healing light. "Talia, Hellfire is part of the Creation. It will take more than an archangel to destroy the Hellfire in this wound. We need Pravuil here. Now."

Anahera laid her hand on Talia's shoulder, squeezing. "I'll send Daidrean to get him."

Reaching up, Talia squeezed Anahera's hand. "Azrael's gone after him, but get Daidrean anyway. In case we need another swift errand."

Anahera rushed onto the terrace and in a moment, Daidrean

blinked over the round room and landed on the stone floor, looking frightened.

A moment later, Azrael descended through the portal. With Pravuil beside him.

Pravuil, dressed in casual white robes, short white hair shaggy and windblown, gold eyes owl-bright, his expression intense as he took in the room, a large white satchel slung across his robes. Talia knew they all looked a sight with their burnt wings and…wounds and…she pulled in a pained breath.

And Jack…

"Pravuil!" Talia cried. "Hurry…we need your help."

Pravuil moved over to the bed, satchel creaking. He frowned when he saw Jack motionless on the bed and everyone trying to heal him.

"Azrael said Jack's very badly hurt," said Pravuil as he blinked over to her, a hand on her shoulder. "What's happened?"

Lucifer nodded toward the knife lying on the bed. "Take a look at that blade, Pravuil, ol' boy. That's our problem."

"This is the blade that stabbed Jack?" Azrael asked, worry spreading through those charcoal grey eyes.

"Kesien brought it back from the cavern," said Muriel. "He wrapped it in cloth and didn't touch it."

Pravuil looked shocked as he picked up the hilt with thumb and forefinger using the cloth, holding it up to the light that poured in through the ceiling portals.

"What the devil?" his brows furrowed, mouth pursing as he turned the blade in the light, his gaze fixed on the glowing symbols.

"It's Demonaic, Scribe," said Lucifer, calling up more healing light and drenching Jack's entire body in it. "The word is fire. Short for Hellfire."

Pravuil whirled around, his gold eyes as big as a barn owl's eyes. "Hellfire?" He wrapped the blade back in the fabric and set it on the bed. "Are you telling me that this blade…"

"Yes, Scribe," Lucifer continued. "That this blade is tempered with Hellfire."

Pravuil crowded in between Talia and Lucifer, calling up a white healing light that wrapped around his fingers like cotton. Gently, he pressed the light to Jack's wound. Pravuil's healing light wrapped around Berith's and Talia's gold healing light and then braided itself with Lucifer's. When it had gathered up all the strands of healing light, Pravuil's healing light twisted into a tight coil and unwound into Jack's wound.

He pulled his hand back, studying the wound.

Talia had no idea what he was looking for, but she knew that Pravuil's healing light was some of the most powerful healing in Heaven. Cherubim healing was stronger, followed by seraphim. And finally, the Maker's healing light was the most powerful in existence. And somewhere in there was Lucifer's healing powers.

Jack's wound stopped bleeding and began to close.

"Scribe, look!" Talia pointed at the wound. "Look, it's closing!"

The Scribe smiled, looking pleased until Berith's gasp shook him out of his celebratory expression.

"Pravuil, no..." Berith pointed at the splintered light fibers bubbling up, separated by droplets of blood as Jack began to bleed again.

God's Scribe tried again, crafting a stronger weave of healing light that he wrapped with Berith's, Lucifer's, and Talia's healing lights again.

All of it was absorbed by the wound and it stopped bleeding again.

But as they let their healing lights go dark, Pravuil's weave of healing light splintered like the last one and leaked out as the bleeding slowly resumed.

"Blast it!" Pravuil shouted as he turned to Talia, looking defeated. "Talia, forgive me. I can't heal this."

Talia snapped to her feet, burnt wings trailing as she moved toward Pravuil, grabbing hold of his arms.

"Scribe, please...who *can* heal this?"

When he didn't answer right away, she gently shook him.

"Scribe, please! This is Jack. Help me. Help him!" The tears funneled down her cheeks and she couldn't stop them this time.

To her surprise, Lucifer was on his feet beside her. In Pravuil's face.

"Then who, Scribe?" he demanded. "Who in all of Heaven can destroy the Hellfire infecting Jack's wound? Cherubim? Seraphina? Father?"

Pravuil's tone was quiet and that terrified Talia.

"Lucifer," Pravuil said, shaking his head as he put his arm around Talia and hugged her. "Berith has Seraphina's healing fire in that gem she's using on Jack. And you know that I just used the most powerful healing light I possess on him. Neither Seraphina or I am strong enough to heal this."

Lucifer winced, smashing his eyes closed as turned back to Jack.

"You know as well as I do, Lucifer, that the cherubim's healing would also be useless here."

"Then who, Pravuil!" Lucifer shouted, turning around again, his eyes brimming with moisture. "Who in Heaven can save him? Who?"

Pravuil reached into the satchel he carried at his waist and lifted out a large, dusty hardcover book. Stars drifted across the midnight blue cover that had the words, *Book of Life and Death: Jack Seeger Casey* on it.

Talia gasped, her hand trembling as she touched the cover, more tears trickling down her cheeks.

Jack's Book of Life and Death, like all humans' books, was the book that every angel of death had access to...so they would know when a story ended. In order to cross the human over to the afterlife.

She shook her head, backing away.

No. No...she couldn't open that book and look at its last page. The last line of his story. That was ending right before her eyes as this cruel tome was already writing that very last line as she stood here staring at it. At him.

She swallowed a painful breath.

As Jack's life slipped away.

"Pravuil, no..." she cried, her voice breaking. "I can't. Please...don't make me crossover the love of my life. The man I was supposed to love…now until forever." She shook her head, backing away, trembling from wing tip to wing tip. "My happily ever after."

Pravuil's expression was dire, his eyes brimming with emotion as he let Jack's book float, pages flicking open until the movement stopped.

On the very last page.

An unseen pen was already in motion, black flourishes and broad strokes beginning as the last line of his story began to appear on the page. This was it.

Jack was dying.

"I'm so very sorry, Talia," said Pravuil. "The beginning of Jack's ending has begun. As the Hellfire burns deeper, his soul is beginning to leave his body." The heaviest sigh she'd ever heard Pravuil heave echoed through the deathly quiet round room. "And I can't stop it. I took this to the Maker. It looks like Jack is still humanly mortal, even though he's stopped aging. Soon, an angel of death will have to cross his soul over. I'm so sorry."

The Scribe's words were swords through her soul, tearing her heart into shards that crashed against every word Pravuil spoke. No. This wasn't real. This wasn't happening.

"Can't the Maker make him immortal?" she asked, wiping away the tears that kept falling as she felt the light inside her dim and fade.

She barely felt Muriel's arm slide around her waist, holding her up because her knees were buckling.

Pravuil wiped a tear out of his eye and shook his head. "I will ask. But Talia, your time with Jack's human form is short. Use this time to tell him the important things while you still can."

She smashed her eyes closed. Tell him the important things? How did she tell him a lifetime of important things in moments?

How could her love story with the most incredible man she'd ever met end like this?

"Like what, Scribe?" she said, her voice breaking. "That I love him more than my own existence. That I can't live without him? That I can't survive being apart from him?"

She sank to the floor, the stones gouging her knees.

Azrael was at her left side, his eyes brimming with tears as he put his arms around her, steadying her.

"I'm so sorry, Talia," he whispered. "I'd give my last flicker of light to be able to heal Jack. We all would."

"He'll rise, Pravuil—won't he?" said Talia in a hoarse voice. "And go past the portal? Can we be together there? For eternity?" She pulled in a breath, another flood of tears burning down her cheeks. "Like the Maker said we could be together?"

Pravuil winced, his gaze drifting to Azrael like he needed help explaining all of this, but it was achingly clear to her.

"For visits, Talia."

Azrael's arms tightened around her.

"Talia," Pravuil continued. "You are first and foremost an angel. It won't be like now with Jack. You can pass through the portal, but you can never be with him again like you are now."

She smashed her eyes closed, clenching her hands into fists, and pulled away from Azrael and Muriel. She blinked over to Jack and wrapped him in her arms, holding him close enough to feel his heart beating against her chest. He weakly slid his arms around her.

"Tal…" he said in almost a whisper.

She cradled him, the sobs bubbling up, and she couldn't hold them inside.

This was what the Maker meant by mortal eternity, wasn't it?

Why hadn't she understood that? Why hadn't she protected him better? Now, he would just be a soul she saw in passing on the occasional times she slipped through that portal. With an incorporeal touch that didn't sizzle against her skin. That didn't burn her mouth with soul-searing kisses. Or light her heart on fire and send her soul soaring. He would never again be a constant presence beside her. He'd be almost like a ghost…like Tre Sheridan.

She wanted to die.

She laid her face against Jack's cheek. "Why can't I still love him? Be with him?" she demanded. "I have a human soul. Can't we still love each other? As two souls?"

Pravuil knelt down beside her, a hand against her shoulder.

"Talia, you're immortal. Jack's Book of Life and Death shows that he is very much still mortal—even though he's stopped aging. Even with the seraphim and rare powers. The wings and halo. Once humans cross over as souls, it all changes. I'd give anything in Heaven to have the power to make him immortal for you. But his soul is leaving his body. It's too late to stop it. I don't have the power to stop it."

She could barely see through the flood of tears. "Even for the Maker?" she asked in a tight, broken voice.

"I don't know," said Pravuil. "I'm still waiting for the Maker's reply. There just isn't time, Talia. I'm so, so sorry."

He was sorry. She felt it. And she would pay for that with an eternity without Jack at her side. With only stolen moments through the risen portal. The love of her life.

And she couldn't stop it.

"Well, I'm going to do everything in my power to stop it!" Lucifer raged.

He dropped down beside Jack again as Pravuil blinked backward. Berith knelt beside Lucifer, the seraphim healing gem in her hands.

To Talia's surprise, Lucifer began calling up basketball-sized orbs of healing light that appeared between his hands. The moment one orb appeared, he guided it onto Jack's wound as Berith kept the seraph's healing light steady.

"Pravuil!" Lucifer shouted.

"Yes, Lucifer?" said the Scribe as he plucked Jack's Book of Life and Death out of the air.

"Tell my father that I want to see him. Now! That it can't wait."

"I'll blink to High House and tell him immediately," said Pravuil, a flicker of possibility in his intense gold eyes.

Lucifer turned his full attention to Jack and began to unleash a firestorm of energy that made everyone stand back. Except Berith. And Talia who held Jack tight against her chest, sending him every drop of healing light she possessed.

And holding onto him with everything she had.

11

Outside the terrace's round room, the entire guard kept vigil, lighting the braziers along the terrace and kneeling in the grass. Sending up words of healing and calls for assistance to the Maker. For Jack.

Talia's squad kept vigil in the round room near Jack, also calling to the Maker for help. Muriel stayed five feet from the bed and hadn't moved from her spot as she continued to ask the Maker to heal Jack. The rest of the squad knelt behind her. Kesien's moods shifted from sorrow to rage. Anahera refused to hide her sorrow, wearing it like armor. Talia was moved by the guard's calls for Heaven's and the Maker's assistance.

Lucifer and Berith stayed with Talia, right at Jack's side. Berith looked devastated as she kept healing Jack's wound with the seraphim healing gem. But what surprised Talia most was Lucifer. He had not left Jack's bedside, his moods running from despair to fury as he threw every sort of healing power he possessed at Jack's wound. He was wild, furious—intense. Desperate.

Talia sat at the head of the bed, holding Jack's weak and fading body in her arms, cradling him as she pressed healing light against his forehead. The thought of never again seeing his sexy smirk or the devastating temptation of his pale green eyes made more tears fall.

She ran her fingers through his light blond hair, unable to comprehend not lying beside him, holding him close while he slept. She winced. Trying to decode his JackSpeak or hear him call Azrael dude. Or simply spending her days beside him. Hearing him call her babe or Mrs. Casey.

For her, there was no life after Jack Casey. She'd rather not exist if it meant feeling his constant loss, this pain for eternity.

As the sunlight dimmed and angelic night began across the lower Heavens, Lucifer grew weary-eyed and frantic, still throwing everything he had at Jack's wound with a despondency she'd never seen in him before as he tried to destroy the Hellfire killing Jack.

"Why isn't it working!" Lucifer shouted as he blinked against the wall and struck it with his fists, eyes burning red, blood red halo spinning like a top as his shiny black wings trembled in frustration. Anguish.

He looked feverish as he whirled around, holding out his hands that dripped with pale white light, Jack's blood staining his fingers.

"I've hit him with every single power I possess! With the seraphim powers. With Pravuil's bloody powers. Your bloody rare powers! Why isn't it working!"

He punched the wall again and slid down it, covering his face with his hands.

"Jack doesn't deserve this!" He turned his gaze toward the ceiling. "FATHER! Do you hear me? Jack Casey doesn't deserve this!" He shuddered and pulled in a heated breath, hands smashed into tight fists. "Why can't I heal him?"

He blinked to his feet and began pacing the chamber, wringing his hands as healing light dripped onto the white stones with every step. He was so angry. Wild. Frantic for anything that would heal Jack as he made circles around the room. Ideas raced from his lips as he mumbled possible powers he hadn't tried or healers they hadn't called to Jack's bedside yet.

Talia had called them all. But none of them had the power to burn away the Creation's Hellfire from Jack's cursed wound.

She felt so helpless, her rage giving way to despair.

"Wait!" Lucifer shouted, rushing back to her, a hint of light in those bloodshot, glowing red eyes. "Abaddon! We haven't brought in Abaddon!" He blinked to the doorway of the round room. "Azrael! Get in here! Now!"

Azrael appeared in the doorway, his expression dire as he glanced at Jack and then at Lucifer's frayed appearance.

"You have an idea?" Azrael asked. "I went to Seraphina, asking for healers that could heal Hellfire. She said only the highest echelon of angels had that power. I asked about the Throne angels, but she said they had no direct capacity to heal anything in the Creation."

"Dammit!" Lucifer shouted. "What about Abaddon? We haven't tapped him yet and…"

"Sorry, Lucifer," Azrael said, bowing his head. "Abaddon has the connection to Creation and Hellfire, but he possesses no healing light."

Lucifer grabbed hold of Azrael's forearm. "Azrael…please. He's dying. We can't stop the bleeding. Our combined healing lights have only prolonged the inevitable. He won't last much longer. An hour at most before he bleeds out."

Talia couldn't believe it when Azrael laid his hand on top of Lucifer's.

"We've done everything wc can," said Azrael, his voice breaking. "And more. I've been on my knees for hours, begging the Maker to intervene—like the entire guard. The Maker does not respond. Lucifer, I'll do anything. Call on any angel. Go before High House. Anything…"

Lucifer smashed his eyes closed and turned away.

Talia hadn't stopped sending up her desperate appeals to the Maker, to High House, to any angel listening, but not a single angel note returned to her on the wind. It was as if all of Heaven had stepped away, knowing there was nothing to be done. No way to save Jack.

He had gone quiet, no longer responding to her touch. He was like a rag doll in her arms. Like the dying humans she carried out of crumpled cars, hospital beds, and dark alleys, their last moments spent unresponsive and unconscious. Even his last words had been taken from her. She'd never hear his beautiful, hot caramel voice say her name again or call her Mrs. Casey. And with every raspy breath he took, she died a thousand deaths, her human soul breaking into pieces.

"Well, it looks like Father is the only one who can save Jack," said Lucifer, defeat aching through his voice.

He staggered over to Jack's bedside and stared up at the rooftop, at the stars overhead.

Unfurling his wings, he let the shiny black wings curl around him as he dropped to his knees beside Jack's bedside. And called up burst after burst after burst of healing light, each gold burst of healing paler than the last.

Talia's own healing energies had dried up to trickles, but she kept pressing them to Jack's forehead.

"Where's Berith?" Talia asked, realizing she wasn't applying the seraph's healing gem to Jack's wound anymore.

"High House," said Azrael as he knelt beside the bed and called up his healing light to Jack's wound. "To get two more healing gems."

It seemed like hours had already passed, Jack's heart beating so softly that she had to hold him closer to feel it. Her healing light was only a drip or two now, but she kept applying it.

She wouldn't stop until she had nothing left.

Lucifer looked panicked as his last cast of healing light barely lit Jack's skin when he pressed the light to the wound and held it there.

"My healing light is almost gone," said Lucifer, wincing.

"Mine, too," said Azrael, a heavy sigh shuddering through him.

"There's only one thing left to try then," said Lucifer.

Closing his eyes, he bowed his head and put his hands together, shocking Talia as Lucifer, the former King of Hell, the Prince of Darkness began to pray.

Azrael gaped as he watched Lucifer. "Are you praying?"

Lucifer nodded.

"I never thought I would ever see a time where you actually prayed to the Maker," said Azrael.

Lucifer bowed his head lower and sang a lament of angel notes that brought a new flood of tears to Talia's eyes. Jack's heartbeat was weakening. His beautiful, big heart that had never stopped loving her, never stopped trying to find the good in people—even when it hurt him the most.

"Hang on, Jack," she whispered. "Please. Don't let go of me."

"Father," said Lucifer, his voice thin and ragged. "I have used every bit of my returned powers. I've brought every healer in Heaven to his side, but you and I both know it isn't enough. Only you hold the power to heal him. So, come down here! From that bloody high perch of yours where you've locked yourself away from all of it and heal him!"

Talia glanced around the room, where her squad still knelt, asking the Maker to heal Jack, but no column of Heavenly light descended from the upper Heavens. No procession of angels landed to lay hands on her beautiful, wonderful husband of almost one year.

"I know you hear me!" Lucifer yelled, his voice rising. "Can't you hear all of bloody Heaven asking you to heal this one little human? I know you hear us."

He gritted his teeth as his eyes snapped open and he stared at Jack a moment. Remorse and pain burned in those red eyes, blood red halo spinning wildly, shiny black wings shifting nervously.

"Father!" he screamed. "This little human defied all of Heaven's judgment against me and voted to spare me. After every terrible thing I did to him. After every wrong—and there were so, so many—and every attack, he found a way to move past it. His was the only voice, Father. The only one that insisted I be given a chance at redemption. Redemption I don't deserve."

Lucifer laid his hand on Jack's arm and squeezed. "I can't bear to watch Talia suffer for eternity without him…like I watched Berith pine for Azrael for millennia." His eyes were wet with tears, moving Talia to more tears.

Jack's breaths began to slow. Coming farther and farther apart.

She held onto him, tightening her arms around him, trying to keep his soul in his body. She couldn't cross over the love of her life.

She couldn't!

"Father! I beg you…save him. Jack Casey does not deserve this. I have no more healing light left to give. No more powers. Nothing but what I am. So, I beg you, take my essence. My life force. I freely trade it in exchange for Jack Casey's existence. Me for him, Father."

"Lucifer!" Azrael cried. "What are you doing?"

"Fixing this, archangel," said Lucifer in a tired but intense voice. "I had already resigned my fate to the Lake of Fire. So, please…take my chance at redemption and keep Jack's soul in his body. He deserves to live and I've—done enough damage."

Exhausted, Lucifer collapsed against the floor, most of his energies and powers emptied.

Talia glanced at his face. He looked as heartsick as she and the rest of Eolowen felt.

"My life for his, Father. It's the only thing I have left to give."

Talia listened for a response, for a cacophony of angel notes erupting across Heaven, responding to Lucifer. But only the sound of the wind and Jack's raspy breathing touched her ears.

A pained shout tore from Lucifer's throat as he arched his back, hands clenching into fists. He tossed his head back, blood red halo wobbling and spinning out of control as his wings folded flat against his back.

Again, he screamed, flailing against some unseen force.

"Lucifer?" Talia cried, holding Jack tightly. "Lucifer, what's wrong?" Her gaze shot to the archangel who slid across the floor to Lucifer. "Azrael? What's happening?"

Azrael glanced at her, shaking his head. "I have no idea. Lucifer? What's the matter?"

Lucifer writhed against some unseen force and collapsed against the white stone floor, shaking and shuddering, his wings furling and unfurling. Like he couldn't control them. Shiny black feathers began to fall, littering the white stones as his halo spun so fast, Talia thought it might take flight.

Another scream tore from Lucifer's throat, red eyes burning bright as pure white Holy fire ignited across his wings and the feathers began to burn away.

Lucifer threw his arms across his face as the high-pitched whine began, coming from his halo that spun faster and faster. Until it caught fire, white-hot Holy fire so bright that Talia had to shield her eyes.

Azrael put his arm over his face, forced back from the heat.

A sonic boom shook the grand hall as a massive blast of Holy fire rippled through the round room. Lighting up the entire grand hall with the brightest white light Talia had ever witnessed—not even when the Maker had appeared on the judgment dais in High House.

For a moment, she was blinded, but slowly, the room dimmed, the soft even glow returning to the lower Heavens.

But she gasped when she looked at Lucifer.

Gone was his blood red halo. Burned away were every last shiny black feather of his wings. Not a trace remained of that red glow in his eyes, leaving them only a pale, bright blue. Perched above his gold curls was a spinning halo of pure white light. And at his back were the most beautiful pair of radiant white wings she had ever seen.

Lucifer struggled to his feet, staring at the piles of ash surrounding him.

"What happened?" he said, looking dazed. "Why am I still here?"

"Lucifer!" Azrael cried. "Your wings!"

Lucifer's face contorted. "They're gone," he lamented. "Burned away to ash."

"Lucifer, no…they've—evolved."

He flexed his wings, surprised that something was still at his back, and curled the wings around him. They glowed with white Heavenly light almost as bright as the Maker.

"They're…white," he said with a gasp.

"So is your halo," said Azrael.

Pravuil blinked through a portal in the ceiling, Berith behind him.

He still carried the satchel with Jack's book, his archangel wings folding against his shoulders, gold eyes intense. But at the sight of Lucifer, they froze.

"Heavens preserve us!" Pravuil shouted.

Berith was wide-eyed, staring at Lucifer, an incredulous look on her face.

Even Talia's squad was staring now.

"What's happened to me?" said Lucifer, turning his hands over and over at the sight of the soft glow clinging to his skin. Even his black Hell armor had turned pure white.

Pravuil rushed at him, grinning.

"By the Maker, Lucifer! I don't know what you did, but you've become Heaven's Lightbringer!"

Lucifer looked aghast. "The Lightbringer?"

Pravuil nodded, his expression brightening. "What did you do right before this?"

"I...I called out to Father. On my knees. Begging him to heal Jack. When he didn't respond, I..." Lucifer pulled in a deep breath of air as the realization hit him. "I asked him to trade my life essence for Jack's existence and I gave back my chance for redemption. To keep Jack's soul in his body."

"A selfless act if I ever heard one!" Pravuil exclaimed. "Directed at a human. By the King of Hell. That must have been enough to unlock your Lightbringer energies! The Maker always intended that title for you, but you never showed you were worthy of it—or its powers. That epic sacrifice transformed you."

Lucifer held out his hands. "Then I have Lightbringer energies?"

Pravuil nodded. "And the power to heal Jack, Lucifer."

At last, a grin rose on his face.

"Lucifer, hurry!" Talia cried. "Jack's heart is stopping."

Panicked, Lucifer rushed to Jack's side and laid both hands on the knife wound. Closing his eyes, he called up the new healing energies he carried.

"Hold on, Jack!"

Like a firehose, white light poured from his hands into Jack's back until Jack's skin began to glow.

Talia kept holding Jack as the most powerful healing energies she'd ever seen or felt sank into his wound.

Light shot up through the deep, jagged gash and to Talia's surprise, flames shot up and then ash began to bubble up from the wound as the bleeding slowed. And finally stopped.

"The bleeding's stopped," Talia shouted, the tears rushing down her cheeks.

She waited. Holding her breath. Watching the wound. But not even a droplet of blood oozed up.

"Lucifer…it's really stopped."

Lucifer looked exhausted, but he smiled.

"Only ash is surfacing from that deep puncture now. The Hellfire must be cooling."

Berith leaned over Talia and placed her seraphim gem against Jack's forehead, letting the warm gold light wash over him. She pressed her hand to Jack's chest and Talia held her breath as she continued to cradle him.

"I feel his heartbeat, Talia," she replied, the hint of a smile on her face. "It feels…stronger. But he's going to need some time to heal."

Talia closed her eyes and focused her angel senses on Jack as she held him against her body. She knew the signs of a soul about the leave the body by feel and moments ago, his soul was beginning to float free.

"Pravuil!" she called, opening her eyes. "Jack's Book! What does it say?"

Pravuil hurriedly pulled out the Book with its midnight blue cover, stars moving across it, and thumbed through the pages until the book began to float. He let go of it as it bobbed gently on the air currents in front of him. Pages turning to the last one.

An unseen pen nub was busily scrawling words onto the paper. And Pravuil smiled as more pages began to appear behind what had been the last page.

"Would you look at that? Talia, more pages are appearing. The words are continuing his story. It's telling how Jack began to heal from his injuries after coming within a heartbeat of bleeding out. But because Lucifer has transformed into the Lightbringer, Jack's wound was cleansed of Hellfire and is currently healing."

Berith reached out and stroked Jack's face. "Then he's going to be okay," she said.

Pravuil glanced up from the Book as another page appeared after the last one.

The Scribe grinned as another page appeared. And another. "It's still recording information and all, but Jack's Book says he's beginning to heal. And more pages keep appearing. Thanks to Lucifer." He grinned when yet another page appeared at the back of the book. "And new pages are still materializing. Talia, Jack's going to be okay."

Unable to halt her relieved shout, Talia sang out angel notes that Jack was going to be okay. She let new happy tears roll down her cheeks as she continued to cradle her husband of almost one year. They would get to celebrate their first anniversary after all. And hopefully, many more.

"Lucifer," said Talia, her voice quivering. "I have no adequate words to thank you for giving Jack back to me. Thank you seems so trivial, but I am eternally thankful."

He turned to Talia as he sat down against the wall and slid down it, looking exhausted.

"Without this little human, I would no longer exist, so believe me when I say that the pleasure is all mine."

Muriel laid her hand on Talia's shoulder as she studied Jack's wound. "So, is Jack really going to be okay?"

Talia wiped away tears as she hugged Muriel. "He is, Muriel. His Book of Life and Death says so."

Muriel whooped and rushed over to Kesien, Deemah, and Anahera. "You hear that, squad? Our vanguard's going to be okay!"

"Thank the Maker," Kesien said, exhaling sharply as he got to his feet.

"No," said Talia, glancing at the former King of Hell who had at last been restored to his full glory. "Thank Lucifer and the Maker."

Anahera grinned. "Thank you, Lucifer. I'm so relieved. There's only one vanguard for this squad."

Talia nodded. "For me, too, Anahera. And that's Jack."

"And for the guard," Azrael added and suddenly, the whole mood of the round room shifted from a wake to a celebration.

Muriel reached down and ruffled Jack's hair. "And now, you owe Lucifer your life, Jack," she said, chuckling.

Lucifer shook his head. "I think I still owe Jack a few favors after his solo stand for me at the tribunal."

Jack took a deep breath and shifted against the bed, his breathing even. Steady. Not so labored. And his heartbeat was stronger. Rhythmic.

"Okay if we tell the guard?" Muriel asked, nodding toward the rooftop. "They're probably all still out there calling for help on Jack's behalf."

"Of course," she said. "But make sure they know that Lucifer healed him."

Talia leaned back against the wall and slid a pillow underneath Jack's head, his breaths louder now. He was in a deep, peaceful sleep. Only then did she relax and let the tension unwind from her body.

Jack was going to be okay.

12

*J*ack awoke to a cool breeze blowing through the quiet, empty round room, making him shiver. He tried to sit up, but the heat and pain in his lower back made him reconsider.

He glanced around the chamber, at the sun-washed white stone floor, bright blue sky peeking through the rooftop portals. The scent of honeysuckles and jasmine wafted through the room as an occasional angel flew over Eolowen's quiet rooftop. Headed toward the meadow.

How long had he been out? And how'd he even get here?

He shivered in the cool breeze, dressed in only a pair of grey boxer briefs, a heavy bandage wrapped tightly around his lower back. He pulled the crisp white sheet up to his chin. The fabric smelled like warm linen and rain, but it was thin and he felt chilled.

Where was Talia? And the squad? Had they defeated the Nephions and traitors from Samael's guard? And Lare Dumont? He had only hazy memories of those moments after they'd landed across the lava river with charred wings. And then, those shadowy Nephions and their creepy spider movements crossed behind them, attacking. Along with the douchesquad.

He remembered taking down some Nephions with a load of murder marbles. The concussive force had ruptured both his eardrums and everything went silent. Then white-hot pain pounded through his back as the world got fuzzy. He'd been stabbed and he remembered bleeding a lot until everything went dark.

Now, all he had was pain, a gap in his memory, and lots of questions.

But he was so tired, his eyelids barely staying up. He must have lost a lot of blood. Were all the angels still in Hell fighting? Cleaning up Samael's mess. Was Talia okay?

He had to see her. Make sure she was okay.

And where were Zanth and Tre? He remembered Lucifer's black tower and sending Zanth and Tre back here to Eolowen with two Watchers. But he had no clue whether they'd gotten here safely or not. Or if Berith had even agreed to treat Zanth who'd been repeatedly assaulted by that asshalo, Samael.

Before long, Jack fell back asleep, waking up later to a soft white quilt across him and the room looking all dim and oozy. Like he had fever. He couldn't quite open his eyes this time, but he felt angels in the room. And someone holding his hand.

"But why is he running a fever, Berith?" asked the familiar, musical voice of his wife. "I thought the wound had been healed."

Talia!

"Lucifer said the last remnants of Hellfire still need to burn out of the wound," said Berith. "Give him a little more time, Talia. Pravuil says that Jack's Book is still busily adding entries and pages, so he's doing fine."

What did that mean? What had he missed by being unconscious? And why was Talia so worried?

But he was already sinking back into cool sleep.

The next time he awoke, the room's temperature felt comfortable when he opened his eyes. He found Berith seated by the bed, a book in her hand. Probably from Azrael's library of human books.

"Jack!" she cried, leaning over him. "You're awake!"

"Hey, Berith," he said, his voice sounding raspy and sandpaper rough like he hadn't spoken in ages. "What's happening with Samael and his spawn? After our staycation in Hell."

She smiled. "Samael and Raum are still in holding cells at High House. And Lord Kushiel has been quite busy interrogating Samael."

"Wish I'd been there to watch them rehearse for the Lake of Fire championship toss. Any luck getting anything out of him?"

Berith shook her head. "Not much. But at least Lord Kushiel is enjoying himself. Azrael actually saw him smile the other day."

Jack chuckled. "I like a prosecutor who really enjoys his work. Glad it's Samael he's interrogating. Couldn't happen to a nicer douchebag."

"Agreed."

"So, where's my smokin' hot wife?" he asked, sitting up in the bed.

"I had to shoo her out of the room for a while," said Berith, setting her book on the bed. "She hasn't left your side since Azrael brought you in."

Jack leaned forward until he saw the cover of the very old book. *Pride and Prejudice.* He chuckled. Made sense. A heroine who redeemed herself. Right up Berith's alley.

"Where is she now?"

Berith straightened the covers on the bed and folded them neatly across his bare chest.

"She and Azrael are discussing plans to round up the remains of Samael's army. Any Nephions left. And Reptev, Lix, and Pharzus. They escaped with Lare Dumont, but—"

"That bastard escaped, too?" Jack said with a growl. "Figures. I'll find him."

"Jack," said Berith in a sobering tone. "Lare Dumont's dead. He fell into the lava river while trying to escape."

Jack froze for a moment. Lare Dumont was dead?

Jack bristled. He had developed a healthy hatred for his former co-star and former best friend. That meant he was really in Hell this time. Where he belonged. But it ticked him off that those three traitors got away. He had no memory of it.

"Guess he's really in Hell now," said Jack finally. "And those three traitors are back on the To Do List. I'll bet Kesien's chewin' through walls trying to go after them." He laid his head back against the stack of downy white pillows behind his head and shoulders. "And Deemah's probably expanding her shield collection—to bash all of these douchebags into another form of existence."

Berith's smile widened. "Kesien and Deemah have both volunteered to go after them, as you have already guessed, but Azrael's wary about sending them—considering their history with these monsters. And what happened in Hell."

Jack flinched. What did happen? He didn't know because he couldn't remember. Not all of it anyway.

"But Berith, Kesien and Deemah have earned the right to hunt down the douchesquad and bring them in," said Jack, folding his hands in his lap.

"They have," she replied, laying the back of her hand against Jack's forehead. "But Azrael wants to give Kesien and Deemah both time to cool down a little." She sat back down in her chair and retrieved her book. "Get a level-headed plan underneath their wings. But Talia will be so happy to see you awake, Jack. It's been days."

Kesien was probably still murderous over his old squad turning and Deemah probably hadn't thought past that first shield bash. Not that he could blame them. He'd have felt the same way.

"Makes sense." He studied Berith a moment as she settled back in the chair and opened her book again. "Berith?"

She didn't look up from the book. "Yes, Jack?"

"What happened with Zanth? I sent her and her soul toy, Tre with two Watchers when we sprung her out of Samael's chains. Did they make it safely here?"

She nodded, looking at him over the top of the book. "Zanth was in a bad state when the Watchers brought her here. I did what I could, but she needs time away from that horrible place, some distance before I can help her heal." She frowned.

"Are you okay with healing an archdemoness?" Jack asked. "I'm sorry. I should have checked with you first."

"It's okay, Jack," Berith replied, setting her book in her lap again.

"I know, she's an archdemoness who has probably inflicted more than her share of pain and suffering on humanity and angels, but the way I see Zanth is she didn't have a choice. She was made for her role. Forced to perform those tasks or be destroyed. And now that she wants out of that life, I'm sympathetic. I want to help her heal."

Had Zanth slipped away with Tre somewhere? Hiding until Samael was in custody?

"Where is she?"

"She's still here," said Berith, gazing at him with a calm expression. "We setup a small private room here in Eolowen for her and Tre. Right next to the hellhounds."

Hellhounds! Azrael and Lucifer were watching over them. He couldn't help but grin at that news.

"Zanth needed privacy and time. When you're back on your feet, I'll take you to her. She'll be glad to see you. She's been through a lot. And she's been asking for you."

"I just couldn't leave her chained up down there," said Jack, frowning as he twisted the sheet with his fingers. "Not with Lord Kushiel about to flip that place. Besides, she's helped me and the angels more than once. That should give her a chance at redemption, too."

"It will, Jack," said Berith. "You seem to have a knack for finding celestials who deserve a chance at redemption."

Jack shrugged. "I just know she didn't have to help us and she did. And she took me to my dad in purgatory. When I'm back on my feet, I'll go see her."

Then his brain backed its way through the conversation, settling on when she'd snuck the hellhounds into the conversation.

"And back to the hellhounds..." he said, his gaze narrowing as Berith smirked, book in hand. "You just quietly slipped that in, didn't you?"

Berith frowned. "Slipped what in?"

"About Zanth being next door to Cerby and Orthy," he said. "And don't think I didn't notice." He tried to do a fist pump, but the pain was like a linebacker slamming into his body and he let his arm drop against the bed.

"Careful, Jack—don't you dare reopen that wound. It was too hard to close."

"Sorry, just relieved they're okay," he said in a pained voice and leaned further back on the pillows.

She smiled. "You and those hellhounds. Yes, they are both here and fine, Jack. Azrael even let Lucifer put them temporarily here in Eolowen. No one wanted you to wake up and find them missing." She gave him an annoyed stare. "Especially since your daring rescue of them—that almost got you killed."

"Hey, I stuck the landing."

She tried to give him her sternest look, but she couldn't erase the smile.

"Yes, you did. Lucifer said you blinked across the cavern with an arm around each one. Got them to the other side."

"I couldn't watch them get torn apart by those Nephions, Berith. The Nephions were really embracing their demon side...or Samael's side...maybe both. So, I blinked Orthy and Cerby across the river."

Berith still looked annoyed at him.

"You do realize that, if your timing had been even a little off, you'd have plunged headfirst into that lava river, Cerby and Orthy right behind you."

He'd never even considered that happening. He just kept imagining him and the hellhounds sailing across the chasm and landing on the other side. If he'd thought about that possibility, it would have probably crippled his reaction time. Good thing he was an optimist who hated being told no.

Berith's gaze snapped toward the rooftop portals and she smiled.

Either she'd heard angel notes or someone was about to drop some mana cakes down through the portals. Or he'd bored her enough that the thought of escaping through the ceiling was the only thing keeping her alive.

"Planning your escape route, Berith?" he asked. "Did I bore you that much?"

She gave him that don't make me smite you look that Heaven's angels had been perfecting since he'd first stepped foot in Heaven. At least he'd done some good up here.

"It was Talia," said Berith. "Asking if you were awake yet."

"That's a tune I wish I could hear," he said.

Berith lifted her chin and opened her mouth, but Jack couldn't hear a single note.

"What'd you tell her?" he asked.

"I told her you were wide awake and in rare form. She'll be here shortly from High House. And she can't wait to see you."

He grinned. At last. He ran his fingers through his bangs and tried to smooth his blond hair, but it probably looked terrifying after lying here unconscious for days.

"My hair look okay?" he asked.

Berith chuckled. "Like you just woke up as the romantic lead in one of your Earth movies, Jack. She'll love it."

He shrugged, unsure if that was good or bad, and waited for Talia. It seemed like forever before she, Azrael, Muriel, and Lucifer dropped through the rooftop portals into the room. Talia wore a short grey robe beneath her Eternean armor.

"Jack!" Talia shouted, blinking across to room.

He held out his arms. "My smokin' hot wife," he said. "At last."

She blinked into his arms and wrapped them around his bare chest.

"Oh, Jack," she cried, her eyes watery. "I'm so glad to see you!"

"Tal..."

He held her as tight as he could manage, until the wound in his back began to throb, forcing him to relax his hold.

But he compensated by pulling her mouth to his in a long, frantic kiss that made him a little dizzy as she kissed him back hard on the lips, her hands anxiously touching his face and his bare chest and then slid across his bare shoulders. Her touch sizzled across his skin in fevered waves and he wanted to hold her forever.

She sat up, her hands still traveling across his face, down his chest, and around his waist. Checking his bandage, he realized with a grimace.

"When Lare Dumont stabbed you in the back, I thought I was going to explode!" she cried, fingers sliding through his hair and caressing the side of his face, thumb brushing across his lips.

His gaze narrowed. "Wait. That douchebag Lare Dumont stabbed me? In the back!"

She nodded. "With a cursed knife."

"Like *Smile* and *The Ring* kind of cursed or an F-bomb in front of the Maker kind of cursed?" He frowned. "This is Lare Dumont we're talking about. At least he's in Hell where he belongs now."

Talia glanced at Jack, still smiling, and shrugged. "I don't know what those first things are."

"Horror movies, Jack?" Lucifer replied. "They used to be great icebreakers for introducing wagers to humans."

Muriel walked over to the bed and rumpled Jack's hair. "Not just horror movies though, Lucifer," she said. "Those two horror movies are both about curses, so yes, Jack. The first kind of cursed. Only more Biblical."

Jack's eyes widened. "Like Raiders of the Lost Ark kind of cursed?"

Muriel nodded.

"Oh, I get it now," said Lucifer. "Yes, definitely more Biblical, Jack. The knife had been tempered in Hellfire."

"That's it?" Jack replied. That didn't sound so bad.

"Jack," Talia cried, stroking his hair. "Hellfire was created to consume humans, body and soul."

"Talia's right, Jack," said Lucifer. "And once the Hellfire entered your body, it was literally consuming your blood and flesh. You were only a breath away from crossing over."

Talia nodded and held him tight as she laid her head against his right shoulder. She looked terrified.

"Your Book of Life and Death was writing your very last line, Jack," said Azrael. "We all saw it trying to record your ending and we couldn't stop it."

"I almost lost you," said Talia against his ear, her voice breaking.

And then he realized they weren't just yanking his chain. They meant it. He almost died.

"Wow, glad I missed that part," he said. "If I thought for even a blink that you and I were being separated, Tal, I'd have been begging the Maker for a reprieve."

Lucifer burst out laughing as he approached the bed. "I had the very same thought, Jack."

That's when Jack realized that Lucifer had changed. Drastically.

"Whoa…dude…your wings. What happened?" He gasped when he saw the halo of white light encircling his head. "And your halo's been bleached or something."

"When my father didn't respond," said Lucifer, not quite meeting Jack's gaze, worrying Jack. "I offered my life essence up as a trade, Jack. For your life."

Jack sat up and leaned across the bed, frowning at Lucifer. "You did what?"

"I offered my life force up for your existence, Jack. You didn't deserve to perish because of my mistakes. And Talia didn't deserve the punishment of being without you for eternity, either. So, I offered up my redemption."

Jack gasped. "Your redemption? For me? Why?"

Lucifer put his hands on his hips and looked away from Jack. "Because I've learned to love this stubborn little human who completely changed me. At times, against my will. I hated humans. I blamed them for everything that had ever happened to me. Until one convinced me he was worthy of love and respect. And my sacrifice."

"And that sacrifice, Jack," said Azrael, stepping to the foot of the bed. "That sacrifice transformed Lucifer into the Maker's Lightbringer, a role they had sought for their firstborn angel since the Creation came into being. You were dying, Jack. The Lightbringer's powers were the only thing that could have saved you—besides the Maker."

"That's why your wings and halo changed?" said Jack in surprise.

Lucifer nodded, looking a little overcome with emotion, something Jack had never seen in him before.

"Dude…how do I even thank you?" His arms tightened around Talia and he pulled her closer. "Talia and I would have been separated. For eternity." He pulled in a breath, shaking now. Knowing how close he'd come to losing the one thing he could never lose. The love of his life. Talia.

Lucifer had changed in so many ways. He was blown away by the statuesque, radiant angel that stood before him now. Lucifer's red eyes were gone. So were his shiny black wings and that blood red halo that spun wildly whenever he got angry. Which was most of the time. Even the faint white scar across his forehead was gone, healed by the limitless glow of Lightbringer powers that radiated from him.

He had become Lucifer the Morning Star. The Bringer of Light.

"Thank me?" Lucifer turned around, looking shocked as he dropped down beside Jack's bed. "After everything you did for me. After everything I did to you. And you want to thank me? It is I who should be thanking you, Jack Casey. Without that big mouth of yours and that total lack of fear at the most inappropriate of times, I would have already ceased to be. Disintegrated in the Lake of Fire. The thanks are all mine."

The room went quiet as Lucifer patted Jack on the shoulder and stood up, looking emotional in a way that Jack had never witnessed before.

"Did you guys get to interrogate Samael?" Jack asked, breaking the quiet.

Azrael shook his head. "Alas, that privilege belongs to Lord Kushiel. No, but we did get to witness the interrogation of Raum and Samael though."

"Both are stubbornly unrepentant and refuse to acquiesce and admit fault," said Lucifer. "Much less change their ways. No, Samael will end up in the Lake of Fire for this. He refuses to accept blame. Or defeat. Quite strange if you ask me."

"So, Azrael, what is the plan for going after Kesien and Deemah's former squad?" Muriel asked as she leaned against the wall, dove grey wings folded against her shoulders, sable hair hanging to the middle of her back.

She still wore her Eternean armor and looked like she'd been training with the guard.

Jack's gaze shot to Azrael who crossed his arms against his Eternean breastplate, charcoal grey eyes sharp with anger.

"I want all of Samael's loyal guard in custody," said Azrael, his features tightening. "And any angel who would openly fight for demons and traitors like Samael. So, we will be going after them. We've got a flurry of Watchers out there combing Earth and the Heavens for these idiots. But the Nephions are a different story." He began to pace, a worried look spreading across his taut features. "They will be very difficult to locate and apprehend. It will take a lot of time to hunt them all down. And we don't even know how many of them are left."

Lucifer nodded at Azrael. "I am working with Abaddon and Kushiel to locate the Nephions. And when Zanth is feeling better, I will be discussing them in greater detail with her. She has much to say on the matter."

"I hope she gets dibs on releasing the trebuchet arm that propels Samael into the Lake of Fire," said Jack.

Chuckling, Lucifer nodded. "Oh, there is already a line forming for that honor, but yes, Zanth should have first go at the bastard. Followed by Azrael, Kesien, and Deemah for starters."

Jack tried to sit up, but the wound in his back shot fresh stabbing pain through his legs and rib cage. Groaning, he laid back against the pillows.

"Careful, Jack," said Talia, rubbing his shoulders.

"Too late," he said with a groan.

"Oh, that reminds me, Jack," said Lucifer, turning toward the terrace doorway, white curtains billowing. "I brought you another healer."

Lucifer sang some angel notes that Jack couldn't hear. A moment later, a cherub blinked through the curtains.

Talia gasped and got to her feet, looking shocked as the cherub's lion form faded into short dark hair and dark skin, her yellow eyes bright. Jack sat up, a heartbeat ahead of a knife thrust of pain that shot through his torso.

He yelped and grabbed hold of his side, shocked as he recognized this cherub.

"Oseira?" he said in a pained voice.

Talia moved toward Oseira and stared at her a moment and then hugged her. Muriel rushed over and hugged her, too. Followed by Berith. And then Azrael.

"Using my Lightbringer powers, I spent one entire angel day searching for a glimmer of her light in the High House rubble. There wasn't much remaining, but I found it. And brought her back."

"Thank you, Lucifer," said Oseira.

He shook his head. "Don't thank me for correcting a horrible act that I committed, with you as my actor, Oseira. I hope that someday, you will forgive me."

Oseira nodded. "In time."

"All I can ask for," said Lucifer, motioning toward Jack. "In the meantime, if you could heal Jack and then work with Berith to heal an archdemoness seeking redemption, I would be grateful."

Oseira looked frightened. "An archdemoness? Here? In Heaven?"

"Clientele has expanded a little now that Heaven is upholding its tenets," said Azrael. "And you've got Jack to thank for that."

Jack shrugged, not sure if Oseira wanted to fly away or stab him with a flaming sword. But she was back from oblivion. Something he hadn't expected from Lucifer.

"Hey, they're your tenets," said Jack. "I just read them back and asked for clarification."

"Love frees all," said Talia.

Jack nodded. A philosophy he intended to live by.

"My next project is to locate the lost seraphim," said Lucifer. "And keep searching until I've brought back everyone lost at High House. While I work with the fallen in Hell and find paths back for them. They really do want to redeem themselves and come home. Even Procel."

"Could you skip Raziel?" Jack said. "For me?"

Everyone laughed.

"Pretty sure we're doing Raziel a favor by not bringing him back, Jack," said Azrael as Oseira moved across the room and silently conferred with Berith.

"How's that?" Jack asked.

Azrael smiled. "If Lucifer brought him back, Kushiel just would convict him of treason and toss him into the Lake of Fire."

"Agreed, Azrael," said Lucifer. "Raziel made it quite clear he was unrepentant when he joined forces with Samael and me. And it was also clear that he was working entirely for himself."

Berith moved into the center of the group. "All right, everyone," she said. "Jack needs his rest. Let's clear out and let him get some sleep."

Muriel stepped over to the bed and squeezed Jack's shoulder. "Rest up, Jack. We still need our vanguard."

"Thanks, Muriel."

Muriel blinked up through the ceiling.

"Give that wound time to heal, Jack," said Lucifer. "The Hellfire did a lot of internal damage. Give my Lightbringer powers time to work."

"Thanks, Luci," said Jack as Lucifer blinked to the rooftop. And disappeared on those silky white wings.

Oseira followed Berith out of the round room and into Eolowen. Probably to evaluate Zanth. Leaving him alone with Talia.

Smiling, she walked over to the bed and pulled off her sabatons. Piece by piece, she unfastened her armor and laid it on the floor beside the bed.

"Angel armor striptease," he said with a smirk. "You had me at angel."

She dropped the last piece beside the bed and clad in a short, thin grey robe, she crawled underneath the covers with him, enfolding him in her arms.

"I love you, Jack Casey," she whispered against his ear. "And I almost lost you."

He felt the pain and anguish rush through her body as she began to tremble.

"The very last line of your Book of Life and Death began writing itself into your book, Jack. I almost lost you forever. Your soul was a breath away from leaving your body. The Maker had already let me pass through the risen portal, but our relationship would have been reduced to occasional visits."

Occasional visits? He felt sick, wishing he'd known that before taking on all of Hell. One wrong move and he'd have lost her forever.

"I love you, Talia," he said, holding her tight. "Now until forever. And I'd give my soul to stay with you."

He kissed her.

"Jack, I don't know how much time we have left together, but I never want to be apart from you again. I don't know what's happening on Earth, but whatever path you choose, I will be there right beside you. No matter what Heaven says."

He felt her shaking and the tears clinging to her cheeks.

"Well, we may have to leave the beach house if I can't find another acting job."

"I'll follow you anywhere, Jack Casey."

He chuckled. "You may have to. We may have to couch surf here in Eolowen until I figure out where I'll be landing after The Cinderella Hour."

She frowned, tilting her head in confusion. "Couch surf?"

"I'll explain if it comes up," he said. "But right now, I don't want to think or deal with any of that."

"No?" she said, sliding against him, her head against his chest as he snuggled closer.

Jack's wings shifted to the edge of the bed as he folded them tightly against his shoulders. He shook his head, smiling.

"No. I just want to have white hot angel sex with my smokin' hot angel of death wife. Is that too much to ask?"

Talia glanced up at the ceiling, over at the curtains leading into Eolowen, and finally the curtains leading onto the terrace.

"Probably is, Jack," she said with a smile. "Communal space and all."

"Seriously," he said with a growl. "That's it. I'm warding the room.

Maybe Orthy and Cerby can guard the entrances until we've had our —quality time. It's almost our first anniversary."

She looked conflicted.

"You think I'm bluffing?" he said. "Throwin' down the river card and bettin' the pot."

He pointed at the ceiling and cast a white seraphim ward across the ceiling. With another flick of his hand, he called up a seraphim ward across the Eolowen-side entrance. He took a deep breath and filled the terrace doorway with a blaze of white light from a third seraphim ward.

Talia giggled and pulled him under the covers as Jack slid the robe over her head.

13

Three angel days later, Jack was shakily on his feet but under close watch by the entire guard because he was still unsteady and lightheaded from all the blood he'd lost. And the damage that the cursed Hellfire blade had caused. But, despite his difficulties, Berith finally allowed him to see Zanth. Talia stuck close to his side, making sure he was okay and didn't reopen his delicately healing wound.

"Talia, are you all right?" he asked as she blinked him down to the opposite end of the grand hall's long nave, not allowing him to do it himself.

They paused in front of a heavy white door with a glowing crystal doorknob. Berith's idea since so many of the rooms had become occupied. So, a glowing doorknob meant the room was in use.

"Of course," said Talia, reaching up and tenderly brushing a lock of blond bangs out of his eyes. "Why?"

He smirked when she frowned at the grey short robe he'd tucked into his jeans like a shirt. She turned him around, her hand against the small of his back. Making sure his wound wasn't bleeding. And to Jack, it felt like she was getting her kid ready for the first day of school, but terrified to let him go.

"Because! That's so extra!" he said, turning back around, motioning at her. "I've got my lunch money and I won't miss my bus stop."

She frowned, a confused look on her face.

"Babe, you're treating me like a little kid. Or an in-patient. I'm worried about this out-of-pocket helicopter angel behavior. It's not like you."

Her eyes got watery and she bit her lip, sliding her arms around him. Holding him close. He felt her shaking.

"I'm so scared, Jack," she said in an aching whisper.

"Aw, Tal," he said and pulled her into a protective hug. "It's all going to be okay. I won't let these douchebags steal our happily ever after. Or make us afraid."

She pulled away from him, fear so bright in her eyes that it made his stomach ache. What exactly happened while he'd been out?

She motioned at his head. "Jack, despite that halo, all your rare angel powers, your wings...and the seraphim powers, you are still very, very mortal." She gripped his hands and she was still shaking. "I almost lost you because of a Hell-cursed dagger. Something I never saw coming. For eternity, Jack. It was the end!"

Tears rolled down her cheeks, turning into crystals and pearls that scattered at her feet. He stiffened. Whatever happened rattled her to her core.

She began to pace, hands in motion. "I watched, helpless, as the last line in your Book of Life and Death began writing itself. To finish your story, Jack. In a place where I could only visit."

He slowly steered her back into his arms and held her, but the tears kept tracking down her face.

"I'm not sure I deserve you," he said, laying his head against hers.

She jerked back from him, eyes like embers. "Don't you dare say that!"

He gripped her hands. "Babe, I'm just an out of work actor. And all I have to offer you now is me. All of me. And this strange cosmic luck that keeps keeping me at your side. I'm not sure that I'll ever be worthy of you, but I love you. And I will fight for you, fight to stay right here in your arms to my last breath." He held up his left hand and tagged his ring finger with his thumb. "And this ring is that promise to you. For the rest of my days."

She kissed him hard on the lips and held him so close that he felt the flow of air through her heart as it beat against his chest. "But I want forever, Jack."

He sighed, nodding. He had to stay alive because seeing her occasionally for eternity was a hell he couldn't imagine. Now, he understood her panic. And it made him ache all over.

"None of this was your fault, Jack," she said, a little calmer, the tears fading. "Yet in a heartbeat, Lare Dumont almost took you from me. Forever. And if it hadn't been for Lucifer's sacrifice elevating him to the Maker's Lightbringer, you would have died."

She said that like it was the direst event in her existence. And it humbled him.

"Cosmic luck held, Talia. Even if it hung by an unraveling thread, it still held."

"How can you be so optimistic, Jack? Can't you see the constant mortal danger you're in? Of us losing each other for eternity?"

He shook his head. "No, because when all I want to do is spend all my days with you, I can't help but see the upside here. I have to see that light or I'll go crazy. And somehow, I'll find a way to spend my eternity with you."

She kissed him again, urgently, and stepped back, gripping his hand.

"And that's why I can't let you out of my sight, Jack. It makes me crazy with worry."

He squeezed her hand. "Then I'll just shut my mouth," he said. "Because I'm the luckiest guy in the universe that you want to be this close to me all the time."

He reached out and wiped away the last of her tears.

"I love you, Mrs. Casey," he said and brought her clenched hand to his mouth, kissing it. "No matter what."

At last, she smiled. "Happily forever after."

He kissed her again. "That's exactly what I want, Mrs. Casey. Now, let's check on Zanth."

He motioned toward Zanth's room. Berith had placed her and Tre in a small room farthest from the terrace, thinking the sounds of angels sparring might be unsettling for them. She was always thinking about the comfort of others. So different from his mother who only thought about her own comfort.

Talia nodded and he knocked on the door. "Zanth, it's Jack and Talia."

"Enter," said the muffled but sultry alto voice.

The room was small and austere, but pleasant with windows that looked out onto the Archive spire. Only a chair against the wall and a white bed with a rectangular mattress stood in the center of the room, made up with white sheets, white pillows, and a white blanket. It faced the wall of windows overlooking the Archive. The room had a smoky scent to it, traces of honeysuckle and dried roses hanging above the lit brazier that stood beside the bed. It had an almost campfire smell to the burning oil. A hint of sulfur clung to the air. Bet the guard loved that.

Zanth huddled in the bed beneath the covers, looking tired and ill, a short grey angel robe clinging to her thin frame. Her red eyes were weak, shadows dusting her ashen complexion, making her already chiseled face look thin. Her bat wings were tucked tightly against her shoulders.

Tre sat on the bed beside her, looking confused and tense, like the last place he wanted to be was in Heaven, surrounded by angels. Guess he'd been with Zanth and the other demons too long. Jack knew that Zanth had to be feeling the same way, but she had to feel relieved at being free from Samael's assaults. She was an archdemoness and she'd been Lucifer's executioner for longer than he could even comprehend. She had always been a hardened, seasoned soldier with razor-blade precision. Yet, in her eyes, he saw distress. Pain. And the hollowness of someone who had survived something horrific. And for an archdemoness, that was a level of suffering that Jack couldn't comprehend.

And it made him furious. He knew Zanth. Knew how much she had changed. How she had devoted herself to doing the right thing. Her and Tre. And all these months of horror she'd suffered. He gritted his teeth. All of it had come from an angel. An archangel—one he wanted to throat punch…for starters.

He forced down his rage. Had to keep his head clear.

"Zanth, I'm came as soon as they let me out of bed," said Jack as he moved with slow footsteps toward her bedside.

Zanth gave him a puzzled but concerned look as she sat up in the bed and leaned against the low white headboard. And Tre. "What happened to you, Jack Casey?"

Talia steered him to a stool beside the bed and he sat down heavily, studying Zanth. Wanting to apologize even though he had nothing to do with what that douchebag Samael had done to her.

"Lare Dumont backstabbed me with a cursed knife. Long story."

She opened her eyes to slits. They glowed red as she stared at him for a few moments, like she was trying to gather her thoughts.

"It has to be," she said in a quiet, velvety French accent, her smoky alto voice resonant. "Because you would never let that connard sneak up on you." Her eyes opened wider, a sad look on her face. "You look so pale, but I am so glad to see you."

The fire and arrogant confidence she'd always had were absent. Now, she seemed small and frail, her ashen skin making her look almost doll-like, not the poised, haughty archdemoness about to throw down destruction. It almost made him sad.

Zanth reached out a bone-white hand to him, her long red fingernails all broken. He held her hand, gently squeezing as he took inventory of her injuries. Except for some bruises and cuts, she looked physically okay. On the outside. But he knew the bulk of her injuries would remain hidden. For demons, injury was weakness and vulnerability, so they kept those things concealed.

Jack knew she would hide anything that made her a target. So, he had no idea what Samael had done to her psyche. Demon, angel, or human—what Samael did to her would have scarred all of them. If that bastard had touched Talia like this…a white-hot burst of fury burned through him and he gritted his teeth to hold it inside.

After he'd fought down his rage, he found his voice again.

"Zanth, I'm so sorry…I want to destroy that pompous bastard for what he's done to you."

With Tre's help and another pillow, she sat up straighter in the bed, her thin frame still covered by that thick white quilt, grey angel robes hanging on her.

"I am okay," she said in the most unconvincing tone he'd ever heard from her.

Red eyes filled with tears, her voice sounding fragile, bordering on breaking. It trembled when she relaxed her iron grip on her emotions even a little. For a demon, that was huge. No, the damage was done inside, where he couldn't see to heal it. Regardless, he'd do his best to try and help her—even if it was just to listen and tell her she did nothing wrong. That was the truth. All of this had been done to her. Against her will.

"You don't sound okay," he said softly. "Look, I only know a little about what that bastard did to you. But Talia and I are here to help you get through this, Zanth. Even if it's just to listen and call Samael a bastard, we're here."

He wanted to tell her that the angels supported her, but he knew that would make her appear weak to other demons. So, he kept that part to himself.

Zanth nodded, her smile not quite reaching those red demon eyes.

"Merci, Jack, Talia," she said. "I appreciate that you both got me out of Hell."

"You know we grabbed Samael and Raum, too, right?" Jack said with a smirk. "Brought them both in for interrogation. Kushiel's got them. They're so screwed."

He tried his best to act normal and make her feel calm.

Like nothing had changed even though he knew having that douchebag in custody would give Zanth some closure. Especially since Zanth had been repeatedly violated. She was a demon, so what?

But she was hurting and wanted out of that life. He would listen and help her get better.

It icked him out that Raum was her son, but Jack had no idea how much contact she'd had with this beast of prophecy like the angels called him. Was he her son or did she just bring him into the world?

"Did Samael abduct you?" Jack asked. "Or try to recruit you?"

She lowered her gaze to the covers. "He tried to recruit me at first. Convince me to willingly help him create the other side of a monster."

"He kept promising her all these things," said Tre, his voice sharp and angry. "And she knew there was no way he could deliver any of it. Like she was too stupid to know he was lying."

"I knew he could not deliver anything and frankly, I wanted none of what he offered," she said, glancing at Tre. "I started to walk away, but he surrounded me with Holy fire and slapped those…those chains on my wrists and ankles." The muscles in her cheeks tightened. "And then he forced himself on me."

Tre punched the wall, a frustrated shout escaping through his gritted teeth.

Her voice was so small and quiet that Jack barely heard the words, but it didn't make them any less powerful. Or painful. He bristled, wanting to shield-bash Samael a couple million times in his ugly, douchebag face.

He took a moment to cool down.

"Forgive my ignorance, Zanth, and feel free to ignore my question if it's way too personal," he said as he chose his words carefully, not wanting to hurt Zanth more by asking her to talk about what happened. But no matter how he said it, the words just came out all kinds of awkward. "But how are Nephions created?"

The touch of a smile rose on her lips, a sparkle in her red eyes.

"Surely, your parents explained this to you, Jack?"

He felt his face burn as Talia and Tre burst out laughing.

"I'll explain it all to him later," Talia said with a chuckle, her arms sliding around his neck as she gently kissed his cheek.

Burn. He sighed, hanging his head a moment and then looked up at his angel of death wife. "Promise, Talia?" he asked, flashing her his most devilish grin.

She gave him an emphatic nod. Sweet!

"Walked right into that one," he said, turning back to Zanth. "No, I was…just hoping there'd be a demon stork or something. A vulture maybe? I really didn't want the image of Archangel Samael doing the Time Warp in my head. Eewww." He shuddered, feeling shook. "So, you carried each and every Nephion and gave birth to them?"

Zanth violently shook her head no. "Non. Jack, please!"

"Thank God," he said.

"Indeed," said Zanth. "Since I cannot thank Lucifer anymore." She bowed her head. "Have they thrown him into the Lake of Fire yet?"

She sounded sad, regret in her scratchy alto voice.

"What?" Jack's eyes widened.

"Samael, that connard, said Lucifer had been found guilty of all charges and the Maker had sentenced him to…*oubli*." She pulled in a pained breath. "Oblivion."

She smashed her eyes closed, grief rising in her red eyes, her mouth flattening into a taut line. She obviously cared a lot about Lucifer.

"That asshalo's a lying sack of…of…archangel," said Jack. "No. Luci was given a chance at redemption, Zanth."

Her head jerked up, a shocked look on her face. "What? The Maker…*racheté*…how you say…redeemed him?"

"The Maker gave him the chance at redemption," Jack said, correcting her. "He's taken some major steps toward it, too. Fought beside us in Hell. Helped us free you. He even saved my life, healing me, a sacrifice that lifted him into the role of Lightbringer."

Zanth gasped. "Lucifer has ascended to the Lightbringer?"

"Tal, sing Luci in here," he said and she turned toward the door.

He couldn't hear the notes, but Talia turned back to him after a moment or two and hovered beside him again, wings in a gentle motion.

"Wings and halo have turned white, red eyes gone. He's changed a lot, Zanth."

The knock on the door was almost immediate.

Talia blinked to the door and opened it. Smiling, Lucifer floated into the room in all his Lightbringer radiance.

"Hello, Zanth," he said and moved beside Jack. "Forgive me for just now coming to see you. Things have been rather—hectic since my trial."

"Lucifer!" said Zanth with a gasp. "You are not obliterated like Samael said." She stared in awe at his white wings and halo.

Lucifer looked unfazed. He leaned down and gripped Zanth's hands, making her smile widen.

"That ignorant prat has no idea where one lie stops and the rest begin. No, Zanth. Thanks to Jack Casey here, I have been given a chance to redeem myself. And I am working hard to show Jack and my father that this chance has not been wasted."

Zanth motioned at Lucifer and then at Jack with her index finger. "The two of you are...*amis?* Friends?" she asked, eyes wide, brows raised.

Jack glanced over at Lucifer and finally nodded. "Yeah. Luci and are I friends now. After he stopped trying to kill me."

Talia looked frightened until Lucifer chuckled and bowed his head. "Who knew that a forced truce with my biggest enemy would end in friendship? Yes, Zanth. I now consider Jack my friend. Anyone who fights beside me in battle and watches my back like he has can only be called a friend. Especially one who saved me from the abyss."

"Thanks, Luci," said Jack with a smirk.

"I also consider Talia, Azrael, and the death angel guard friends, too," said Lucifer. "They are much more than colleagues after standing beside me in that battle. And Zanth, I wanted you to know that Raum is also in custody."

Zanth's expression didn't change. "He was the first Nephion, one I gave birth to, but he was immediately taken from me to train up in Samael's image. Many of the other Nephions were created from Raum. Until Samael sought...changes."

She shuddered, no doubt remembering the assaults in vivid detail and Jack wanted to bust that douchebag into little archangel shards.

But he was relieved to know that Zanth hadn't birthed every single one of the hordes of Nephions he saw and had fought in Hell.

"Jack," said Zanth. "Raum is no more my son than the Watchers who carried Tre and I to Eolowen."

He felt relieved because if Raum was as unrepentant as Samael, he would end up in the Lake of Fire, too. Especially being this beast of prophecy.

"Good to know," said Jack.

Lucifer sat down on the edge of Zanth's bed and folded his wings against his back.

"Let me heal you, Zanth," he said.

She nodded.

Gently, Lucifer laid his hand against Zanth's shoulder and closed his eyes. A soft white light enveloped Zanth. She closed her eyes, lifting her chin, and settled into the radiant glow for several moments until finally, it began to dissipate.

"There, that should heal the physical injuries that Samael caused you," said Lucifer as he sat up straight again.

Zanth's red eyes looked sad. "Can it also...how you say—redeem me?"

"Only you have the power of redeeming yourself, Zanth," Lucifer replied in a quiet voice. "And you've got that chance now. Jack, Talia, and I have all vouched for you."

"But where do I start?" she asked, glancing from Tre to Lucifer.

Jack stepped toward her bed.

"Zanth, you've already started," said Jack. "You helped me and the angels both in purgatory and during the apocalypse. And now, you helped reschedule Armageddon. Talk to Berith. She's been through it."

"Zanth's scared," said Tre.

"Tre, no!"

"Jack, Zanth and I have nowhere to go," Tre continued. "I'm a renegade soul, escaped from purgatory. She's an archdemoness, escaped from Hell. With no place to go."

Jack sighed. "Part of that is my fault. I couldn't leave you in Hell when Kushiel got there to remake it alongside Abaddon. So, that's why I pulled you out of there." He turned to Lucifer. "Luci, where can they go?"

Lucifer stared at them a moment, shaking his head. "That's a tough one. For one thing, Tre's incorporeal. And that's my fault for deceiving you. And Samael's."

Leaning across the bed, Lucifer, pressed his hand to Tre's forehead. Tre gasped and wilted, sinking to the floor.

"Tre!" Zanth shouted as she sat up board-straight in the bed. "Are you all right?"

Groaning, Tre Sheridan pulled himself out of the floor. And when he stood up, he had physical form again.

"Dude!" Jack shouted. "You're…you again!"

"What?"

Tre grinned as he turned his hands over and over again. He slapped his hands against his face and balled them into fists. Then his gaze shot to Zanth. He plopped down beside her on the bed.

"Oh, Tre…" she whispered as her hand lifted to his face.

Smiling, she caressed his cheek and ran her hand down his arm. "I can touch you again," she said, her voice quivering.

"Like this," Tre said as he put his arms around Zanth and held her.

"Much better than my healing light," said Lucifer as he glanced at Jack. "I am liking these Lightbringer powers." He fixed Tre and then Zanth with his gaze. "Now then, Zanth, I will be returning to Hell and working with the fallen to bring them home. Act as my assistant and I will add your path to theirs. And now that Tre is human again, you and he can live on Earth for now."

Jack leaned toward Zanth. "I know where there's an incredible deal on an L.A. studio apartment. If you don't mind hellhound claw marks on the hardwood and a squeaky Murphy bed."

"It's got a comfy bed, a nice shower, and a small patio with a great view of the Heavens," said Talia, leaning against Jack. "If you know where to look."

"Jack, Talia, Lucifer—merci," said Zanth, looking overwhelmed. "It sounds like…chez moi." She sighed as a smile rose on her lips. "Home."

"Send me the contact info?" said Tre as he held Zanth close and then sighed. "When I get a phone."

"Done, dude. I'll write it down for you."

The knock on the door startled Zanth.

"Enter."

Archangel Azrael floated into the room, his gaze on Talia.

"Talia, Lord Kushiel has asked to see you and Jack. Pardon the intrusion, Zanth."

"Of course, archangel," said Zanth.

Jack frowned. "Kushiel? What for?"

Talia's wings began to twitch, her halo spinning faster. "Why?" Talia demanded.

"He wants to take both your statements about Raum and Samael," said Azrael. "A debrief after the battle and captures. He's still interrogating them."

Azrael didn't look distressed. This seemed basic. Like a standard angel thing.

Lucifer waved his hand dismissively toward the windows. "I just returned from giving my statement, Jack, Talia. No worries. It's painless."

At both Lucifer's and Azrael's response, Talia relaxed, her wings flattening against her shoulders.

"All right," she said. "Jack and I will head right there."

"Feel better soon, Zanth," Jack called to her as Talia led him out of the room.

Talia gripped his hand and pointed up at the rooftop portal. And blinked them to the roof.

"Seraphim blink, Mrs. Casey?" he asked, motioning toward the High House spire.

She wrapped her arms around him and kissed him. "Please."

He held out his hand, pointing his index finger at the High House spire. He pulled in a deep breath, holding it, and blinked.

14

Talia tightened her hold around Jack as they blinked through the High House portal. Inside, the tiny alcove stood at the edge of the spire's vertical gallery that ran the length of the spire.

"Up or down, babe?" Jack asked, glancing around.

She pointed above her head. "It's up. The holding cells where Lucifer was kept."

"Lead the way," he said, close enough that she smelled his warm, cottony and cedar scent, a touch of jasmine and cool rain clinging to the short grey robe he'd tucked into those faded Levi's that hugged his body in all the right places.

She chuckled. That angel robe was anything but a T-shirt, but the celestial grey folds draping across his lean body made it look like a hot Roman toga. His pale green eyes were luminous, the corners of his mouth quirked into that sexy smirk as she blinked them up through the gallery. And into the block of cells glowing with white wards that stood just below the courtroom and the Cloud Chamber.

Lord Kushiel leaned against the wall, fingers twined, those massive red-tipped white wings curving around his lanky frame. Gone were the shadows that had surrounded him when she'd first encountered him—all caused by Raum's control. Kushiel looked less like an angel of death and more like the legendary angel royalty he had become. His shaggy white hair was longer, his dark eyes looking brighter in a pale gold-grey hue.

"Talia, welcome," said Kushiel in his raspy, precise tone, motioning her toward him. "And Jack, thank you for coming."

Jack seemed to relax at Kushiel's welcoming demeanor. Kushiel seemed a lot different now that Raum's influence was no longer affecting him. Patient. Calm. Angelic.

"Lord Kushiel," said Jack with a nod as he followed closely beside Talia. "Azrael said you wanted to see us?"

Kushiel nodded toward the holding cells. "Yes. I require both of your statements regarding the capture of these two traitors."

"Gladly," said Jack.

Lord Kushiel motioned them toward the wall where a bright white light pulsed across a translucent square. "Place your hand here to record the events through your eyes."

Talia nodded and pressed her hand to the glowing panel. Its light flashed and rolled for several seconds and then went out.

"Jack, put your hand to the light as well," said Kushiel.

Nodding, Jack pressed his hand to the light square. It roiled with light for a few seconds and went dark. Jack stared at the square a moment and then stepped backward.

"Do you think either one will repent?" Talia asked Kushiel.

"Repent?" Archangel Samael cackled, shaggy black hair in his eyes. Raum joined him in a deep, guttural laugh as Samael leaned against the wall of his cell, looking calm, collected, and self-assured. Amused. "Oh, I won't be here long enough. Besides, I'll never be that weak—not like Lucifer."

"You mean the Lightbringer? Most powerful angel that's ever existed?" Jack said, glaring at the archangel. "And since when is electing not to be a douchebag a sign of weakness?"

"Repentance is for cowards and prisoners," said Raum in a taunting voice.

Jack laughed, arms folded against his chest as he approached Raum's cell.

"Let's see…cell block, check. Locked cell door, check. Shackled douchebag prisoner in denial, check." Jack shook his head. "If ever there was a time for repentance, this is it, dude."

"If you still want to keep on existing," said Talia as she stood beside Jack, glaring at this deluded monster who thought he was above it all. "And want to forego a swim in the Lake of Fire. You'd be wise to repent."

"Oh, I'll never repent," said Raum, looking amused as he pressed his palms against the cell's inside walls, a smug look on his Nephion face. "And I plan to continue existing here in the Heavens."

"Stuffed or in a jar?" Jack asked. "Or maybe part of the angel potpourri in those angel statue bowls?"

Talia shook her head "That would never work, Jack," she said.

"Why's that, Tal?"

"Because they reek of betrayal and cowardice." She was almost an inch from Samael's face now, only the holding cell's clear frame separating them. And she didn't crack a smile. "So, Raum and Samael would just stink up the whole spire."

"Good point," said Jack as he stood closer to Talia, arms still crossed.

Samael's leering grin didn't waver.

"Keep your pet winged rat on a short leash, angel of death," snapped the archangel.

"Just long enough to strangle this colossal douchebag, please, babe," said Jack.

Samael glared at Jack and returned his gaze to Talia. "Don't worry, we won't be in Heaven long enough for any of this to matter, I assure you."

"Planning to reunite the band, Samael?" Jack asked. "Launch a new world reunion tour? Trust me, traitor, no one's buying that T-shirt."

Samael settled back against the cell's far wall, arms folded against his chest, black feathered wings gathered around his shoulders, halo dim as he stared at Jack and then Talia, his gaze unsettling. Talia wondered what this monster had planned. He seemed so confident that his time in here was temporary.

"Reptev's got it all under control," said Samael. "You'll see."

"Reptev?" said Talia with a bitter laugh. "Who has never been anything but your spineless errand boy?"

Samael didn't flinch, that stupid smile still stretched across his face. So confident that she wanted to shield-bash that leering smile off his face. Or watch Lord Kushiel use his wrath to remove it.

"Soon, Reptev and my army will break us free of these cells," said Samael, continuing his delusions. "And we'll meet you and Heaven on the battlefield. At Armageddon. And destroy you."

Jack shook his head. "Dude, you're delulu. That show's been cancelled. And we bricked your army."

"Delayed," Samael corrected him.

"Samael!" Talia shouted, banging the front of his cell with her hand.

Startled, the archangel's gaze snapped toward her.

"Your army's been reduced to some minions and three rogue angels of death who couldn't cross a street without someone else leading the way!"

Was Samael really this clueless? Or was his denial that complete?

Talia couldn't believe how he was sticking to this fairy tale ending. Maybe it was because he'd managed to escape prison here in Heaven before—and when the guard pursued him into purgatory. But he'd never faced Lord Kushiel any of those times. Shouldn't that be his clue that the game was over?

"Dude, the rest of your army?" said Jack, shaking his head. "It's just a handful of confused Nephions and an out of work actor with the emotional range of a hand puppet! Or was. Because Dumont's currently backstroking the lava river around Hell's Gates." He glanced at Raum and then Samael. "And Armageddon's been canceled and returned to the warehouse. The seventh flight never touched down on Earth. So, enjoy your swim in the Lake of Fire, dudes. Better bring a towel...made of tungsten."

Lord Kushiel stepped toward Samael's cell.

"I will remind you, Samael," said Kushiel, red-tipped wings rustling against his shoulders as he paced around the cells. "Your tribunal before the Maker begins in two angel days. With punishment to be carried out immediately following the tribunal."

"Two angel days?" said Raum in a quiet voice.

Samael laughed it off. "You jest. That's not even time to assemble the judges."

"The judgment dais has already been filled with the Maker and your peers, Samael," said Kushiel.

"Who dares to sit in judgment of me?" Samael roared, the smile fading from his face.

Kushiel looked unaffected by Samael's shouts.

"Besides your Maker?" Kushiel asked. "Archangel Pravuil. Lord Abaddon. Archangel Turiel. And the Lightbringer. And testifying will be Archangel Azrael, Archangel Sidriel, the archdemoness Zanth, angel of death Kesien, and angel of death Deemah." Kushiel motioned to Talia and Jack. "And I have already gathered statements from Jack Casey, Talia, and her squad."

Talia couldn't halt the grin from spreading across her face. Jack burst out laughing and then stood in front of Samael's cell.

"Dude, you are so chopped," said Jack.

"Unless you'd like to repent," said Talia. "And we'll know if either of you is lying."

Jack tapped his index finger against his wrist. "Hope Reptev can tell angel time, because when the big doom hammer's on twelve and the little doom hammer's on six, it's free swim time at the Y." Jack stepped back from the cells.

"I guess this is goodbye, Samael," said Talia. She glanced over at Raum. "And Raum. I doubt either of you will be here when I return to High House." She turned to Lord Kushiel. "Did you need anything else from us, Lord Kushiel?"

"No, thank you, Talia, for your statement." Kushiel turned to Jack. "And thank you as well, Jack for giving a statement. They will be added to the judgment dais' records."

"We're done here," said Talia, wrapping her arm in Jack's.

She led him out of the cell block and into the vertical gallery, down to the small alcove, and out the warded portal.

"Blink us back to Eolowen?" she asked, hovering beside Jack, his silvery grey wings in motion beside her as they floated in an updraft. She still had her right arm wrapped around his left.

"You got it, Mrs. Casey."

Jack extended his right arm toward Eolowen and pointed his index finger. Blinking them across the square, past the parks, along the white cobbled streets, and over Eolowen's rooftop. Onto the terrace.

A grin lit his face as his gaze shot toward the meadow.

Azrael, Lucifer, and her squad were out in the grass, throwing two balls almost the size of basketballs. Cerberus and Orthrus barreled through the meadow, fetching the balls in one of their mouths and bringing them back.

Already, Jack was grinning.

Talia poked him. "Well, what are you waiting for, Jack?" she said, trying to hold back her smile. "Blink us into the game."

He grabbed her by the hand and blinked across the meadow.

When Cerberus and Orthrus saw him, they barked and rushed at him, knocking him into the grass. Orthrus sat on his chest, licking his face while Cerberus ran around him, barking and nudging Jack's hand for pets.

"Careful with that wound, Jack!" Lucifer called. "Now that you've completely corrupted the guardians of Hell's Gates."

Talia checked to make sure there was no blood on Jack's robe. Just a bit of hellhound slobber and some grass stains.

"How'd it go?" Azrael asked as Jack hugged Orthrus and scratched behind his ears—all four of them.

"We both gave our statements to Kushiel," said Talia. "And then he let us into the cell block as he began another interrogation."

Jack's laughter floated across the meadow as Cerberus jumped on him, too. Jack scratched behind his three sets of ears. And Talia couldn't help but smile.

"Samael still thinks Reptev and his army—what's left of it—are coming to break him and Raum out of High House." Talia shook her head. "Refuses to repent. Like Raum."

Lucifer's eyes darkened. "So, deluded to the very end."

Kesien nodded. "Doesn't seem to realize that unless he repents, in two days, Kushiel will toss him into the Lake of Fire. Not that I'll shed any tears. His choice."

"He just can't understand that his luck's run out," said Deemah as she set one of the balls in the grass. "Good riddance."

Azrael put his hands on his hips. "Deluded? Lucifer, he is in complete denial."

"With no one to speak for him either," said Lucifer in a quiet voice.

"Can't speak for someone when they've done nothing redeeming," said Talia. "And not only do they refuse to acknowledge it, but both Raum and Samael refuse to change."

"Quickest way into the Lake of Fire I know of," said Muriel. "But it's all his doing. He only has himself to blame."

Azrael nodded.

Lucifer looked pensive. Humbled.

But Jack's laughter brightened their mood.

Talia tossed one of the balls to Jack.

"You ready to fetch, Orthy?" Jack said, dangling the ball over his head. "Cerby? C'mon! Let's fetch!"

Both hellhounds, once the fiercest guardians that Hell had ever borne, ran in circles, tongues wagging, tails pounding the grass as they waited for Jack to throw them a ball. Jack Casey had forever changed them. Like he'd changed all of Heaven and its angels. He had no clue how much change he'd caused. Just by being Jack Casey. And she loved him for that.

Jack tossed the ball and the game began again as everyone gathered around, tossing out the second ball. Talia moved beside Jack, laughing as he threw himself into the game with the hellhounds.

"Think Jack will fetch one of the balls if I toss it?" Lucifer asked and everyone laughed. "He is part golden retriever, you know."

They played for a long time until they managed to exhaust Cerberus and Orthrus. And Jack who'd expended way too much energy. He was visibly tired as Azrael and Lucifer rounded up the hellhounds. Lucifer led them back toward Eolowen.

"Bye, boys!" Jack shouted as Lucifer blinked them across the meadow and into the grand hall.

He made a funny face and grabbed at his right jeans pocket, pulling out his phone. He glanced at it and his face went from relaxed and elated to tense and brooding.

"Jack? What is it?"

"Text from my sister, Meredith. Saying she'll...uh, talk to me on Friday."

"Your sister?" Talia cried. "You haven't talked to your sister for a long, long time, have you?"

He shook his head. "Not since she called me a week or so ago. Before that, it had been years. It's not her text though...it's the one under it." He looked up at her and he looked nervous.

"What text, Jack?"

"A text from...Evan Bellows," he said in an anxious, surprised voice.

"Your former director?"

He nodded.

"The one hiring your costars?"

He nodded again.

"Is something wrong, Jack?"

Jack shrugged. "He wants to meet with me on Friday. That's the day we're having our first anniversary party."

They'd sent out invitations to everyone weeks ago. They were having it at their new beach house. And she refused to reschedule a party because Evan Bellows had finally decided to contact Jack.

"So, invite him to the party, Jack," she said with a shrug. "Or tell him to call you on Monday. We are not rescheduling our party."

"That's a good idea, Tal," he said.

His thumbs flashed across his phone as he typed out a response. He sent the text and kept staring at the screen.

"Why's he want to talk to me now?" said Jack, beginning to pace through the meadow. "He's already recast my old show. He looking for my blessing or something? Is he gloating that he's cast all my friends?"

Talia let him try and work through his anxiety of not knowing. She didn't think a professional like Evan Bellows would be that petty. And he had always seemed to like Jack...or at least appreciate him, even when Jack had turned down the part that made him famous.

She put her arms around him and led him toward the terrace. "C'mon, Jack. You need to let that wound rest after running around with the hellhounds. No matter how Evan responds, it's out of your hands. Okay?"

He nodded, distracted, and tried to be part of the conversation, but she knew that would be impossible for him until Evan had responded. And she knew that Jack would probably brood about this all night. She smiled. But she had a few ideas on how to keep him distracted.

Berith stepped out of the round room, headed toward him.

"Jack, we need to change your bandage," said Berith.

"Can we do it later?" he said, pulling his phone out of his pocket again, glancing at the screen, and then returning it.

"Now, Jack," said Berith.

Berith took hold of his left wing and led him into the round room. Talia followed behind, cutting off his blink path if he decided to bolt.

Berith sat him down on the bed.

Jack's gaze immediately shot to the small gold plate with two glistening mana cakes on it.

"Mana cakes!" he shouted.

Berith smiled as Jack untucked the grass-stained grey robe he wore and pulled it over his head.

"It was the best distraction I could come up with," she said and laid the dirty robe on the floor beside the bed.

Talia chuckled. So, she wasn't the only one trying to distract Jack.

She hovered at the foot of the bed as Berith gathered her fresh bandages and sat down behind him, cutting away the old, bloody bandage. The wound had bled a little. Talia wondered if he'd exerted himself too much with the hellhounds. And that frightened her.

Berith made a face and took a white cloth from a basket at her feet. She tipped a clear glass bottle of celestial spring water onto it and returned the bottle to the basket. The celestial spring ran alongside the pergola at the edge of Eolowen's meadow and meandered through all of the lower Heavens. Purest water in Heaven. With remarkable healing properties.

She cleansed Jack's wound and then used the seraphim healing stone while he devoured the first mana cake, his face dusted with golden sugar.

"So good," he said, closing his eyes.

By the time that Berith finished wrapping his lower back in the fresh bandage, Jack had eaten the second mana cake.

Berith fluffed the pillows at the head of the bed. "Now, get some rest, Jack."

His eyelids looked a little droopy despite the sweet rush of the mana cakes. Finally, he nodded, kicked off his beat-up blue Vans, and crawled over to the pillows, settling himself against them.

And that sexy smirk lifted the corners of his mouth, those pale green eyes sparkling with devilish light.

"Cuddle with me, Mrs. Casey?"

She blinked onto the bed and settled herself beside him, her arms sliding around his neck.

"Thought you'd never ask."

She laid her head against his bare shoulder as he leaned over and kissed her.

He settled against her, his eyelids getting heavier. Until they closed. Opened. Closed. Yawning, he pulled the white quilt across his jeans.

But something shook him wide awake.

He shot upright and hit the floor, fumbling his phone out of his pocket. A new text message had arrived.

Talia held her breath a moment as he read the text on the screen.

"Tal! He said he'd love to come. He'll be there."

"That's great, Jack!"

But brooding Jack had returned and even though he climbed back into bed and laid his head against her shoulder, sliding his arm around her, she knew his thoughts were a million miles away. And they would stay there until the party on Friday night. At their newly renovated beach house.

15

On Friday, Jack and Talia left Eolowen and flew back to Earth, down to the Southern California Coast, just past Pacific Palisades. Just off Pacific Coast Highway where a dilapidated old beach house had been resurrected from the dead. It was right on the beach. Three bedrooms, two baths. Two car garage and a concrete patio. Two thousand square feet. With his beautiful angel of death wife, Talia at his side—it was everything he'd ever wanted. The bungalow had been renovated by the show and most of the money he'd saved.

He'd had the keys to the place for a while and had already arranged delivery for his things from the apartment. Which wasn't much. Just Dad's dresser, a nightstand, some boxes of books, kitchen stuff, and clothes. And his SUV. The bedroom and living room had already been renovated, the house transformed by white baseboards and trim and the cornflower blue and pale aqua walls that Talia loved. A huge, curved blue-grey sofa, driftwood coffee table, glass lamps, and a large flat screen on a driftwood stand now filled the living space. Porcelain wood-grain tiles the color of driftwood covered the floors.

And the patio that faced the ocean had been decked out like a Hawaiian lanai with white rattan furniture and soft cushions in cornflower blue, lavender, and aqua. A fire pit stood in the center, surrounded by four white rattan sofas and four cushioned rattan chairs.

He'd used the last of his savings to renovate the kitchen into a European style kitchen with grey lacquer lower cabinets and pale aqua upper cabinets. Brand new commercial appliances had already been installed, all stainless steel. With white quartz counters and a colored glass tile backsplash like one Talia fell in love with that looked like pastel sea glass.

Four barstools stood around the bar end of the countertop and a sleek, oblong Alder wood dining table with a crystal chandelier stood between the kitchen and the living area.

For the party, he'd hired a caterer who had already delivered the appetizers and wines. All he and Talia had to do was set out the appetizer plates, beer mugs, and wine glasses he'd had delivered that morning. And champagne flutes for the case of grand cru champagne he'd gotten to toast their first anniversary.

"You're gonna love it, Tal!" he said as he unlocked the tan ranch house's white wrought iron gate and then its bright turquoise door.

It had an unremarkable tan exterior, only one gable over the two-car garage that created a vaulted ceiling in the living room. But the house was right on the beach and nestled a comfortable distance from the endless line of cramped beach house properties nearby. To the north, along the beach, Pacific Coast Highway curved along Topanga Creek to the next house. It was perfect.

"I can't wait, Jack!" Talia cried, her wings rustling in the wind as he opened the door.

Talia started to walk in, but he waved his arms and stepped in front of her.

"Wait!"

"What's wrong, Jack?"

He smiled. "I want to carry you over the threshold."

"So romantic," she said and held out her arms.

Gently, he lifted her into his arms and carried her inside, the smell of new wood and fresh paint in the air as he set her down on the porcelain tiles.

He stepped inside and closed the door, holding out his arms, wings extended as he turned in a circle.

"Welcome home, Mrs. Casey! Designed according to your choices and ready for our first anniversary party."

He just hoped she'd like his gift. Meredith and Whitney, with Jenna and Tara who had joined them somewhere between Kansas and Colorado, got into L.A. last night. He'd paid for the appointment to get the car washed and detailed before they brought it tonight to surprise Talia. He couldn't wait! He hadn't been in the same room as all four of his sisters for years. And they couldn't wait to see him either.

"We're going to have a house full of people soon," said Talia as she moved through the open concept space. "But Jack, it's just perfect!"

The grin on her face radiated light.

"Did I really do this?" she asked, looking so surprised as she rushed over to the sofa and ran her fingers across it.

She touched the newly painted walls and lingered in front of the wall of windows in the back, that led onto the lanai…and to the beach.

"Everything here is decorated according to what you chose, babe, and you did an incredible job."

She rushed over to him, kissing him tenderly, her wings curving around him.

"Even the kitchen?"

He chuckled. "Well, maybe not the kitchen. I took the colors you liked and tried to match them with the beach house kitchen you liked so much when we were filming The Ever After Hour."

She slid her arms around him. "I can't wait to cook with you, Jack."

He pulled her close, kissing her again. "Looking forward to it, babe. It's going to completely change my suppertime."

"How?" she asked, running her fingers up his back and through his hair.

"Well, there'll be more on the menu than pepperoni pizza from Pizza Playpen."

Suddenly, Talia gasped and stared at him, a fearful expression pushing away her joy.

"What's wrong, Tal?" he asked, frowning.

"The party!" she cried. "We'll need to cook food for our guests, won't we?"

He shook his head. "I had it catered. Wine and appetizers are in the fridge. With some microbrews, too. No, we're good, babe."

"I don't even know how many people are coming."

He smiled. "All of them, babe. Every angel, demon, and human we invited is coming. Confirmed. Especially since this is the last time we'll see each other like this again." He sighed. "With the show cancelled and everybody going their separate ways."

She reached out and cupped his face. "We're not, Jack."

"Thank the Heavens for that," he said. "I couldn't have survived that, but Gianni's my best friend. And it'll never be like it was on the show again." He sighed again. "Now that he's gonna play Drumm. Banks, too. They'll both move on to SanFran Confidential without me and pretty soon, we'll be polite strangers again."

Talia stroked his face. "Not after everything you went through with Armand and Mark, Jack. And if things start to get distant, you'll have to make it a priority. Work to keep their friendship."

He nodded. "You're right, of course. I'll just have to try harder."

"We'll make sure we invite them over once or twice a month, Jack." She let him go and wandered into the kitchen, opening doors and cabinets. "I don't want to lose touch with Izzy and Morgan either."

He followed her, watching her confusion, until she turned around, staring at him.

"Look at all the colors!" she cried. "So soft and delicate. They remind me of Heaven." Then she paused, opening all the upper cabinets as she worked her way past the island with its farmhouse sink and stainless-steel sprayer and tall curved faucet. "Jack, all the cabinets are empty."

He smiled. "That's because we'll need to buy things for those cabinets. Plates, bowls, silverware—glasses. Coffee cups even. I've got some stuff I kept after Rachel walked out on me. Just need to unpack it and put it away."

"What about the fridge as you call it?" she asked.

"No, that's fully stocked by the caterer I hired. All we have to do is uncover everything, heat the hot appetizers, and serve it all."

At last, her smile returned. "Then we can buy those things together?"

"You bet we can. It'll be fun." Especially when she saw all the kitchen gadgets that would give her lots of little mermaid moments. And he looked forward to every single one.

He led her through the house that still smelled like fresh paint, past the two empty bedrooms to their master suite. With its large walk-in closets and oversized glass shower with sea glass tiles on the blue-grey walls and cobalt blue glass tiles on the floor of the shower. A brand-new king-size bed stood against the wall that faced the beach, another wall of windows capturing the orange, pink, and gold lights brushing like watercolors across the clouds as the sun dipped toward the horizon. It wouldn't set until almost eight o'clock. When the party was in full swing.

And they had a little over two hours before it started.

Still, he couldn't get Evan Bellows' text out of his head. What did Evan want from him? His blessing on the casting choices? To gloat? To finally get closure on their working relationship? Would it be awkward with Gianni, Banks, and Rachel here? Dude hadn't even talked to his agent yet. And sadly, Jack couldn't decide if that was good or bad. It meant there wouldn't be any negotiations, so returning to his old show was probably off the table. He groaned, wondering if there was a Pizza Playpen location nearby...that needed a delivery driver.

Regardless, he'd just have to suck it up and pretend that whatever Evan wanted didn't hurt. It was his and Talia's first anniversary. No matter what Bellows wanted, he'd pretend it was all good. While he was still an actor. He was not going to let this ruin his and Talia's first anniversary celebration.

After touring the house, he and Talia changed into some casual clothes for the party. From the things they'd kept in the studio trailer. Talia wore a short jean miniskirt, some sort of gold angel jewelry that fit around her right leg and spiraled up to her thigh. She put on a sheer purple blouse with a lavender tank top underneath and black flats.

He put on a clean pair of faded Levi's, a pale green and white striped oxford shirt, and his old blue Vans. And together, they set out an iced silver tub of chardonnay and pinot grigio on the patio. Jack carried out some bottles of red wine and lined them up on the outside bar along with oversized red wine glasses and a couple of folded bottle openers with burgundy handles. He filled another tub with microbrews and covered them in ice.

He set out the bowls of potato chips and pita chips on the bar. Along with plates and napkins. He'd wait for actual guests to arrive before he set out dips and cheese trays from the fridge. Or tossed the little egg rolls, mini quiches, and wontons in the oven to bake. He wondered who would arrive first? Angels or humans. Zanth was a demon. She wouldn't show up first—unless there was a fight.

At four minutes past seven, the doorbell rang, a sound so strange to him. He hadn't had a doorbell in a long while.

"I'll get it, Tal," he said and hurried out of the kitchen, through the living area, and toward the door.

He opened it.

Standing there was Armand Gianni and his wife, Izzy. Dressed in a casual charcoal grey sports jacket that Cary Grant would have been perfectly at home in, light blue V-neck T-shirt, Italian leather loafers, and a pressed pair of dark jeans. Izzy wore an orange sundress and tan heels, her bobbed coppery hair dazzling as it caught every last ray of the setting sun.

"Jack!" Gianni said and hugged him.

"Dude! Great to see you. Izzy, you look beautiful! Come on inside. Talia can't wait to see you both."

He hugged Izzy and led them through the space. To the kitchen where Talia was sliding the first trays of appetizers into the oven.

"Tal, look who's here," said Jack.

When she turned around, her face lit with delight.

"Armand! Izzy!" She rushed out from behind the counter. "It's so good to see you!"

Gianni hugged her and then Izzy.

"Happy Anniversary, you, two," said Gianni as he handed Jack a card.

He let Talia open it. It had sparkly angels on the front. "For a match made in Heaven," Talia read. "Happy first anniversary!" Inside was a gift card for a high-end home furnishing company.

"Wow, nice! Thank you, both! Talia and I will have fun picking out something for the house. Won't we, babe?"

Grinning, Talia clapped her hands together. "We sure will. Thank you."

Jack gave them the tour and then led them out to the lanai where he opened some wine. He poured Izzy and Talia a glass of chardonnay and Gianni a glass of malbec. He poured a glass of merlot for himself.

"Jack, this view…" Gianni walked to the edge of the patio. "It's stunning. How'd you end up with such an unobstructed beach view?"

"No clue, dude," he said. "If you'd seen this place before the renos, you'd have said no way in hell. But with a little Hollywood magic and my angel of death wife, we resurrected it."

He patted Jack on the back. "And you and Talia are only a stone's throw from Izzy and me. We are definitely having you both over for dinner soon."

Jack realized that with Lucifer redeemed, Samael and Raum in custody, and Armageddon on ice, he had a lot of time on his hands. Especially until he found another acting job.

"Our schedule is pretty open right now," he said. "So, text me."

Gianni gave him an unconvinced look. "No saving the world on Tuesday?"

Jack shook his head. "Not even on Friday night. We captured Archangel Samael and brought him in, dude. He'll be on trial in a day or two."

"What about Lucifer?"

"Luci?" He smiled and took a long sip of merlot. "At the end of the day, he was more about abandonment issues and anger at his dad. And he wanted a chance to redeem himself. Long story, but Heaven gave him that chance. He's changed a bit."

Gianni's eyebrows raised. "Lucifer?"

"He'll be here tonight," said Jack.

Gianni's face went pale. "LUCIFER?"

Jack nodded. "Yep, along with Azrael, Berith, Pravuil—Talia's squad."

The look on Gianni's face shifted between shock and confusion. "That's a lot of angels, Jack."

"Well, I also invited the cast from Angelic Anniversary Show. Jennifer Collins, Steve Kosinksi, Roy, Rhonda…and Herb. Even Devin Van Fossen. Zanth and Tre will be here, too."

"Jack!" Gianni cried, lowering his voice as Talia and Izzy walked along the patio, examining the new lanai furniture. "You invited angels and demons along with the humans? Isn't that a recipe for disaster?"

He smiled. "Only if Rachel crashes out again." Might as well warn him that Bellows would be here, too. "Oh, and I invited Evan Bellows. He'll be here, too."

For a moment, Gianni looked stunned. Jack couldn't blame him. He'd been so salty over Bellows hiring his costars under his nose to the show he'd made famous. But after everything he'd been through in Hell this time, his anger had cooled. Whatever Evan had to say, he'd deal with it. And cheer his friends on. It was all he could do.

"Why would you invite Evan Bellows, Jack?" Gianni looked confused. He took a big drink of his malbec and waited for Jack's response.

"He texted me, wanting to talk to me today. About something." Jack shrugged. "So, Talia told me to invite him. And I did. I figure the crowd of friends will keep me from losing my shit in front of him."

When he saw Talia and Izzy sit down on one of the outdoor sofas, he pulled Gianni behind the bar and lowered his voice to a whisper.

"Listen, my four sisters will be here tonight," he said. "They brought my dad's old 60s convertible here—out of storage in Indiana.

It's the most personal thing I could think of to give Tal for our first anniversary present."

"You're giving her your dad's car?"

"That car was his baby, Gianni," said Jack. "And I have such great memories of him driving us around in that car, the wind blowing through my hair, the rumble of the engine as we blew down country roads with the top down. Fresh mown grass and sweet clover filling the air. In that car, he was the dad I loved and the dad I remembered. And I want to share that with Talia."

Gianni patted him on the back. "Jack, that's beautiful. She'll love it. And she'll finally get to meet your sisters."

"All four of them," Jack said with a nod. "They ignored my mother who poisoned them against me. They want to reconnect with me."

Gianni's smile brightened. "I can't wait to meet them," he said and lowered his voice to a whisper. "And see this car."

"She's a beauty. We call her the Firechicken."

"Firechicken?" he said, laughing. "Why Firechicken?"

"Because she was nothing but bare bones when dad found her. Once a Firebird, he rebuilt her into a pristine state. Rise of the Firechicken."

Gianni took another sip of wine as Jack led him toward the sofas. But then the doorbell rang again.

Jack excused himself, rushing to the door.

Banks and Morgan stood on the stoop, Banks dressed in faded jeans, loafers, and a long-sleeved chambray shirt. Morgan wore a pink and white sun dress and white sandals. Morgan handed him a card in a yellow envelope.

"Banks! Morgan! Come on in! Thanks for the card."

"Happy Anniversary, Jack," said Banks.

Jack hugged them both and led them on a quick tour through the house, fearing Morgan might crash out when she saw it. She'd been so pissed at him for snagging this place. But he'd had the lowest budget. For months, she'd made snide comments about it—and him —from the start of last year's filming. He hoped she was over it now.

"Jack! This place…it's incredible! Mark, just look at that vaulted ceiling."

He exchanged a worried look with Banks, but Banks gave him a reassuring nod, his spiky hair catching the golden sunlight streaming into the place from the western wall of windows.

"This way. Gianni and Izzy are on the patio."

They followed him out to the lanai and he got them drinks. They greeted Gianni and Izzy and sat down on the sofas, chattering away about their new roles. On Jack's old show—the one that made him a star. Making him feel a little left out.

He excused himself when his phone dinged, reminding him to pull the first tray of hot appetizers out of the oven. Besides, he didn't want to make his best friends feel badly about these great career jumps. Made without him along for the ride this time.

The flutter of wings startled him. He turned.

Muriel, Kesien, Anahera, and Deemah blinked into the center of the house.

"Hey, Jack!" Muriel replied, dressed in a lavender sun dress and gold sandals.

Anahera wore a chambray blouse, white shorts, and sandals. Kesien and Deemah both wore faded jeans and sandals, Kesien in a light blue Property of California T-shirt and Deemah in a teal green camp shirt.

Jack grinned. He'd never seen them dressed like humans before. But they were angels, so they fit right in with any L.A. crowd.

"Wow, Muriel!" he said. "Look at you…smokin' hot in that dress."

She blushed and stared down at her sandals. "Thanks, Jack."

Jack held out his arms. "And look at my squad. Wearing human armor for a change."

"We're here on holiday," said Kesien with a laugh as he glanced around the house. "Wow, nice renovations."

Deemah leaned against a bar stool as Jack slid the mini quiches, wontons, and little egg rolls onto a serving tray with containers of sweet and sour sauce.

"Talia said it was beautiful," said Deemah. "Look at that sea glass backsplash!"

Anahera and Muriel slipped around Jack into the space, admiring all the finishes as Jack set a turquoise oven mitt on the sand-colored countertop. Jack watched Kesien crowd in beside Deemah as they marveled at the commercial refrigerator and stove. It felt surreal to have Talia's angel squad admiring kitchen appliances after battling Nephions and demons beside them, in full angelic armor.

Only in Hollywood, he mused. The thing he loved most about this little corner of his world.

"Wine?" Jack asked them.

They glanced up from the backsplash.

"Uh, yeah, Jack," said Muriel.

The others nodded.

"White or red?" he asked, reaching for wine glasses that were lined up on the counter.

"White," said Muriel.

The others nodded.

"Red," said Deemah.

"Chardonnay or pinot Grigio?" Jack asked.

"Surprise us," said Kesien.

He turned to Deemah. "Merlot or Malbec?"

"Malbec," said Deemah.

Jack filled four wine glasses and passed them around.

"Come on," he said, motioning them toward the terrace, the tray of appetizers in his hand. "Gianni and Izzy are here and so are Banks and Morgan."

He carried out the hot appetizers through the buzz of conversations as he led Muriel, Kesien, Anahera, and Deemah out to the patio. He set the tray on a table by the sofas that had a stack of appetizer plates and turquoise paper napkins.

Gianni and Izzy jumped to their feet, rushing over to greet the squad. Banks and Morgan were right behind them.

"Muriel! Kesien!" Gianni called, hugging them and then Deemah and Anahera. "It's great to see you all."

"Hi, Gianni," said Anahera with a shy smile as Deemah hugged Izzy.

"Hey, Muriel, Kesien," said Banks, hugging them as Morgan hugged Anahera and Deemah.

They were all old friends now after dealing with the archdemoness hunting him and Talia on their honeymoon and then the apocalypse when Zanth became part of the squad.

"I hear you had interesting times together this week," said Izzy, glancing at Talia who looked smokin' hot in a jean skirt, black flats, and that sheer purple blouse over a lavender tank top.

And that gold spiral angel jewelry made her legs look so sexy.

Kesien ran his fingers through his black curly hair, shrugging. "It was quite a battle. But Samael's in custody."

Gianni looked almost envious. "You finally got him? Wow…wish I'd been there."

"So is Raum," said Deemah.

"Trust me, Gianni," said Jack as everyone got some appetizers and sat back down on the sofas surrounding the electric fire pit that guttered in the twilight. "This one was brutal."

As Gianni asked for details, Talia grabbed a bottle of white and red from the bar and began refilling everyone's glasses. Along with hers.

Doorbell rang again.

"I got it, Tal!"

Jack rushed back inside to the door.

Rachel Daniels stood beside her stocky body-building financial planner fiancé, Eric Saunders. He was dressed in jeans, black leather slip-ons, and a long-sleeved black button-down shirt. Rachel wore a pale pink sundress and matching heels, and prominently displayed her baby bump.

"Hey Rach," said Jack. "Eric. Come on in. Wow, Rach…showing already."

She nodded. "We can't wait."

"Congratulations, both of you," said Jack.

He shook Eric's hand and hugged Rachel who handed him a card in a turquoise envelope.

"Happy Anniversary, Jack," said Rachel.

"Yeah, Happy Anniversary, man," said Eric, his gaze shifting around the house. "Wow, this place turned out great."

"Don't worry, baby," said Rachel, leaning up and kissing Eric. "Ours looks like this, too. Wait 'til you see it on television."

Jack smiled. "Does that mean you and Eric are the reno winners?"

She nodded. "Yeah, we found out Tuesday. They're finishing the last changes and then we film the winning segment next Wednesday."

"Congratulations again," said Jack. "You guys earned that win."

Rachel was smiling, a faraway look on her face. "Yeah, we did, didn't we? Will be a big help until filming starts for SanFran Confidential."

Jack did his best to let that go by him without wincing.

"I've got some bottles of non-alcoholic sparkling cider in the fridge for you, Rachel," he said.

"How sweet, Jack, thank you," she said as he stepped into the kitchen and pulled one out of the fridge, opening it for her. "Eric, there's beer and wine on the patio," he said and as the oven timer went off.

He handed her the cider and moved back to the oven, sliding another pan of appetizers out with the oven mitt and filled another tray. He glanced up, surveying the house.

Expecting demons to slip through the walls and attack him, he realized. But only Eric and Rachel stood beside the barstools, smiling at him. God, it felt surreal. He wasn't used to a mundane night like this. It made him jumpy.

He carried the appetizers outside and into the growing crowd. Rachel and Eric followed him, Eric grabbing a microbrew from the bar and then joining the conversation. They all knew each other. He smiled. All of them even knew the crowd was half angels and half humans. Well, except Eric.

But Jack's mind quickly circled back to his meeting with Evan Bellows. To his old show—and his costars all moving on to it. He tried to focus on the conversation, his anniversary, but not being part of the cast ate at him as he stared at this beautiful beach house he may have to sell.

He always found a way to chop his own life. Would he have to go back to doing commercials? Take a second job? He winced. Teach acting classes at one of the community colleges? Or start over again? He shuddered. Go back to college and finish his degree?

The rustle of wings shook him out of his thoughts. He excused himself and went inside.

Azrael, Berith, and Pravuil stood in the living room, wings folded against their shoulders. They were dressed in human clothes, too, Azrael and Pravuil slappin' in linen suits and ivory shoes. Berith wore a short, smoldering white sheath and matching heels. He couldn't quite handle seeing the archangels in human clothes. It was just... weird.

Now, angels had the humans outnumbered.

"Hey, Azrael, Berith, Scribe...thanks for coming." He glanced around. "Where's Lucifer?"

"Had to pick up something," said Berith.

Jack frowned. The former King of Hell turned Lightbringer had to pick up something? A human sacrifice? A bucket of Holy fire? A gallon of milk?

"Okay, now, you're scaring me," said Jack.

Azrael smiled. "Don't worry, Jack. It was something for Talia."

"Something for the house? Like the Ark of the Covenant? The Holy Grail?"

Azrael shook his head. "Think it was a package. From someplace called Beverly Hills."

Jack busted out laughing. "He get a new suit or something?"

Pravuil rolled his eyes. "Wouldn't surprise me. Just to outdo our snappy linen suits."

"Come out to the patio," said Jack. "There's wine and food."

"You're singing my song, Jack," said Pravuil in a gruff tone as Jack led them outside and got them glasses of wine.

"As long as there isn't a trailer I have to piece back together," Azrael said with a growl.

Jack laughed. "No trailers. I promise."

The archangels and Berith quickly blended into the conversations, fitting right into everything. He gazed at Talia who sat with her squad and Gianni and Izzy, laughing and sipping wine. She looked so happy. He just hoped he wouldn't screw this up and lose the beach house.

FOR THE NEXT FIFTEEN MINUTES, Jack went back and forth to the door at every ring of the doorbell or rustle of wings.

Herb arrived with Jennifer Collins, Steve Kosinski, and Devin Van Fossen. Herb wore tan pants and a blue and gold Hawaiian shirt, Jennifer in grey leggings and a purple belted shirt, no clipboard in sight. Steve wore jeans, loafers, and a long-sleeved jean shirt. And Devin wore grey pants and a cream-colored dress shirt. Jack barely recognized him because he'd let his hair go dark and he'd left out all that crunchy gel. His hair looked a little windblown and natural. Best he'd ever seen Devin look.

A moment later, Roy and then Rhonda arrived, both in jeans and T-shirts from *The Ever After Hour*. They each handed Jack a card as they entered the house.

Jack set the stack of cards in a kitchen drawer and led everyone out to the patio, carrying out more appetizers. He passed Talia entering the house as he went toward patio.

"More appetizers," she said, leaning out and kissing him.

"Hungry crowd tonight, Mrs. Casey," he said, tasting chardonnay on her lips.

The crew of his former show mingled with its former cast and some of Jack's favorite angels. Conversations filled the patio as the sun sank closer to the horizon. In less than thirty minutes it would set. His sisters were supposed to be here at 8:15 P.M. with the car. And somewhere in between, Evan Bellows would show up.

The flutter of wings whispered behind him. He glanced inside the house.

Lucifer. With Zanth and Tre.

Lucifer wore a champagne silk Tom Ford suit and black slip-ons, looking like he'd stepped out of *GQ Magazine*. Zanth wore a red tank top dress and black heels, Tre dressed in jeans, grey sneakers, and a white silk shirt. Lucifer had given him his soul back, so he was human again, his arm around Zanth's shoulders. She looked a little fragile, but having Tre back in human form had given her something hopeful.

Lucifer carried a small black box in his hand about the size of a sandwich that he showed to Talia who grinned them and led them all out to the patio.

Lucifer paused beside Jack, a smile lighting his face. It was equal parts celestial and up to something. But nothing the King of Hell would do. More prankster than Prince of Darkness. Guess he'd find out when he sat down on a whoopie cushion or picked up a leaking wine glass.

"Hello, Jack," said Lucifer, that prankster smile a little unnerving. "Happy Anniversary."

"Thanks, Luci," he said and motioned toward the bar. "Help yourself to some wine or some microbrew."

Lucifer shook his head and nudged Jack over to the bar. From his jacket, he pulled out a bottle of whisky that looked older than dirt.

"I brought you a bottle of whisky for the occasion."

Lucifer set it on the bar along with two tulip-shaped glasses.

Jack glanced at the label. Frowned. Looked again. And then his mouth fell open as he turned back to Lucifer.

"Macallan 1926?" he said, glancing at the label and then back to Lucifer. "Valerio Adami?" He swallowed a breath. "This was sixty-year-old scotch in 1926!"

"Very good, Jack," said Lucifer as he carefully opened the dusty bottle and poured him and Jack a glass. "I knew you would appreciate this bottle. It was the least I could do for the man who gave me a chance at redemption. A toast to a happy anniversary."

Lucifer motioned for him to pick up the glass.

Jack lifted it and Lucifer clinked his glass to Jack's and took a sip.

Jack closed his eyes and drank a sip, rolling it over on his tongue as the taste of black cherries, dried fruit, and sherried sweet oak rolled over him. He let the mouthful stay on his tongue, tasting a touch of sulfur, sugary treacle, and warm caramel until he swallowed. It was intense and complex, delivering flavor after flavor against that sweet sherry oakiness.

And he was hooked.

"That's the best testing whisky I've ever had. Incredible!"

Lucifer nodded toward the bottle. "My gift to you, Jack. Keep it safe and we'll have another glass later."

"I'd like that," said Jack as Lucifer moved over to Zanth and Tre who were talking to Gianni and Izzy.

Jack chuckled. Zanth was probably apologizing again for ruining their honeymoon on San Juan Island, back when she was trying to kill him and Talia. And anyone who got in the way.

He took another amazing sip of the Macallan as he marveled at how well they were all mingling together. All his friends. Demons, angels, and humans. Incredible.

He looked up. The sun was quickly disappearing into the Pacific, the oranges, pinks, and purples intense now, lighting the clouds and the sky with neon stripes of color that burned across the darkening sky.

The doorbell rang.

He grabbed his glass of Macallan and answered the doorbell on its second ring. His stomach dropped, mouth going dry as his fingers went cold.

Evan Bellows.

His former director stood on the stoop, dressed in a navy-blue suit, pale blue dress shirt, black shoes, and yellow tie, thinning dark hair a little windblown, brown eyes intense.

Business attire.

Jack froze.

16

"*E*van...good to see you."

Jack felt the air rush out of his lungs, a burst of cold fear and apprehension surging through his body. Dude was finally here. And Jack had no clue why. The other shoe was finally about to drop.

"Hello, Jack," said Evan, looking anxious, nervous as he fidgeted with his car keys that jangled in his perfectly manicured hands.

"Come in, Evan," said Jack, motioning his former director inside. "Thanks for stopping by."

"Happy Anniversary, Jack," he said as Jack led him through the bungalow and out onto the patio.

"Thanks. Glass of wine? Red or white?" Jack asked as he led Evan to the bar.

Okay, it was two folding tables with turquoise tablecloths covering them. The wine glasses, small white appetizer plates, and bottles of red wine stood on the left beside a stack of paper napkins in aqua, turquoise, and lavender. A metal tub filled with iced microbrews and some Coke Zeros sat beside the tables. Another tub filled with iced bottles of chardonnay and pinot grigio sat at the other end. In the center were the trays of vegetables and dip, cheeses, bowls of chips, and a big fruit plate with bright green kiwi slices, plump red strawberries, and juicy, golden pineapple chunks with a yogurt sauce.

"Or maybe you prefer beer," said Jack. "Got some great local microbrews."

"A cold chardonnay would do wonders," said Evan as he wiped his forehead with a napkin and leaned against the bar.

"Got you covered."

As if on cue, Gianni and Banks approached the bar, each grabbing a red, white, and blue can of Stone Pilsner out of the iced tub as they talked quietly and grazed on wontons. They both looked shocked when they saw Evan standing beside the bar.

"Uh, Evan—hi!" said Gianni, stepping back as Jack reached for a bottle of chardonnay out of the nearby tub. "What brings you out here? To…Jack and Talia's anniversary party?"

"Hey, Evan! Good to see you." Banks moved beside Gianni, gaping at Evan and giving Gianni sideways glances as his relaxed demeanor turned tense and anxious—like Gianni. "Didn't know Jack invited you to the party."

Banks gave Jack a sideways glance that was all nerves, Gianni still looking like a deer caught in headlights.

Did they know something about this meeting? Something they'd neglected to share with him? They looked worried.

"Should have known I'd see you both here," said Evan, smiling as he shook Gianni's hand and then glanced over at Jack. "Yes, Jack graciously invited me to the party after I asked him for a short meet."

Banks shook hands with Evan, can of Pilsner still in his left hand. He still had a surprised look on his face.

Now, his and Evan's conversation felt way more awkward than Jack expected as he poured Evan a glass of chardonnay and handed it to him. Then he slammed his last sip of Macallan, set down the glass, and grabbed the half-full glass of merlot he'd set aside for the Macallan.

Gianni and Banks were still staring as they not-so-nonchalantly excused themselves and shuffled away from the bar. They hurried over to Talia, Morgan, and Izzy by the fire pit, but their gaze was still on the bar. And Jack.

Jack could almost hear the frantic whispers as he felt their stares bore into the back of his head. He wondered what they knew that he didn't and it made him a little sad that they hadn't bothered to at least warn him. Maybe they didn't know anything? But they were freakin' actors. How much of that had been a scripted performance?

Guess he was about to find out.

"So, how you been, Jack?" said Evan, his gaze traveling around the patio.

Picking out Gianni, Rachel, and Banks, no doubt. Just before the Hollywood hammer dropped to kneecap him and wish him well at his new pizza delivery job at Pizza Playpen. And a reminder for him to watch all his friends on the *SanFran Confidential* reboot on that new 75-inch flat screen in his living room.

"Doing great," Jack said. "How are things with you, Evan?"

God, he hated small talk. Especially small talk they'd already covered.

But the look on Evan's face told him that Evan didn't believe him for even a moment that he was doing great.

"Okay," said Jack, setting down his glass of merlot as Evan took a drink of chardonnay. "Let's turn over the flop and be done with it." He kept his voice quiet. "Everybody here knows my show's been cancelled. So, let me just say that things could be better."

Evan's expression softened. Appreciating the truth, as always.

"Let me play my hand, too, Jack," said Evan, making a sour face. "Can we go inside for a moment? So, I can hear myself think?"

Jack nodded and grabbed his wine glass. "Sure."

He felt Gianni's and Banks' stares follow him as he led Evan back inside and over to the barstools in the kitchen. Jack slid one out and sat down. Evan sat down in another one, sighing as he set his wine glass on the counter. Jack fidgeted with his glass as he glanced at Evan, waiting for him to speak.

"Where were we?" Evan asked.

"Playing our hands," said Jack.

"Right," said Evan, bowing his head with a deep nod. "As you know, with Lare Dumont's continued erratic behavior and now, another sudden disappearance, nothing I've done has kept the show afloat."

Jack wasn't surprised by that. Hard to keep a show going with its star AWOL. He nodded for Evan to continue.

"All the main characters that our audience loved are gone." Evan swirled his chardonnay around in the glass and took a slow drink, his gaze returning to Jack. "Daniels, Dumont, …you. Stories now involve guest stars that our audience has never met or minor characters they don't know. Or care about." He stared into his glass again. "New characters with the charisma of potatoes because our writers no longer understand the story. How could they? With no stars, there isn't one. Regardless, it's killed the show. Ratings are in the toilet, as you might guess."

Jack nodded. "I get that, Evan. Believe me."

Evan glanced up and fixed Jack with his gaze. "I have one shot at saving this show, Jack. One."

"That why you hired Rachel back? And Gianni and Banks?"

Evan nodded. "I want to retool the show by rebooting it. With a major motion picture and a comeback season for the show."

Wow, no wonder Gianni signed on…a major motion picture? That meant a big budget summer release. That had been his dream once. What he'd hoped to someday achieve when he moved to L.A.

And it had always been just out of his reach.

Banks must be the new Drumm. Did that make Gianni the new Davy Pierson? Jack's chest tightened.

Gianni was his best friend. Jack had to be happy for him. Besides, *SanFran Confidential* hadn't been his show for a few years now. It was time for him to let it go. And wish his two best friends the best of luck. Gianni and Banks had earned this shot at stardom. And after years of fighting for her, he had Talia.

That was enough for him.

"Can't go wrong with those actors, Evan. I'm sure you'll be back on top in no time."

Evan looked panicked. Jack frowned.

"Jack, your show was a huge hit, but you and I both know that Armand Gianni, Rachel Daniels, and Mark Banks aren't enough to save SanFran Confidential. You know that."

He fixed Evan with his unblinking gaze. "Then what *will* save it, Evan?"

Why was Evan talking to him about this? What could he do? Did Evan want him to do spots to endorse the show? Endorse his successors? Of course, he'd do that for Gianni and Banks.

"If you need me to do endorsements," said Jack. "Say the word."

Evan stared at Jack for several unnerving moments, his gaze unwavering.

"No, Jack. I need Jack Casey returning as Davy Pierson. That's the only way to save this show."

Stunned, all Jack could do was stare at Evan. His voice had left him.

"Jack, you don't have to make a choice anymore! Your show's been cancelled. Lare Dumont's gone. You'd be the top-billed star. It would be your show! And the chemistry between you and Gianni is fantastic. So much better than you and Dumont ever had! Gianni will make a great Drummond if you come back as Davy Pierson. And you'd be the highest paid actor on television."

Wait, Evan was asking him to come back to the show?

Again? After Jack had already turned him down? Turned down the role that made him famous? For obscene amounts of money? Now, Evan was asking him to star in a major motion picture and reboot of the series. Giving him, finally, his chance at redemption. To fix the screwup that still haunted him, even now.

"Jack, please don't say no!" Evan gripped Jack's sleeve. "Listen…I want to cast your wife, too. As Detective Kenzie Wylder, Davy's new love interest. Creating a love triangle between her and Rachel's Charmaine Steele who's now the District Attorney. Mark Banks would take on the role of new police captain, Wynn Archer."

Jack couldn't halt his smile. "You want Tal, too?"

Evan gave him a huge nod. "Jack, the reason The Cinderella Hour blew up so big is because of that chemistry between you and Talia

Smith. And that rivalry between you and Rachel. And the rival-turned-best friend with Armand Gianni. I want to tap into all of that for SanFran Confidential."

Evan pulled a folded letter (on studio stationery) and a pen out of his jacket pocket and laid them on the counter.

"I know this isn't standard protocol," said Evan, motioning at the letter, something Jack hadn't dealt with before. "I should be negotiating with your agent, but Jack, I'm out of time on this. We can hammer out the entire contract later, but here are the important numbers and details."

Jack leaned toward the paper. A letter of intent. Agreeing to star in a film called *SanFran Confidential: Presidio Blowback* and the television series, *SanFran Confidential*.

The salary figure staggered him.

And so did the offer of salary plus ten percent of the first dollar box office gross on the film. Plus, residuals on the series. Terms were subject to contract negotiations to include Phil Getz, Jack's agent.

No fine print. No ancillary clauses referring subclauses of subclauses. It was surprisingly straightforward—and it felt almost like something divine had crafted it. He'd have to check with the angels later. See if any of them had something to do with this.

"Gianni has already left Crossing Paths, his daytime drama," Evan continued as Jack tried to process the biggest deal of his acting career. "He has signed on to star in the film and the series, but only if you sign aboard, Jack. Banks and Rachel have already signed on for the film and the series, too."

Jack gazed at his former director for a moment. "Evan, are you sure you want me back on the show? After all the shit I pulled? All the grief I caused?"

"Jack," he said, leaning toward him. "Honestly...I never thought you'd make it as an actor after I fired you. Because of everything that happened. The shape you were in with the coke... But Rachel came clean about who was actually at fault when she signed onto the show again. Told me everything."

Rachel confessed to Evan? Jack held his breath.

"What?"

"Rachel confessed everything, Jack. Told me how she and Lare had targeted you from the beginning. Trapped you into getting addicted to blow. Withholding it, sending you into withdrawal, gaslighting you, and causing all that bad behavior. You're to blame for some of it, but most of it was caused by Rachel and Lare. And then you gallantly took the fall for all of them, so they wouldn't get fired. That's real character, Jack."

Evan knew.

He finally knew all about what Lare and Rachel had done to him. How he'd taken the fall for the cast and crew. But he would own his part in it, too and try to be better this time.

"I take full responsibility for my part in it, Evan," he said. "And I can assure you I have changed."

"You have, Jack." Even replied. "I've seen it. And I've watched you every season on that new show. You were not the actor I fired from my set that August day. You'd become the actor I never knew you could be. And you've proven that to me, over and over again. So, yes, I would hire you back in a heartbeat, Jack. You're not that actor anymore."

Jack looked up to see Talia heading inside. Her gaze was intense as she hurried into the kitchen.

"Jack, people are asking for you," she said, her gaze shifting from Evan to him. "Oh…hi…Evan Bellows, right?"

"Yes, hello, Talia," said Evan, turning toward her. "Happy Anniversary."

"Thank you."

Her gaze was still fixed on Jack.

"Talia," Jack said in a shaky voice. "Evan has offered me the helm of SanFran Confidential. Starring role in a major motion picture and reboot of the series. With top-billing on the reboot. He also wants to cast you as my love interest."

Her expression brightened, but her surprise was still evident.

"Me?" she said. "As your love interest?"

"You'd be a detective on the show. Gianni would be cast as Drummond Turillo. It's funny. It's sort of a…"

Jack groaned. Would she go ballistic when he told her about the love triangle with Rachel Daniels?

"Of what?" she asked.

"Of a…love triangle…between uh—Rachel Daniel's character, yours, and mine."

He winced. Oh, please don't let her smite him in front of Evan Bellows.

"Talia," said Evan, butting into the conversation—before her eyes turned to white flames and she threw Holy fire at him. "Rachel was Davy's love interest in the old series, but I'd be bringing on your character as the woman Davy wants, but Rachel is trying to break them up."

Talia frowned, still no Holy fire or wildly spinning halo. She didn't completely want to murder him yet.

"Sort of like The Prince Charming Hour," said Talia. "And every season that followed. In real life. Until she fell for Eric Saunders?"

Jack laughed. Talia didn't mince words.

Evan nodded, looking uneasy again. "Yes, like that."

"What do you say, Tal?" Jack asked in a timid voice. "He wants me to sign this letter of intent. Tonight."

She moved over and read it, the silence painful.

"When does filming start?" Talia asked finally, her gaze moving back to Jack, but he couldn't tell what was going through her mind right then.

Maybe the urge to smite him *and* Evan Bellows?

"The movie will film in and around L.A. and San Francisco in a few of months," said Evan. "After Rachel delivers her baby."

Talia moved around the barstools to Jack and laid her hand on his neck, caressing. "Lover, is this what you really want?" she asked.

He didn't need to think about it, not even for a moment. He already knew his answer. This was his chance at redemption. Even though he'd proven himself on *The Cinderella Hour*, returning to *SanFran Confidential* still mattered to him—now that he wouldn't screw over one show for another. Especially if he could work alongside Talia, Gianni, and Banks.

"It's what I really want," he said, smiling at her. "Especially with you on the show."

Talia picked up the pen and handed it to him.

"He's in, Evan," said Talia as she pulled Jack into a steamy kiss.

Jack kissed her hard on the lips and then grabbed the pen, grinning as he signed the letter.

He'd never seen Evan Bellows look so relieved in his entire life. He drank the rest of his chardonnay in one gulp.

"Welcome home, Jack," said Evan, extending his hand. "And I sincerely mean that."

"Thanks, Evan," said Jack, shaking his hand. "It's good to be back. With actors I can trust."

"I'll let Gianni and Banks know that you've signed on. They'll be thrilled—and relieved. And Talia, I'll be in touch about your contract soon."

"Sounds good," she said. "Thank you, Evan."

Evan rose from the barstool and slid the letter in his pocket. He pulled out his phone.

"Sorry to leave so soon, but with you back on the show, I've suddenly got a bunch of things that I can't wait to do. Like send out a presser about you, Talia, Gianni, Rachel, and Banks—together again on SanFran Confidential. It's gonna blow up social media."

Grinning, Evan practically floated out the front door, leaving Jack and Talia alone in the kitchen.

Jack took her in his arms. "Did I ever tell you that you're the best wife ever, Mrs. Casey?"

She kissed him. "You have. And I love you for it. Because you are the best husband I could ever have, Jack Casey. And I will always be at your side. Now until forever."

"Emphasis on forever," he said as the patio door opened.

Herb, Jennifer Collins, Steve Kosinski, and Devin Van Fossen came in, moving toward the front door.

"Jack," said Herb, extending his hand. "I've already thanked Talia, but I wanted to thank you for the wild ride one more time. Thanks for those years at the top. I'll never forget them."

Jack shook his hand. "Thank you for giving a washed-up actor one more chance. What will you do now, Herb?"

"I'm retiring, Jack," he said, sounding relieved. "But I have agreed to do some guest directing for Evan Bellows. So, I'll get to see you and Talia rise to the top of the charts again. Along with the rest of my cast."

Jack gave him a funny look.

Herb held up his phone. "News travels fast." He smiled. "Evan just texted me."

"That's awesome!" Jack said with a smirk. "Can't wait to work with you again."

"You, too, Jack. Both of you, take care."

Herb stepped back as Jennifer and Steve moved toward Jack, looking excited.

"Jack, is it true?" Steve asked, his dark brown ponytail shifting against his shoulders.

Jack nodded.

"Congratulations!" Steve shouted.

Jennifer clapped her hands together. "And more news! Steve and I got hired as part of the SanFran Confidential crew this week."

Jack smiled and hugged Jennifer. He shook Steve's hand.

"It'll be a regular family reunion on set."

Jennifer nodded as Talia hugged her and then Steve. "Can't wait. Oh, Roy and Rhonda have joined the camera crew, so it'll be like old times."

"Jennifer, that's amazing," said Jack as Roy and Rhonda walked inside and headed toward Herb.

"Happy Anniversary, you, two," said Roy, waving. "And welcome home, Jack—Herb's got a loud voice."

"Seeya in a few months on set," said Rhonda, nodding. "Studio 18 this time."

"Thanks for coming to the party," Jack said as he and Talia walked them to the door, giving them a hug goodbye. "Looking forward to working with all of you again."

Devin extended his hand and Jack shook it.

"Good to see you again, Devin. Thanks for coming."

"Thanks for inviting me, Jack," said Devin. "Hope to see you around the Four Acre Studio lot. I'm emceeing a new fall talent show called Coast-to-Coast Talent that films in Studio 33."

"That's a big upgrade for you," said Jack. "Congratulations. Will definitely see you around the lot."

He and Talia waved goodbye as all six of them headed outside to a large blue SUV parked against the curb, twilight darkening as the last intense remnants of the orange and pink sunset faded to deep violet against the Pacific's steel-blue waves. The air smelled of eucalyptus, warm asphalt, and sea salt. Jack slid his phone out of his pocket. Almost time for his sisters to drive up with the car.

He closed the door and with Talia on his arm, returned to the patio. To his tribe. Most of the people left on the patio were his closest friends—except maybe Rachel and Eric Saunders who looked shell-shocked. And Tre, but he'd seen it all as a soul trapped in purgatory.

Laughter pealed across the patio, the group clustered at the edge, admiring the view. Where the sea grass met the sand and the Pacific.

Where Kesien and Lucifer stood in the sand. Jack grinned. With Cerby and Orthy running in circles around them. Orthy ran up to Gianni who offered him a couple of turkey sliders. The two-headed hellhound devoured the sliders, letting Gianni pet him.

"What the hell are those things?" Eric demanded, looking terrified and confused.

Rachel laughed as she petted Cerby who ran after a neon yellow frisbee that Lucifer found on the beach.

"Eric, it's such a long story," said Rachel as she gripped his hand. "They won't hurt you, I promise. And I'll tell you all about it when we get home."

Lucifer fixed Jack with his gaze. "Initiates, Jack?"

"'Fraid so," said Jack. "Go easy on this one though," said Jack, patting Eric on the back. "He's about to become a dad."

Lucifer held up his hands. "There's nothing I could do that would cause more havoc than living with Rachel Daniels. And coming from the former King of Hell, that's a lot."

Everyone except Eric, who looked unnerved, laughed.

"Or living with me, an ex-archdemoness," said Zanth as she slid her arms around Tre. "You are in for trouble now, Tre Sheridan."

Everyone laughed—even Rachel. Eric still looked confused.

"Tough call on that choice," said Lucifer.

Jack nodded. "Couldn't agree more."

Jack tossed the frisbee, watching the hellhounds chase it across the sand. They barked and tackled each other, trying to bring back the frisbee until finally, Orthy snatched it out of one of Cerby's three mouths and brought it back to Jack. He threw it again and they raced off, claws clacking against the concrete patio and thumping against the hard-packed sand.

Jack's phone vibrated. He pulled it out of his pocket, grinning at the text.

We're here, Jack. Let us in.

"Be right back, Talia," he said, hurrying inside to the front door.

When he opened the door, all four of his sisters crowded around the doorframe.

"Happy Anniversary, Jack!" they shouted in unison and rushed at him, hugging him, ruffling his hair, kissing his cheek.

"Mere!" he shouted. "Whit!"

They both favored his mother with dark hair and tall, willowy builds. Meredith was the tallest, about Talia's height, her hair in a longish shoulder-length bob. Whitney was a little shorter, her hair in a long French braid down her back. Meredith wore blue leggings, tan sandals, and a white V-neck T-shirt that hung past her hips. Whit wore a pair of khaki shorts, red canvas sneakers, and a yellow camp shirt over a red tank top.

"Hi, Jack," said his third sister, Jenna, who was shorter than Whitney and more petite like the youngest of his sisters, Tara.

Jenna had straight, dark blond hair and wore a purple tank top dress cut above her knee. Tara wore jean shorts, black and white checked canvas sneakers, and a white UCLA sweatshirt that hung off one shoulder. Her blond hair was a few shades darker than his and cut in a short pixie.

"Jenna! Tara! My God…it's been ages."

He hugged them both.

"It's so good to see you, little brother," said Tara, shaking her head. "You haven't changed a bit."

Meredith nodded. "You still look like that high school kid who drove out of my driveway in Dad's convertible. Bound for L.A. Seems like yesterday."

His wings shifted against his back and he felt the spin of his halo, knowing just how much he'd changed since that day. They couldn't see his wings and halo, but he wondered if they somehow felt the changes in him. It had been more than three years since they'd last seen each other. And somewhere after filming *The Ever After Hour*, he'd stopped aging.

"It's so great having you all here tonight," he said. "For my first anniversary."

"So, are you ready to give Talia your gift?" Mere asked, a smile widening on her oval face.

He nodded. He couldn't wait to see Talia's face when he gave her the car. "Let's do this."

"We parked the car where you said," said Jenna. "I'll drive it in. You just text me when you're ready. Then we can have some wine and catch up."

"I'd really like that, Jenna," he said.

Jenna hurried out the front door.

"The rest of you, come on," Jack motioned them through the living room. Toward the patio. "I'll introduce you to the love of my life. And all my friends."

Meredith gripped his hand as he led them through the house to the patio.

"Everybody!" he shouted. "Your attention please."

The patio fell quiet as Kesien hurried up from the beach and slid next to Muriel, Deemah, and Talia. Lucifer stood behind Azrael and

Berith, Pravuil seated on one of the sofas. Gianni, Izzy, Morgan, and Banks sat on another sofa, Rachel and Eric seated on another sofa. Zanth and Tre stood behind them.

Jack glanced around for Cerby and Orthy, hoping he wouldn't have to explain that surprise to his sisters. But Kesien—or Lucifer—had thankfully hidden the hellhounds from view.

"Everyone, I want you to meet my sisters," he said, holding out his hand as he motioned toward them. "Meredith, Whitney, and Tara. Jenna's here too, but she's dealing with the car."

The group started toward him, but he put up his hands.

"Wait! Before everyone mingles..." He walked toward Talia and took her hand, leading her to the edge of the patio, where the sea grass met the sand. "Talia, I wanted to give you my gift for our first anniversary together."

Talia's smile brightened, those grey eyes sparkling as he held both her hands, turning her back toward the beach.

"Talia, you are the love of my life," he said. "And I've never fought harder for anything in my existence than to make you my wife. And after a year at your side, I want you to know that I'd do it all over again. I'd fight for you to my last breath."

He laid his hand against his heart and held out his hand to her. Offering her his heart.

She reached out and closed her hand into a fist. Pressing her fist against her own heart. Accepting his as her eyes brimmed with tears.

"Jack Casey, you mean everything to me."

"I thought a long time about what I could possibly give you for an anniversary gift. What do you get the an...woman who has everything? But there was one thing that means so very much to me. So, I had to give it to you. As a symbol of my love."

He pulled out his phone and hit send on a text.

"Your phone number?" Talia replied.

Everyone broke up laughing, including Jack.

"No, that's how I got you into this mess in the first place," he said.

A horn honked.

He motioned over her shoulder and Talia turned toward the sound.

As Jenna drove up in his dad's 1969 cherry red Firebird convertible, top down, freshly detailed. Jenna parked it and hopped out. She hugged Jack and handed him the keys, joining his other sisters beside the bar. Where they'd found the wine and poured themselves each a glass of chardonnay.

Jack pressed the keyring into Talia's hand, a silver set of angel wings.

"A car, Jack?" she said, looking confused.

He frowned. Had he let her down?

"Not just any car, Tal," he said. "That was my dad's car. He loved that car and passed it down to me. It brought me here to L.A. and I drove it to my first audition. And to the call back for SanFran Confidential."

Her eyes got glassy again.

"This is your father's car?"

He nodded.

Tears slipped down her cheeks as she threw her arms around him. "Oh, Jack, I'm so touched that you'd give me your father's car."

"And Talia, he would have rather lost a limb than that car," said Meredith from the bar.

"Thank you, Jack!" Talia cried, kissing him. "I'll treasure it."

"Can't wait to teach you how to drive it," said Jack, kissing her back.

He started to step away, but Talia pulled him back to her.

"Jack, I have a gift for you, too."

"For me?" he said, intrigued.

What would his angel of death wife get him as an anniversary gift?

She turned toward Lucifer who handed her that small square black box that now had a gold ribbon on it. She held it out to Jack, her hand trembling.

She was nervous! What was in the box?

He glanced at her as he untied the ribbon, the breeze catching it from his hand and carrying it off. Slowly, he lifted the lid. A silver and gold wristwatch. It was beautiful.

"Thanks, Tal," he said, a little surprised that she'd choose such a mundane gift, but he kept his actor's mask in place.

But the fact that Talia had given it to him made it special. And he'd cherish it.

"Tal, it's gorgeous! Thank you!" He leaned over and kissed her.

"Go ahead," she said. "Put it on."

He lifted the watch out of the box. It had a stretch band with gold and silver links. He pushed it over his left hand and onto his wrist. Comfortable. Sleek.

But a burst of heat shot up his arm and exploded through his entire body. He shuddered, staggering a moment, and then found his balance again.

"Better lay off the merlot, Jack," said Lucifer. "And the Macallan."

Everyone laughed as conversations returned.

Dazed, Jack frowned and leaned toward Talia, whispering. "Babe, what just happened?"

She pressed her mouth against his ear.

"My gift to you wasn't just a watch, Jack," she whispered.

"You got them to throw in a little electrocution, too? Hoping there won't be a second anniversary?"

She shook her head. "I asked Lucifer to use his Lightbringer energies. He infused the watch with immortality, Jack."

He frowned, staring at her, the words sinking in…immortality.

Now, she looked unsure. Frightened.

"After almost losing you, I couldn't bear the thought of being separated from you for eternity, Jack."

Immortal. The word hung there, scaring the hell out of him. He was now immortal?

"Jack," she said in anxious whisper. "Please tell me you're okay with it. That you're not mad. I know, I should have asked you first, but I couldn't go through watching you die again."

He'd already stopped aging. He had wings and a halo. Seraphim powers. And Talia's rare powers. Even though he still saw himself as a typical human, without all those things, there was no denying the fact that he was anything but typically human. Not now. He'd been given the ability to pass through the risen portal, so he would never be separated from his sisters, his friends, or even his dad if he ever found his way out of purgatory.

From there, immortality wasn't such a big step. It was the last step. And it meant that he and Talia could never be separated.

He leaned against her, pressing his mouth to her ear.

"Best. Gift. Ever."

She threw her arms around him, kissing him like it was the first time she'd ever kissed him. He twirled her around in his arms and set her back onto the patio.

"I love you, Mrs. Casey. Happily forever after."

Lucifer moved toward them. "Oh, and Jack," he said. "My anniversary gift to you…well, it's from me and the entire guard. And Pravuil."

Azrael, Berith, and Pravuil stood beside him now as Muriel, Anahera, Deemah, and Kesien crowded in on his left.

"Don't talk him to death, Lucifer," Pravuil grumbled. "Just tell him."

Azrael smiled and nodded for Lucifer to continue as Berith squeezed Jack's shoulder.

"Jack, Talia and I went to see your dad in purgatory," said Lucifer. "He called for us."

Talia caressed his cheek. "Asked the angels to lead him home." She smiled. "He's risen, Jack. When you're ready, you can go see him. Any time."

Jack tried to stop his bottom lip from quivering as his eyes stung with moisture. And he wondered how much of that his sisters had heard.

"He's…he's in Heaven?" he choked out, biting his lip to keep it from quivering.

Talia nodded, anticipating his worry like she always did. "Only you heard this. Not your sisters."

Jack smashed his eyes closed and threw his arms around Talia, trying to rein in the flood of emotions that were washing over him. He could see his dad again! Any time he wanted!

"Sorry," he said in a tight voice as he let go of Talia. "You angels really know how to wreck a dude."

"It puts all the fun in angeling, Jack," said Lucifer. "Something I've missed."

Talia brushed the hair out of Jack's eyes. He leaned over and kissed her. "Thank you, babe." He turned toward the flock of angels surrounding him. "Thank you...all of you."

"You're not going to kiss us, too, are you?" Lucifer asked making a sour face.

"No," he said as he motioned toward his sisters. "But I am going to have all four of my sisters join the party."

His sisters hurried over and a dozen conversations exploded around him as stars began to glitter overhead, the soothing rush of the ocean tide touching his ears. It had never been a more perfect night.

Talia led him onto the beach, away from the crowd. She gripped his hands.

"Jack, I just want to make sure you're okay with my gift. I saw the look on your face."

He needed a little time to wrap his brain around it, but if it meant keeping Talia at his side forever, he was more than okay with it.

"Don't act your way through this, Jack. I have to know that you're okay with it. I shouldn't have just thrust it on you like that. I'm sorry."

He held her face in his hands, caressing her cheek. "Talia, it's fine. I never want to lose you. If being immortal is what it takes, then that's what I want, too."

The tears threaded down her cheeks and she was shaking now.

"Jack, you don't know what I went through after Lare stabbed you in Hell. Nobody could heal you and I felt your soul slipping from your body. I'm angel of death, Jack. I'm used to crossing over souls." Her voice broke and she pulled in a breath. "But I could never cross over your soul, knowing I could never love you again. I just couldn't."

He held her. "And now, you'll never have to, babe. You're stuck with me now. For eternity."

"At last," she said. "I've never wanted anything more than you, Jack Casey."

Jack held her hand as they walked back onto the patio. He pulled her toward his sisters who stood between Lucifer and Pravuil, talking to Muriel and Gianni. Already, he heard Meredith's voice, at least three glasses of wine loud now, in rare comical form. So much like dad. And him.

Jack snickered. Meredith had no idea she was telling a priest joke to God's Scribe and the former King of Hell. And an audience of angels of death.

"What's so funny?" Talia asked as Jack leaned against her ear and whispered.

"My sister's telling Pravuil and Lucifer her best priest joke."

Talia burst out laughing. "Best party ever, Jack. And I want to hear this joke."

She tugged on his hand, pulling him into the circle.

Meredith smiled and hugged Talia. "Hi, Talia! It's so great to finally meet you in person."

Meredith was a little over her limit. At least she was a happy drinker, like dad had been. Up to a point. Then things got dark. And real.

"You, too, Meredith," said Talia, nudging Meredith's arm. "Can't wait to hear all your Jack stories."

She chuckled. "There's a lot of them. Trust me."

Jack rolled his eyes.

"But first, the joke," said Talia. "I want to hear your joke."

Rachel slipped between Muriel and Anahera. "Yes, the joke. Let's hear it."

Meredith continued the joke as Jack glanced at Lucifer and Pravuil. They both had devilish smiles.

"So..." Meredith continued. "Then he turns to his congregation and says, so that's what the confessional is for!"

The angels roared with laughter, especially Lucifer and Pravuil.

"I just love a good priest joke," said Lucifer, nudging Azrael. "Hope you were keeping up, Azrael ol' boy? Or do I need to explain that one to you? About the sinning and the demons—a specialty of mine."

Berith smiled as Azrael's mood darkened.

"I've got one," said Rachel, a devious smile on her face. "Okay, these two angels walk into a bar."

"Walk?" Muriel replied, shaking her head. "They're angels. Don't they fly?"

"Work with me here, Muriel," said Rachel as she continued the joke.

Jack stepped away from the group, the voices growing softer as he walked over to the bar. He poured the last glass of merlot from the bottle and set it to the left of the corked bottles. He'd toss it into the recycle bin on his next trip inside.

Laughter erupted across the patio as he swirled the rich garnet wine around in his glass and brought it to his lips.

But a shadow rushed past the edge of his vision, swiveling around the left side of the patio.

For a moment, Jack froze.

He jerked his head toward the shadow, the movement. Nothing there but the slight flutter of an evening breeze through the palm trees framing the small patio.

He glanced toward the house and back at the party, to see if anyone was missing. But everyone who had stayed was still here on the patio, sipping wine and chatting.

Nothing was out of place. He was overreacting.

Finally, he caught Kesien's attention and motioned him over.

"What's up, Jack?" he asked.

"Where are Cerby and Orthy?"

He nodded toward the heavens. "One of the Watchers took them back up to Eolowen." He looked tense as he scrutinized Jack a moment. "Why?" he said, squinting, his gaze tracking toward the edge of the patio. Where Jack had focused his attention. "Something wrong?"

Nothing was wrong. He was just paranoid. He'd had a few glasses of wine. He was happily distracted. What could possibly be wrong?

"No, everything's good," he said.

Kesien nodded, but Jack saw that brooding look pinch Kesien's features as he glanced around the patio. Like he'd felt or seen something well before Jack had said anything.

"Kesien, you okay? Did you see something?"

Frowning, Kesien glanced around as another cool breeze wafted across the patio and then he returned his attention to Jack.

"No," said Kesien. "But something just feels…off. I can't put my finger on it."

Jack swallowed a breath. "Off? Like apocalypse off or still salty about Reptev escaping off?"

Kesien shrugged and glanced around at the quiet beach, the sound of the waves soothing as they rolled onto the sand and softly receded. Wine glasses clinked. Someone laughed. Ice crunched as Gianni rooted through it for another can of Stone Pilsner.

"Sorry, Jack," said Kesien, laying a hand on his shoulder. "Guess I'm still on high alert and keep looking for Reptev to turn up and finish this."

Jack shook his head and took a sip of merlot. "He's too much of a coward to challenge so many angels. Especially with Lucifer and Azrael here."

Kesien was nodding as he stared down at the patio floor, looking like he'd just flown a million miles away.

"True. And definitely not with Lucifer and Azrael here. He wouldn't dare."

"An ambush outside the mall is more Reptev's style, Kesien," said Jack. "But I know that if anyone can catch that traitor, it's you and Deemah."

"Thanks, Jack," he said, looking up. "Appreciate the vote of confidence."

Jack patted Kesien's shoulder who returned to the group, standing behind Deemah, but Jack studied his tense posture and his gaze traveling around the perimeter. He was still very much on edge.

Something moved to Jack's left.

He turned.

Clink! The empty bottle of merlot toppled off the table and rolled across the patio.

Cursing under his breath, but grateful the bottle hadn't shattered, Jack hurried after it as it rolled toward the palm trees and into the tangle of ferns beneath them.

He bent down to pick up the bottle when something rustled in the palm tree above him. Probably a scrub jay.

He retrieved the bottle. But when he stood up, a flash of red drew his attention. He glanced up at the sky.

Red eyes gleamed from the top of the palm tree. But a heartbeat later, they vanished.

He glanced around, expecting a clutch of shadowy ashen-skinned Nephions or a horde of sharp-toothed, leathery-skinned demons to rush him.

Wind rustled through the palm tree branches and ferns again. But it wasn't just the wind. He knew what he saw.

He froze, watching. Waiting for something to attack him.

Nothing moved. Nothing stirred.

Another shadow at the edge of his vision. To the right.

He whirled around, empty bottle raised.

"Jack? What's the matter with you?"

Talia was behind him. Her sudden presence startled him.

"Tal!" He lowered the bottle. "You scared the hell out of me."

"You planning to brain someone?" she asked, pointing at the merlot bottle he held against his thigh. "Or are you just happy to see me?"

He smirked. "Why not both?"

"Did you see something?" she asked.

"No," he said. "Just knocked the bottle into the ferns, that's all." He lowered his voice. "But Tal, I would have sworn I saw red eyes up in one of the palm trees. Guess I'm overreacting."

She had a funny look on her face as she moved toward the palm trees. He felt her call up her omnificence power. She bowed her head, hands pressed together, silent for several long moments. Until finally, she lifted her head, letting her arms fall to her sides.

"Not sensing any demons, Jack," she said.

"Good," he said and set the merlot bottle back on the table. "Because they weren't on the guest list."

When he looked up, Meredith, Whitney, Jenna, and Tara were walking toward him.

"Jack," Whitney called as she stopped beside him, holding onto Meredith who looked like she'd had way too much wine.

Jenna was at Meredith's right side, Tara at the back, looking worried.

"What's wrong, Whit?"

"Too much to drink," Tara whispered in his ear.

Whitney lowered her voice. "Meredith needs to lie down, so we're going to call it a night. The cross-country trip was a lot more tiring than she let on. We'll see you tomorrow though."

Stunned, Jack stared at his oldest sister. She was thirty-nine not seventy. The excuses, the whispers, the bruises...way too many naps. For the first time in his life, he realized that just because Meredith had dark hair didn't mean she wasn't the spitting image of Dad.

Meredith was an alcoholic.

Horrified, he stared at Whitney. "Whit...I didn't know. Oh, God...I never knew."

Whitney put her arms around him and hugged him. "It's okay, Jack. She didn't want you to know."

"Why?" he asked.

Whitney sighed. "She didn't want you to hate her, Jack—after everything you went through with Dad."

It was a gut punch to his soul.

He moved over to Meredith. "Mere, you're like a mother to me," he said in a tight voice. "I could never hate you, especially for this. My addiction got me fired from the hottest show on television. Remember?"

Meredith laid her hand on his cheek, tears in her eyes, and he put his arms around her, hugging her.

"And I'll always be here for you—no matter what. No conditional family holiday dinners here."

Meredith broke down in tears and hugged him. He held her tightly, his gut twisting at his lack of attention to detail. How could he have missed that his big sister was as much an alcoholic as his dad?

"Me, too, Mere," said Whit, stroking Meredith's hair. "That's why I stayed in Indiana. To look after you."

"See you tomorrow, Jack," said Jenna, hugging him and then Tara hugged him.

He walked them to the door, holding Meredith's hand. Whitney hugged him and they held Meredith up as they walked toward a white rented sedan.

Jack felt a little hollow and shaken when he returned to the patio, but he'd be there for Meredith. To help her get through this, if she was ready. If she'd let him.

"You, okay, Jack?" Talia asked, sliding her arm around his waist.

Conversations were still in full swing, but Jack wondered how many of Talia's squad knew his sister was alcoholic.

He shrugged and fixed her with his gaze. "Did the entire guard know?"

"That your sister was an alcoholic?"

"Yeah."

"Some of us just looked at her Book of Life and Death to confirm it," she said. "If we'd looked earlier, we would have known, but no, Jack. Angels don't know everything about every human. Would it have mattered if we had?"

He sighed. No. Of course not. But he felt like a fool for not knowing after all these years.

"No, but I should have known," he said. "I should have known."

"Jack, you couldn't have changed her any more than you could have changed your dad. The only person you could have changed was you." She ran her fingers through his hair. "Remember how hard you had to fight to change?"

He remembered those knife-blade cravings that never went away and the night sweats and how he would have done or sold anything for one more key bump. And even then, it took divine intervention. Maybe he couldn't change Meredith, but he could be there for her when that road got too long and too dark and too lonely. He knew that road well, every bump and every curve.

"I do," he said, nodding. "And tomorrow, I'll tell her that I'll be there to help her if she wants to get better. But regardless, I'll just be there."

"Being there is the best thing you can do for Meredith, Jack," said Talia.

He smiled. "Like you were there for me." He pulled Talia into a hot, lingering kiss.

He moved to the bar and fished out three bottles of Mailly grand cru champagne from iced tub.

"I think it's time to open these."

"I couldn't agree more, Mr. Casey," she said and began lining up two dozen champagne flutes as Jack popped the first cork.

"A toast, everyone," he called out.

The party crowded around the bar. Jack filled glass after glass and Talia handed them out until two glasses remained. He handed one to Talia and held his up to the stars and the heavens.

"A toast. To the love of my life and the best year of my life," he said.

Everyone drank.

He held up his glass again and did a little acting. "And a toast. To the best friends this dude has ever had. And I want you to know that I won't forget my favorite actors as they move on to SanFran Confidential."

Gianni looked upset. He started whispering to Banks who looked alarmed.

Jack waited a moment, letting the words sink in. He'd let Gianni and Banks worry for another moment or two.

"Because Talia and I have just signed onto the show, me in the role of Davy Pierson and Talia as Detective Kenzie Wylder."

Gianni grinned and fist bumped Banks as everyone cheered and drank another mouthful of champagne.

"Thank God!" Gianni and Banks shouted and clinked glasses and then patted Jack on the back.

But the flash of two red eyes gleaming in the dark behind the palm trees made Jack turn. As something shifted onto the patio.

 are Dumont, fresh from a lava swim and a quick death, stepped out from behind one of the palm trees, barefoot, incorporeal, and smelling of sulfur and ash. In spirit form, he wore scorched dark pants and a soot-covered dress shirt. Lucky bastard had the good fortune to die after Lucifer gave up Hell's throne, and his claim on all those contracted souls. Apparently, Abaddon and Kushiel hadn't caught up to him yet.

He glared at Jack and clutched a knife that glowed with red symbols in his fist.

Jack took a step backward.

Lare's shoulder-length brown hair looked ghostly and stringy, his body scarecrow-thin, a snarl twisting his translucent features as he folded black leathery bat wings against his back.

Jack backed away, protectively spreading his wings in front of Talia.

All of the angels surrounded Jack as Talia pulled Gianni and Izzy into the center of the formation. Muriel motioned Banks, Morgan, Eric, and Rachel behind Gianni. Talia moved beside Azrael, both of them unfurling their grey angel of death wings. Lucifer shielded

Pravuil and Berith with his sparkling white wings as Zanth and Tre stepped beside them.

"Surrender, Dumont," Azrael commanded. "You can't win this fight."

"Especially when he's dead," said Jack.

Pravuil took a sip of champagne. "Better listen to him, son. Azrael gets grumpy when fools ignore his best advice."

Jack counted the shadows behind Lare. Five maybe six. No, more than that now.

"Why aren't you dead, Jack?" Lare demanded, shaking the knife at him.

"Why are you such a douchebag, Lare? And dead? Because you just are...like the Creation. And taxes. Rhetorical question, obvious answer. Why aren't I dead? Because you're incompetent. See? Rhetorical question, obvious answer. Got it?"

"Shut up! Shut! Up! I'm so damned sick of your smart mouth. Even the sound of your voice sends me into a blind rage!"

Jack grinned. "I've now found my new purpose in life."

"Jack, stop!" Talia said with a hiss.

"Why, babe?" he said, still grinning. "I'm immortal, remember? This asshat can't touch me. Not even with that stupid cursed blade."

"What?" Lare roared, his red eyes burning infernos. "You're immortal?"

Jack thought Lare was going to start foaming at the mouth.

Screaming, Lare rushed at him, knife raised.

But Lucifer stepped in front of Lare, grabbed the knife out of his hand, and crushed it in his fist.

"There," said Lucifer. "Crisis averted. Not much of a fight though."

Lare stared at Lucifer like he had horns.

"But that was the fabled demon blade of..."

"Of bullshit," said Zanth as she stepped in front of Lare, Tre sliding into the group of angels beside Morgan. "You ignorant fool. Demons have no fabled weapons. We have whatever we have forged in Hell."

Lucifer's eyes narrowed as he folded his arm against his chest. "Bloody hell, Lare. Can't you see that the demons were toying with you? That was a common blade. Standard issue. It's just been cursed with Hellfire—like you've been cursed with stupidity. Now, stop this nonsense and return your damned soul to Hell before Abaddon hunts you down and hands you over to Kushiel for punishment." Lucifer unfurled his massive white wings. "Or I'll deal with you as the Lightbringer. Your choice."

Lare backed away, more shadows coalescing around him.

"Okay," said Jack as he watched the shadows roil around the edge of the patio—their numbers growing. "None of these Nephions were on the guest list."

Talia shook her head. "Oh, I'd remember inviting Nephions. Sorry, Lare, you'll all have to leave. We've already gone through all the champagne."

"And those little spinach and artichoke quiches," Jack added.

Lare continued to glare at him.

"Reptev will be here any minute," said Lare, pointing at Jack. "To deal with you, Jack."

Jack chuckled. "Bring it, Lare. I could use the workout."

But the flutter of wings echoed above the rush of the ocean.

Kesien's face lit up as Deemah grabbed the Eternean shield from her belt. "Looks like more guests arriving, Jack." His grey eyes narrowed. "Familiar ones."

Kesien's old squad.

"Hope they at least brought a bag of chips this time," said Jack as he watched three angels of death traitors land beside Lare Dumont. "Lare here didn't even bring onion dip. Rude. Would it have killed one of you to bring some hummus!"

Reptev, Pharzus, and Lix drew their swords. Lix handed Lare a sword from the sheath at his side as they stood their ground, daring any of the angels to engage them. But the shadows shifting around them had been too many to count, giving Jack a little uncertainty to just throwing down.

"It's the douchesquad," said Jack. "And here I almost booked a bouncy castle for tonight's entertainment. This is much more fun."

"Why isn't he dead?" Reptev asked, glancing at Lare.

Jack rolled his eyes. "Again with the rhetorical question?"

"I thought the fabled demon blade of Hellfire killed anything you stabbed with it," said Lix.

Zanth groaned and stamped her foot. "Idiots! Are humans and angels always this gullible?"

"Just the douchesquad," said Muriel, lifting her Eternean shield. "Welcome to the party, Zanth."

"Oh, I hope so, Zanth," said Deemah, looking like she'd just won a Beverly Hills shopping spree as she tapped her shield with her fingers.

"I'm going to enjoy this," said Kesien, flexing his wings as he held up his shield, looking like he'd won the lottery.

Gianni slid the sword out of Deemah's sheath and stood shoulder to shoulder with Jack.

"I've missed a good demon fight," he said, glancing at Jack, a smile curving across his Cary Grant handsome face.

Talia stood at Jack's right shoulder, flaming archangel sword in her hand. "Me, too, Gianni. It's been at least a week."

Jack clinked champagne glasses with Gianni and then Talia as he turned toward the trash that had landed on his patio.

Lucifer stepped over to the bar and poured himself a glass of Macallan 1926 Amani. "I do love a good brawl," he said.

Berith shrugged and picked up Azrael's shield. "They never learn, do they?"

Azrael shook his head, fiery archangel sword raised. "Afraid not."

One by one, the champagne flutes started appearing on tables and around the patio as angels, humans, and Zanth set them down, preparing to defend themselves.

Banks moved in behind Jack as Anahera handed him her shield.

"Jack, are all these shadows demons?"

"Afraid so, Banks. Well, half archdemons, half archangels actually. Called Nephions. Still bashable though."

"Izzy," said Gianni in a calm voice, his gaze not leaving Reptev. "Take Morgan and Tre and stay behind the sofas until this is over.

Gianni set himself, sword raised as Izzy pulled Morgan back behind the sofas. Tre went with them, Eric and Rachel following.

"There's too many, Jack," said Gianni, glancing around the patio.

"We can't defeat all these demons!" Banks kept shifting right to left, sweat beading across his forehead. "Not even with archangels in the mix."

Jack pulled his phone out of his pocket and opened his demon-splattering playlist. Maxing the volume.

"Talia, a demon bar fight?" he said and smirked. "Best gift ever. You shouldn't have!"

She caressed his cheek a moment. "What do you get the actor who has everything?"

Jack grinned. She was right. For the first time in his life, he had everything he'd ever wanted.

"You're right. I've got everything I've ever wanted, babe—as long as you're beside me. And my friends."

She leaned over and kissed him. "Happily forever after, Mr. Casey. I just love how romantic you get during a demon fight."

Jack smirked as the first raucous electric guitar strains rang out across the patio, echoing above the ocean waves. The electric guitar riff pounded out the rhythm beneath the building chords as Brian Johnson belted out the opening lines to AC/DC's *Shook Me All Night Long*.

Jack rocked his head to the song, champagne glass still in his hand as Lucifer moved to the front of the group and stood beside Gianni and Jack, a devilish grin on his face as the shadows moved toward them, Reptev, Lix, Pharzus, and soul-form Lare leading the advance.

"Jack, there's just too many," said Gianni. "We'll never defeat all of them."

Jack took to a big swig of champagne and tapped Lucifer on the shoulder.

"Luci, hold my champagne," said Jack as he took a step forward.

Lucifer took the glass as he and Talia moved beside Jack, Gianni, and Banks who had moved behind him now.

Lucifer slammed the last of his own champagne and tossed both glasses onto the patio in front of Reptev.

"With pleasure, Jack," said Lucifer, unfurling his crystalline white wings like sails around his shoulders.

Jack called up murder marbles in each hand, then leaned over and kissed Talia. She kissed him back hard, grinning as she called up glowing gold murder marbles in each hand.

"Never gets old," said Jack, grinning as he glanced at Gianni and Banks.

With a nod to Lucifer and Talia, Jack flung the handfuls of glowing gold murder marbles as they advanced on the demons and materializing Nephions to *Shook Me All Night Long*. Talia flung her handfuls next scattering them across the patio's concrete surface as the rest of the angels moved in formation behind them, shields raised.

Shook Me All Night Long started over again. On repeat as Jack shouted, "Supremes formation, everyone! Let's get this party started!"

The End of THE PERDITION PICTURE SHOW

The End of A Game of Lost Souls series

Enjoyed this series?
Try THORN & BLADE next!
Book 1: Curse and Crown
a romantasy suspense series

READ CHAPTER 1 NOW!

Novels by Lisa Silverthorne

A Game of Lost Souls series:
Contemporary Romantasy

THE CINDERELLA HOUR
THE PRINCE CHARMING HOUR
THE EVER AFTER HOUR
THE FALLEN HEARTS SEASON
THE RISING SPIRITS SEASON
THE ETERNAL SOULS SEASON
THE ROYAL WEDDING HOUR
THE HEAVENLY HONEYMOON HOUR
THE DIVINE NEWLYWEDS SHOW
THE CELESTIAL COUPLES SHOW
THE ENOCHIAN APOCALYPSE SHOW
THE ANGELIC ANNIVERSARY SHOW
THE PERDITION PICTURE SHOW

Curse and Crown series:
Romantasy Suspense

THORN & BLADE
STORM & STEEL

The Spiral series:
Dark Contemporary Fantasy

BETWEEN
REPRISE
AVENGE

The Resurrectionist Papers
Supernatural Romystery
GRAVE RECKONING

Standalones:
ISABEL'S TEARS
LANDFALL
PACIFIC BLUE TATTOO

Short Story Collections
THE SOUND OF ANGELS
THE MAGIC OF ORDINARY THINGS
TIMELESS
WINTER'S EMBRACE

Science Fiction Writing as L.S. Silverthorne

Experiencing True Purple series:
RECOMBINANT, Book 1
HELIX, Book 2
SPLICE, Book 3

Standalones:
REDISCOVERY

FORTHCOMING!

Curse and Crown series:
Flame & Dagger, Book Three
Frost & Foil, Book Four
Curse & Crown, Book Five (Series End)

The Spiral series:
Ruin, Book 4
Descent, Book 5 (Series End)

The Resurrectionist Papers:
Corpses Delicti
Stiffed Again

SCIENCE FICTION WRITING AS **L.S.** SILVERTHORNE

Experiencing True Purple series:
Cipher, Book 4
Renascence, Book 5 (Series End)

SNEAK PEEK: THORN & BLADE

CHAPTER 1

1

*S*hadows from Ereth's perpetual dusk eddied in the corners and pooled along the pocked grey stone castle walls battered and scarred from the Hundred-Year Sundering. A century of war with Rohesia to the east. A clash of magic against blade. A hundred years of fading sunlight and growing twilight.

Of dying crops and invading darkness.

Smell of ozone and wood smoke hung thick in the charged air as mages in royal purple silk robes and archers in grey tunics and trousers lined Castle Skystead's ramparts. Magic glowed amethyst and cyan at fingertips and the points of arrows. It felt like all of Ereth held its breath.

Waiting. Waiting for the enemy's arrival from the east under a banner of truce.

Fingers of pallid sunlight withered and receded as torches guttered in the painful silence, thrum of magic rumbling against the castle walls. Filling my heart with trepidation.

Standing alongside the elite magical guard in my violet purple Erethian betrothal gown, pulse racing, I watched the Rohesian convoy's carriages coalesce like an apparition out of the mists and gathering shadows. Toward Skystead. Without swords drawn. Without magic burning the air.

For the first time in a century, Rohesians stood on Erethian soil in the most tenuous truce ever seen in Ereth. The first I'd ever witnessed in all my eighteen years.

I'd never felt warm sunlight on my face—only this tepid glow. And with every passing day, the sunlight receded more, unable to penetrate the mists and shadows that cursed my mother's magic realm of Ereth. And the kingdom of Rohesia, those vile sword-mongering monsters to the east.

Ereth's bitter enemy.

Instead, the blanched, sickly sun rays cast an illusion of warmth in their fading gold hues, more the color of piss than sunlight. Crops died in the fields and leaves fell from the trees in a perpetual autumn.

Either way, this curse had been my doom. It fated me to wed Prince Arence Siridean of Rohesia—and my sisters to marry his brothers. To fulfill the prophecy that would break this curse and save Ereth. Save the world of Kambria. And Rohesia, too—not that I cared.

My life was over.

I held my breath as I watched the royal Rohesian carriage slide out of the mist, carved from dark grey ironwood by the sharpest blades in Kambria, and led by six stocky black Merced roans the color of midnight, coats ticked grey, manes wrapped in red and orange silks that undulated like flames in the wind. The scent of new leather and sweaty horses hung above magic's burnt lightning smell.

Whiffs of sulfur and lime from the torches burning above the gate made me move up wind to keep the smell out of my blond hair as I watched my doom unfold at Skystead's gates. The Rohesian royal red standard bearing crossed swords flew above the carriage. Fluttering like my heart.

It took all my courage to hold back the tears burning in my eyes, a golden hazel as Lady Laurel described them.

Lady Laurel, my lady-in-waiting, stood beside me, dressed in Ereth's long, royal purple mage robes with long raglan sleeves and silky drape. Magical symbols danced with ethereal light across the fabric, brightening and fading as twilight darkened. Already, she was casting. Wards. Protection. Calm.

She slid her arm around my waist and held me close. My blond hair mixed with long strands of her warm brown locks that had begun to cloud with silver and white. She smelled like magic and rosewater.

More mother to me than my own, Lady Laurel had helped me dress in the magnificent royal purple betrothal gown with its beaded lace bodice, off-the shoulder straps, and a delicate purple chiffon cape that floated into a royal train three feet behind me.

Conjured with air magic and finished by the finest Erethian tailors and seamstresses, the dress was a statement to Rohesia. That Ereth was still a rich and flourishing realm (despite this curse that would soon destroy everything). That its firstborn princess was borne of deep and powerful magical lines—and one of the most priceless gifts from Earth.

But I couldn't get past the fact that I was expendable.

I was one of four prices the realm must pay to save the world. My happiness and dreams had been taken from me and gift-wrapped into this visionary and alluring gown meant to enrapture a barbaric prince into marrying me. Where I would exist in a loveless marriage, in a foreign place I would never love, so that the world survived. I had just turned eighteen and my chest ached with the weight and depth of this sacrifice I was forced to make. Even though certain factions of Kambria wanted me—and my three other sisters—dead and this prophecy left unfulfilled.

This marriage was forever. I would never return to my beloved realm of Ereth.

"Chin up, princess," Lady Laurel whispered against my ear. "You are the bravest young woman I have ever met. Both Ereth and Rohesia will make certain you are well-guarded. You will be safe and I will be with you. You won't be alone in Rohesia."

Lady Laurel knew about the threats to my life from across Kambria. It seemed incomprehensible to me that some didn't want this union of realms to take place. And they had pledged to stop it at all costs. To murder me before I ever reached the border between the countries.

Right now, I almost considered that a kindness.

"Your mother chose me as your lady-in-waiting because of my air sorcery's prowess. You will be safe. The hopes of Kambria go with you this day. And all the love Ereth can muster for our beautiful sacrifice."

She was leaving Ereth, too. Making the same sacrifice. Except that she wouldn't be forced to marry a man she didn't love and would probably despise. Prince Arence. Oldest son of Rohesian King Daegal Siridean. I had heard he was at least thirty and as barbaric and bloodthirsty as his father. In a kingdom that despised magic, mages, and sorceresses. The thought of their blades terrified me.

But Lady Laurel's gracious acceptance of her fate was a model I needed to emulate. Hold my head high no matter what.

"My sisters weren't allowed to watch me leave," I said, trying so hard not to let my voice crack or catch in my throat. "To tell me goodbye."

My mother, the queen, wouldn't allow them to witness my departure from Ereth and the only life I had ever known. Because it was their future. Genevieve would leave next spring. Carysana two years later. And finally, Arianwen two years after Carys.

"Even I can feel the heat and comfort of your sisters' magics swirling around you, Annarissa," said Lady Laurel as the creak of carriage wheels echoed in the quiet.

She was right.

I felt their love and magic supporting me. Wrapping around me like a blanket warmed by hearth fires. Gen with her explosive air magic (a fierce warrior princess and assault sorceress). Carys' fiery magic and fascination with daggers (Carys hated magic, a secret she'd kept from Mother—along with the daggers.) And beautiful white-haired Arianwen, blessed with powerful water magic. My sisters' combined magics kept me upright and moving right now when I wanted to collapse against the stone floor. I felt their magic.

And their fear—for me. For their futures.

Following me into Rohesia's dark, wild expanse. Forced to marry our enemies' sons. All princes of Rohesia.

Our freedom—and our love—was the price of peace. But having even one of my sisters near me in Rohesia was a comfort I clung to right now. And Lady Laurel's strength.

It had to be enough.

Besides, the Prophecy of Magics and Blades demanded it. A price dictated after Queen Maelena Thorn and King Onyx Siridean killed each other on a battlefield at Ereth's eastern border. In the aftermath, Lady Ambren Thorn (my mother) and Lord Daegal Siridean were crowned new rulers of Ereth and Rohesia. As the Kambrian peace delegation read the prophecy right there on the bloody, body-strewn battlefield, the newly crowned queen and king were given two choices.

Blood or death.

By blood or death, a sacrifice was demanded of both realms. Queen and king must sacrifice their children. Either they wed Rohesian blades with Erethian elemental magics or face the total annihilation of both realms.

To lift the curse and save the world of Kambria.

That very day, Queen Ambren Thorn put down her wand and staff, pledging the hands of her four young daughters when they came of age. To four princes of Rohesia. King Daegal Siridean put down his sword across wand and stave, pledging the hands of his sons to the sorceresses of Ereth.

It had been the only way to halt the curse stealing Kambria's sunlight and killing all its crops and livestock. Only Xanthe across Covendrie Inlet to the north, a neutral kingdom, still had full sunlight—and could grow most crops. Without the Thorn sisters' and Siridean princes' sacrifices, all of Kambria's people would soon perish when the sun's light went dark across Kambria. And in Xanthe.

As the firstborn sorceress of Ereth, named for legendary ice sorceress Anna Thorn and her fire mage lady-in-waiting Rissa Thorn (my grandmothers), I became Ereth's first great hope. As the heir apparent to the throne, with three sisters in line behind me, I had been trained in battle magic since I could read the family grimoire. But I knew that after my magical confirmation, a ceremony where one (or more) of the elemental magics binds itself to a sorceress, my mother had been so disappointed in my magical inheritance.

And me.

In a moment that couldn't be taken back, I, Princess Annarissa Thorn, the first great hope of Ereth, had become…just an earth sorceress.

Considered the weakest of the four elemental magics, my magical inheritance had been a portent of doom to my mother. But it didn't matter. As firstborn, I had to make the first great sacrifice.

Part of me wanted to die. To escape this banishment and isolation to the west. A barbaric place I had never even seen before.

"Annarissa, it's time," said the stolid, icy voice of my mother who had materialized behind me in the finest royal purple gown in Ereth. Fit for a sorceress queen. A form-fitting color-changing silk, covered in iridescent beading, that flowed around her like smoke, shoulders bare, sleeves dripping with beads and the sheerest lace.

Made for the occasion of giving away her firstborn daughter in marriage. Bet Mother hadn't expected it to happen in this way. I know I didn't.

I wondered how long ago her ice sorcery had frozen her heart. She seemed indifferent to the fact that I was leaving her and everything I loved behind. Forever. That she would never see me—her firstborn— in person again.

Pulling in a deep breath, I squeezed Lady Laurel's hand and reached up to adjust the gold and amethyst Erethian crown I wore. Delicate. Ethereal. Magical as the violet gems floated along the band and elemental symbols gleamed up and down the crown's myriad spikes of raw gems—like sun's rays. A smaller version of the queen's grand crown.

I gritted my teeth. I was a sorceress of Ereth. I would hold my head high and bury my heart this day.

Along with my hopes and dreams—and my love.

I reached for my earth magic. My hand sparkled with purple light as I conjured a handful of stark black soil that smelled rich and loamy like peat. In my other hand I conjured a delicate porcelain white pearl, a symbol of my wish for true love and the prince of my dreams that I had carefully nurtured and protected since I was a small child.

Inhaling sharply, I dropped the pearl into the soil and waved my hand across it. Burying my last hope of marrying for love. Letting it go.

The soil hardened and crumbled to dust.

I blew the remnants of the life I would never have over the rampart and it brushed across the massive, ornate Rohesian carriage that halted at the castle drawbridge.

The three wagons carrying a complement of hired swords behind the polished ironwood carriage creaked to a stop. Using wagons gave the procession a more innocuous appearance than a company of the king's soldiers on horseback riding the roads. The large, sleek roans nickered and fidgeted, stomping, snorting, tossing their long black manes and flame-like silks.

"Open the gate!"

A gruff, stocky man with black and silver hair, dressed in dark trousers and leather armor, climbed down from the carriage, longsword unsheathed, and waved toward the mages stationed above the gate entrance. The heavy wooden and iron gate glowed indigo with magical protection.

The Rohesian blademaster. My bodyguard on the long journey to Rohesia.

Like a rope stretched too tight, I felt the tension intensify in the magic that permeated the castle and the realm. At the approach of sword wielders invading my world. Enemies. Monsters that had slaughtered my people for over a century. The truce had been uneasy at best and having these marauders inside the castle—my home— made my anger spark and my heart race.

Chains rattled. Wood creaked and moaned.

With a loud thump, the massive wooden gate that led into the inner sanctum of Ereth's royal castle, Skystead, began to lower. The castle stood high on a hill, its five towers touching the clouds. The village of Skystead nestled behind its protection. The ramparts shook as the gate groaned and lifted, allowing narrow passage across the dark, murky moat that circled the castle. A moat filled with dangerous water spirits and deadly magics that could drown an enemy fast.

Feeling nauseated, I gripped Lady Laurel's arm and turned away from the convoy.

But the flash of fire made me turn back again.

A hail of arrows burning with fire magic rained down from the surrounding forest that covered the castle's northeastern edge. Killing the man in leather armor, sword still in his hand, and everyone in the carriage. Including the horses.

ABOUT THE AUTHOR

LISA SILVERTHORNE, an award-winning bestselling author, has published over 25 novels and 150 short stories and novelettes in many genres. She is the author of *A Game of Lost Souls* series, *Experiencing True Purple* series, *The Spiral*, *The Resurrectionist Papers,* and *Curse and Crown*. She lives in Las Vegas, Nevada.

Before you go, you are invited to please leave a **review of this book**!

Reviews are a wonderful way to help an author and share your thoughts with other readers, so **please post yours,** in as many places as possible!

 ***ONLINE STORE!***

*For Ebook Bundles, book swag, and beautiful **Special Edition** hardcovers, visit: **LisaSilverthorneBooks.com***

* 9 7 8 1 9 5 5 1 9 7 7 4 8 *